INTO THE HOLLOW

EXPERIMENT IN TERROR #6

KARINA HALLE

To my mom, for always believing in me. And to my dad, for letting so many of those "IOUs" slide.

Copyright © 2012 by Karina Halle

First edition published by Metal Blonde Books

Second edition published 2020

All rights reserved.

No part of this book may be reproduced in any form or by any electronic or mechanical means, including information storage and retrieval systems, without written permission from the author, except for the use of brief quotations in a book review.

Cover: Hang Le Designs

Edited by: Kara Malinczak

1

Whiteout.

That's what I saw when I finally pried my lids open, my lashes stuck together with the glue of tiny snowflakes.

White. White. White.

Where was I?

I rolled over with a groan and felt an explosion of pain in my side. I looked down and as my vision began to right itself, I saw a rock jutting into my stomach, protruding from the cold, snow-blown ground like a weapon.

I eased onto my back, the chill seeping through my jacket. My bare fingers tingled as I ran them over my body. I felt intact, nothing bleeding or broken.

But how did that explain the rich, acidic smell of blood in the air?

I slowly sat up, surveying my surroundings.

I was sitting on the barren, rocky ground up the side of a mountain. Snow swirled in the air from all directions, some of it falling on the icy white patches on the earth, the rest blown away like angel dust.

Because of the infinite white, I could barely make out a forested valley below, and across from me, in the haze of snowfall, a few jagged peaks.

Beneath me the ground sloped off gently, alternating between sudden drop-offs. Vertigo swept through me and I dug my frozen fingers into the hard ground, suddenly afraid I'd roll off the side and fall to my death.

A soft rumbling came from my left. I turned, painfully, my side still smarting, and saw a slight overhang where snow fell off in gentle lumps. My heart sped up a few beats.

I let out the breath I was holding, watching it freeze and catch in the air before drifting away, and noticed a trace of red where the snow had just fallen.

My bones seized with chill.

I peered at the red spot, my eyes widening as it began to spread and bleed across the snow.

Glancing up at the overhang where the snow had come from, I saw another clump of it come sailing down, landing on the red with a poof.

It too had a spot of red in it that slowly spread like a stain on a paper towel. Curiosity getting the better of me, I carefully got to my feet and walked over to the patch of silky wetness. Hunched over, I tried to figure out why the snow was bleeding. I felt a drip on the back of my neck.

I reached back with my hand and when I took it away, it was slick with blood.

Did I even want to turn around?

I did, anyway.

Above me was a limp, lacerated arm, its torn and bloody fingers dangling over the edge of the overhang.

Claws. Teeth. Blood.

Tearing. Gnawing. Eating.

The images and sounds ripped through my head in a flash of smoky darkness.

Dex! I remembered Dex.

My chest collapsed in on itself as I tried to recall the last time I'd seen him.

Where was he?

What happened to him?

I eyed the arm above my head and felt the world drop away beneath my feet.

A HARD NUDGE into the side of my stomach again.

I winced and grabbed it, expecting to find the sharp, snow-dusted rock but instead found a dainty hand and long fingers wrapped around mine.

My eyes flew open. Beside me, Ada poked my side, a quiet smile on her face.

We were in the back of my dad's car. Of course we were.

My father, at the wheel, eyed me nervously in the rearview mirror. My mom sat beside him, looking out the passenger's side window. Ada was next to me, stuck with the bitch seat, as the hulking douchecanoe, Maximus, hunched on her opposite side.

"Are you feeling OK?" Ada asked, keeping her voice low, even though everyone in the damn car could hear her. "You fell asleep there. You were drooling."

I wiped at my mouth and at the puddle on my collar.

"Well, I've sort of had a long day."

My eyes met my dad's in the mirror again. He looked so much older than he did the other day. Was it possible to drive someone to an early grave?

"We're almost home, pumpkin," he said.

I nodded and felt eyes boring into the side of my head. Reluctantly, I looked past Ada and at Maximus, who was staring at me intently.

"What the hell are you looking at?" I sniped.

His expression didn't change and he didn't look away, just kept trying to read me with those green eyes of his.

This is all your fault, I projected at him, hoping he could hear it in some way. It kind of creeped me out that it looked like he nodded in return.

"Perry," my dad warned, though his voice had lost the edge it normally had. I guess when your daughter is borderline psycho and may or may not have just been kidnapped along with your 15-year-old, it's best to use the kid gloves.

I sighed and looked out the window at the darkening Portland cityscape. I thought about Dex and if he was OK. Jail. I couldn't believe it. I mean, the idea of Dex in jail wasn't all too surprising. He kind of seemed made for jail in some ways, but he was there on account of me. On account of my parents. On account of Maximus. The unfairness of it all boiled my blood and heated my face.

After Dex, Ada and I returned home from Idaho and the exorcism. all my fears came to a head right in my parents' front yard.

Dex was hauled off by the cops on suspicion of kidnapping, which was totally bunk considering both Ada and I had willingly gone with him. At first, my loving Dr. Freedman thought I wasn't in my right mind to give consent, so he convinced the police and my parents to take me to the hospital to get checked out. All I wanted to do was holler and fight and scream, but that probably would have only helped his case. I very reluctantly took Maximus's advice to just go along with it. But I didn't believe for a second that he'd have my back when he said he wouldn't let anything happen to me.

Well, I guess he did keep his word because nothing did happen to me, though I won't give him all the credit. The once-over at the hospital proved to everyone how coherent I was. Because, well, I was. The demons weren't haunting me anymore. Abby was long gone. I left them all with Roman in those dusted Idaho hills. I'd be lying if I said I felt a hundred percent better. But that had nothing to do with ghosts or my mental state. I was just extremely tired and felt…off. Like a lot of extra energy was pooling around in my bones with nowhere to go. Two very contradictory feelings at once and it was scrambling things a bit in my head.

Ada also helped me by ruthlessly sticking to her story: that I had been nutso because I was sick and had a terrible fever. In a panic, she called Dex because he would know what to do and he took us to a medicine man who applied a bunch of herbs and shit during a healing session and voila! The fever broke, I was cured. No more crazy Perry.

I could tell that no one really wanted to believe that story, but they had no choice. Like the truth would have made any more sense—the truth is what would have gotten me in trouble. At least with this version, an external and mildly believable circumstance brought on the psychosis. Plus, it was hard to argue with it when I was sitting there in the examining room, forming complete sentences, wholly lucid, acting like myself.

And Maximus, well, he didn't turn on me like I thought he would. He backed up Ada's story and even interjected some observations such as, "I knew there was something physically wrong with her. I just wasn't sure what, and hearing about Perry's history, I jumped to the wrong conclusion." A total lie, but one I appreciated. It didn't mean I didn't want to kick the ginger right in his freckled balls.

And so I left the hospital with a clean bill of health. Dr. Freedman seemed disappointed. It was like he wanted me to be sick. It didn't help that I caught him pulling my mother aside and telling her to watch me very carefully. I had a feeling that he didn't mean for today, or the next few days, or the next few weeks.

He meant for the rest of my life.

My thoughts drifted over to Pippa. My grandmother. It would take me a long time to come to terms with that, even though deep in my soul I knew we were related. Maybe in some ways, I always knew. Maybe I had seen her in my childhood. Maybe you could feel yourself in someone's blood.

It broke my heart to learn what my mother had done to her. Though I wasn't a parent, I still couldn't imagine what it would be like to have your daughter put you away, to condemn you to a horrible life, to a certain lonely death. It made waves of nausea simmer in my belly.

I looked over at my mom, keeping my actions subtle. She was still staring out the window and so I couldn't see her face. That was just as well. I didn't think I could ever look her in the eyes again, knowing everything that I knew now. I wasn't sure how I'd even survive in the house with her watching my every move for the rest of my life, waiting for me to screw up. I had no reason, really, to believe my mom would act the same way with me as she had with Pippa—my grandmother—but ...

My mother always acted as if she was scared of me. I now understood why, to watch the signs of "mental illness" creeping up in your daughter, knowing what might lie ahead. But now, everything had changed. She was afraid of me and I was afraid of her.

"Afraid of her?" Ada asked.

I jumped in my seat and turned to see everyone in the car looking at Ada, including my mother. I quickly averted my eyes from hers to Ada's questioning face.

"Did…I just say something out loud?" I asked, my heart tight. I hoped to God I wasn't babbling on about my mother. That *really* wouldn't have helped.

But while Ada said, "Yes," everyone else in the car said, "No."

Oh, great, now she was acting loony too.

She raised her brows at me and a flash of fear sparked in her eyes. I stared right back, willing her to not say anything else.

Finally, Maximus laughed awkwardly. "I reckon it's been a long day for everyone, myself included."

My mom smiled gratefully at him, then shot her daughters a suspicious look, and turned back in her seat.

No one said anything for the rest of the ride.

∽

A knock at my door roused me out of my dreamless sleep.

"Come in," I groaned, hoping it was someone I wanted to see, which nowadays meant Ada.

It was. She poked her blonde head in my room and squinted at the darkness.

"Sorry to wake you," she said as she came in and gently closed the door behind her. She flicked on the lights.

"Arrrrrgh," I moaned, throwing my arm over my eyes. "Thanks a lot. What time is it?"

"It's almost ten, lazybones," she said. I felt her come over and sit on the side of my bed.

"In the morning?"

"No, at night."

"Then why are you waking me up? Can't a girl sleep?" I mumbled. "I survived an exorcism, you know."

"That's what I came here to talk to you about," she said lowering her voice.

I took my arm off my face and blinked at her. She looked as serious as anything.

"OK, what is it?" I whispered. An exorcism was the last thing we wanted to get caught talking about. I was so paranoid now, and apparently so was she.

"I...I don't know what happened to you when you were... gone," she said. She looked very small and scared. "But it hurt. It was...so terrifying. I didn't know what I'd do without you."

"Oh, Ada," I told her, sitting up. "I'm fine. I came back."

"Did you?" she asked. "You seem different."

I bit my lip. "Well, I feel different. Not in a bad way, but I do. I don't know what Roman did to me."

"You went somewhere..."

I examined her face carefully. Had I talked to her about Pippa, about what I saw in the Thin Veil? I didn't think so. At least, I didn't remember.

"Somewhere?" I asked.

"I know about our grandmother," she said deliberately. "Pippa. I know what happened to her."

My eyes widened, the breath leaving me. "How...did I tell you?"

She smiled, lips tight and closed. "Sort of. I don't know what's going on Perry but...OK, this is going to sound really freaking weird but from time to time, I'm, like...hearing your thoughts."

That threw me for a loop. I almost laughed then I remembered her bizarre question in the car. But...that was impossible.

I looked at her even closer, wondering if she was fucking with me. Not that she would, but there was no explanation that I could grasp. What, I suddenly became telepathic? How come I couldn't hear anyone else's thoughts?

She watched me for a few beats and I asked, "All righty, if that's true, did you hear what I was thinking just now."

She shook her head.

How about now? I asked internally, projecting my thoughts onto her with all the concentration my poor brain could muster.

"Yeah, I heard that one," she exclaimed quietly, her smile broadening with wonder.

I matched her smile in wattage. This...I couldn't even begin to fathom *this* discovery. It was like waking up and finding out you had super powers.

"Oh my God, OK, how about now...OK wait," I said excitedly.

Is Maximus still in the house? I thought with power behind it.

Her expression was open, watching me.

"Well?" I asked.

"I didn't hear anything," she said.

I took in a deep breath and closed my eyes, my insides straining, like I was pushing through a massive headache.

Is the ginger still here? Or has he left? I asked.

I heard nothing so I opened my eyes to see Ada with her eyes closed.

"Still nothing?" I prodded her.

She opened her eyes. "No, I was trying to project my thoughts onto you. The assfart left right after you took your nap. He said he was going back home and he'd call you later."

"Oh freaking joy," I snarled. "Well, I can't hear you. Try again."

We tried back and forth for a while. Sometimes Ada heard me but only when it felt like I was busting a nut. Otherwise, it didn't work and I never heard her.

"Maybe it's a one-way street," I mulled it over. One-way street was better than no way, providing I had the choice of whether she heard it or not. I didn't want my sister to hear everything I thought, no matter how close we had become.

"Maybe," she said. "Do you think Pippa passed something on to you?"

I shook my head. "Wouldn't she have said something?"

"I don't know. Perry, I'm scared."

"About what?"

It was a stupid question.

She sighed and started picking at the blanket. "About everything she told you. How could mom do something like that to her? What if she does the same thing to you? To me?"

I grabbed Ada's hand and squeezed it. "You're going to be OK. You're the favorite here. You've never given mom any sign that you're about to go loco. Keep it like that."

"You never did either until you were my age." Her voice trembled.

"Ada," I said determinedly. "You have the advantage. You now know about everything. You know the stakes. Just keep being yourself and if you ever see anything that doesn't make sense to you, ignore it. Ignore it and talk to me. We'll keep it just between us. No one ever has to know or suspect anything."

"And what about you? You know mom is going to be watching you like a hawk. You don't see the way she looks at you when you're not looking. She has that same fucking look on her face as the doctor."

"She's still our mom," I told her. Though I thought the same thing, I felt strangely defensive. "We can't jump to conclusions and we can't start hating her. I mean, fuck, she *is* our mother. We have to believe she would never do that to us. She's not a monster. And if she wants to spend the rest of her life worrying about me...well...then she can do it from afar."

"What?"

I swallowed hard and looked around my familiar room. For the last few weeks it was a circus of horrors. Now it meant nothing to me at all.

"I've been thinking a lot lately," I told her honestly. "It's time for me to leave. To move out. I'm fucking nearing spinsterhood anyway, it's getting pretty sad that I'm still here."

"No...don't go," she pleaded with those round blue spheres. Her plea was weak though and I knew she was on board with the idea.

"If I stay here, I'll just get worse. How can I function being paranoid as hell at each turn? I couldn't. I can't live here, with her, worrying about the next time I fuck up. I might be fine now, but am I ever really all there, especially now that I'm, what, a bloody telepath? This shit isn't leaving me anytime soon and we both know it. I might not have a demon on my back but I can guarantee I'm not getting rid of my ghosts anytime soon."

She grew quiet and squeezed my hand back, her eyes dropping to the bed. We sat in silence for a minute, both in our own heads. She gave me no indication that I was in hers.

Finally she pointed out, "But you don't have a job. You don't have any money. How are you going to move out?"

I let out a deep breath. "I don't know. But I have to leave. And soon."

"You could move in with Maximus," she suggested innocently.

I shot her a dirty look. "Are you fucking kidding me?"

She threw up her hands in surrender. "OK, well before you bite my head off just hear me out."

I didn't want to but she continued on, "Look, we're both not a fan of his. I know I wouldn't mind shoving my curling iron up his ass and turning it to eleven. But aside from that, he did do you a favor today."

I opened my mouth to protest but she shushed me. "And I know it was a weak favor and that most of this is his fault and that he never had your back and yadda yadda yadda and OK, I really hate him too. But I wouldn't suggest going with him if I didn't think it would be better than you staying here. Move in with him, get a job and move out."

"No way," I said, crossing my arms. "Not happening. Not ever fucking happening. And also, who the hell says he'd want me crashing his stupid apartment?"

She gave me a wry smile. "Perry, it's pretty obvious he still has a hard-on for you."

"Oh Ada," I smacked her arm. "Don't say things like 'hard-on' it grosses me out to hear it from you."

"Fine," she said, taking her arm away from me. "I guess you do have one other option."

I had a queer tightening in my chest and could barely eke out the word, "What?"

She didn't say anything. She fished her phone out of her pocket and started to text something.

"Ada!" I cried out. "What is the other option?"

She put the phone down and smiled at me. She gestured to my window with her head.

"It's outside."

My legs felt like they were encased in cement. I stared at her, bewildered, my mind racing on about something I both did and did not want to think about.

"Go on," she said more urgently.

I slowly got off my bed and eased my way over to the window. My heart thumped hard against my chest and the blood filtered out of my head.

Outside, across the street, a black Highlander was running, its exhaust floating in the night.

"How the..." I said, barely find the words.

She got up and joined me by the window. "Maximus went to bail him out earlier. He's still a twat, of course, but at least Dex isn't jail anymore. It's not like the charges were going to stick anyway."

I took my eyes off of the sight of Dex's car, my heart awkwardly tumbling over itself at the thought of him outside, and looked at her incredulously.

"How did you know? Did you plan for this to happen?"

She grinned. "Remember that whole sometimes hearing your thoughts thing we were just trying out? I already knew you were thinking of making a run for it. Dex doesn't know, I just told him to come here right after Maximus got out. I have a feeling though, let's call it a hunch, that he's got a hard," she paused, catching my eyes flashing, "er, soft spot for you too."

I didn't know what to think about that. Looking out at Dex's car, and the answer she had given me, all I did know is that my life was – yet again - about to change in an incredibly messy way.

2

"Well?" prodded Ada as I stood at the window. "Go say hello."

"Where's mom and dad?" I asked, not taking my eyes off of the running vehicle, feeling like my chest was being torn in two different directions.

"I think dad's still downstairs watching Law & Order. I don't think he'd be too thrilled to see you going out the door right now."

I nodded. "The window it is."

I put my hands underneath the edge and pushed it open. A cold blast of late February wind coated me in seconds and I felt Ada jamming a retro Kyuss hoodie into my hands.

"Thanks," I mumbled and quickly slipped it on along with my Chucks. I was half-way out the window, ready to put my feet on the sloping roof below when Ada called out, "Hey do you think I can take over your room when you're gone?"

I shot her a look.

She shrugged. "What if I meet a guy and have to sneak out too? It's only fair you know."

I sighed and couldn't help but smile. "Sure."

"Awesome. Well, don't be too long…you never know if they'll want to check on you," she warned, heading toward my door.

I nodded and stepped onto the roof. I was lucky that it was such an easy escape route. When I was younger I used to sneak out all the time. In the past few weeks the route had been used twice; once when a demon had led me up there, the other when Dex came in through my window to rescue me. You know, the usual stuff.

Now he was back. And I wasn't sure if I was going to let him rescue me again. I wasn't sure what the hell I was going to do about anything. I had two options and neither looked very promising.

I made it to the tree at the end of the roof and shimmied clumsily down it, my body still a bit sore from the trauma of the last few weeks. The minute I felt the ground beneath my feet, a trembling started around my heart and radiated outward. I was nervous. I was damn nervous. I couldn't find the strength to walk away from the tree and onto the street.

It's just Dex, I told myself. *He's not worth having a panic attack over.*

And yet my lungs were constricting.

I knew it was just Dex but that was the problem. I didn't know which Dex I had or which Dex I wanted, if any of them. That's where the nerves came from. My uncertainty. Everything had changed. And changed again. One second I wanted to run into his arms and thank him for saving my life. Then in the next second I remembered what had happened between us. I remembered the pain, the darkness, the hell I went through. I knew it wasn't fair to blame him for demon possession but sometimes I found myself cursing him for it. If he hadn't left me like he did, had sex with me and just used me like some old dishcloth, I wouldn't have broken in half. I wouldn't have seeped open and left that space for something else to come in.

And the miscarriage. What, for one very brief time, had been a baby. That killed me in ways I never thought it would. I never thought much about kids and lord knows twenty-three is too young for me to be having them but…it really ripped at something deep inside, something I never thought I had. It was a weird sense of loss and something I couldn't even explain.

You'd think I'd be used to that, the unexplainable. But when it came to my feelings, when I couldn't figure out what they even were, that's when I was really scared. That's when my nerves would clamp up my throat, squeeze my lungs and make me feel that standing underneath a bare tree was the safest, smartest option for me. I wasn't in the house, I wasn't in his car. I was just me. In-between.

Eventually though, I found my footing. Some perverse need to choose. I walked out from under the broken canopy and made my way onto the street. There was the car up ahead, parked on the side of the road, facing the other direction, like he had driven past the house first, then turned around at the end. Funny to think that had happened while Ada and I were attempting to be telepathic inside my bedroom.

I stepped quietly, afraid my feet would echo down the street and be carried off by the breeze and into the house. I knew my parents would flip the fuck out if they knew what I was doing. I kept going.

I wasn't far from the car when the driver's door flung open. My insides whirled feverishly, my breath halting. In that moment I realized he still had that power over me, to make my body react when my mind wanted to turn away, and I hated him for it.

Dex stepped out, almost in a hurry. I hadn't realized I had stopped where I was and was just standing on the road, staring at him in a hiccup of time. I only had a few seconds to take him in, his black cargo jacket, his messy, wind-tossed hair and beautifully scruffy face, the flash of emotion in his dark eyes, buried under the furrow of his brow.

Then he was running toward me and for a moment I thought maybe something was wrong and that I should run too. Then I thought maybe something was right and I should run anyway.

He ran to me and engulfed me in his arms, holding me tight to him, raising me a few inches above the ground. I was caught so off-guard, I could only let him hold me. My breath was gone, squeezed out from the intensity of his hug. I didn't think I could hug him back even if I wanted to.

He held me like that, my feet dangling, his strong arms keeping me as close to him as possible. His face buried in my neck and his familiar smell draped over me like a comforting blanket while his breath tickled my skin until my hairs stood on end. I decided to ignore my brain for a second and just enjoyed the sense of being completely embraced.

"Perry," he mumbled, his lips grazing my throat while he spoke. "Perry..."

He never finished his sentence. Instead he eventually pulled his face away, my skin still feeling hot from his contact, and lowered me to the ground. He kept his hands on my arms, keeping me in place, as if he was afraid I'd run away. With his back to the streetlight, his face was encased in shadows but I could still see his eyes glinting. I couldn't read them except that they looked slightly feverish.

I cleared my throat. "Hi."

A quick smile flashed across his lips. "I'm sorry for just dropping by like this, I just had to see you. I was worried sick."

I smiled wryly. "*You* were worried sick about *me*? You got carted off to jail."

"You got carted off to the hospital," he said gruffly. I noticed then he was holding my hands in his and squeezing them. I eyed them with uncertainty and he let go, taking a step back from me as he did so, as if he was only just noticing he was intruding in my personal space.

"I got out," I said reassuringly. "And apparently so did you."

He glanced briefly over my head at my house then said to me, "Look, can we go in the car and talk? I promise not to keep you long."

I nodded and followed him back to the car, wondering what it was that he wanted, wondering how his shoulders got so much broader. I hopped in the passenger side and was met with a rush of warmth from the heater.

I don't know why things felt awkward between us when the last time I had seen him, he was holding onto me, promising that they'd never take me. Of course, that didn't work and I didn't fault him for that. But being apart again, even for just a few days, reminded me of how much had changed between us. And sitting in the dark car, only the familiar glow of the console lighting us up, there was a discomfort in my seat. I wondered if he felt the same.

I tried not to study his face but now that I could see it clearly, it was hard not to. There was a line of worry on his forehead and his brown eyes were searching my face, alternating between washes of sorrow and apprehension. He never lost that unnerving way he looked at me – that would always be Dex. I just hoped he wouldn't look too deep. I felt the walls around me going up slowly, brick by pasted brick.

Finally, I looked away and studied the dashboard as if it were suddenly fascinating.

"I'm surprised the car is still holding up," I remarked, remembering how it had crashed into a tree only days before, bashing the front side and the headlight. It almost hurt to remember when I was wrapped in duct tape, with a terrible darkness inside me trying to get out.

"I'll get it fixed when I go back home."

"When are you going?" I asked, keeping my voice light, still avoiding his eyes.

I felt him pause, growing tense for a second, and I quickly added, "Not that I'm trying to get you to leave."

His smile was tight. "Tomorrow, probably. I just...wanted to see how you were doing. You look better."

"Do I?" I looked down. "I thought I looked slimmer in the duct tape."

Again, that pained smile. "How are you feeling?"

I shrugged. "I'm tired. Sore, still."

He nodded absently, his thoughts elsewhere. I wanted to tell him what Ada and I had discovered but for some reason I couldn't find the words. It was ludicrous but Dex was always the one to believe me when no one else would.

I opened my mouth to give it a shot, but he beat me to it and said, "Listen..."

He looked down at his hands and cleared his throat. The atmosphere in the car changed dramatically from the strange awkwardness to full-on jangled nerves. I watched him closely. He did in fact look really nervous, biting his lip, blinking fast and at nothing.

"What?" I asked.

I could hear his breathing intensify.

"You need to get out of that house."

I shouldn't have been surprised to find out we were on the same page, but I was. I tried to hide it by eyeing him uncertainly.

"What do you mean?"

He lowered his eyes and voice. "You know what I mean. Perry, you can't stay there anymore. After everything that's happened...it's not safe."

"The demon is gone."

"Your parents aren't. And frankly, my dear, I wouldn't be surprised if some other supernatural hitchhiker came and found a ride through you. You're too weak-"

I glared at him. "I am not weak."

He looked at me steadily. "You're the strongest woman I have ever known. Ever. But it, *they*, found a way in. I can't risk that happening again. And like hell I'm going to let you stay in a house where your parents are jonesing to put you away like some animal."

"I wasn't aware you had control over my life."

He sighed and leaned in closer. "I know you're still angry-"

"Huh!" I exclaimed, folding my arms. But he quickly went on.

"But putting that aside for a moment," he continued, "you know you can't stay there. I know you know it. I know your sister knows it. Your grandmother sure knows it. We all do."

"Well what do you suggest I do then?" I asked carefully.

He bit his lip, a gesture I used to find adorable. Now, it didn't do anything for me. Not much, anyway. He let his eyes roam out along the empty street. Either he was deep in thought or biding his time.

Finally, he asked, "Did you like Seattle?"

I sucked in my breath. He wasn't asking me what I thought he was asking me…was he?

His eyes were guarded in the dark but I could read sincerity on his expressive forehead, like part of him was taking a chance that the other part didn't dare take.

"What?"

There he went, biting his lip again. He ran a hand through his thick hair, giving the ends a bit of a tug. I remembered tugging at that hair, vividly.

"I mean," he ventured, looking at me with a hint of anxiety, "I think you should come live with me. In my apartment. In Seattle."

Now, I know it was just what Ada and I had been discussing but I was not prepared to hear the offer come from his own mouth. Dex was asking me to move in with him? What the hell kind of sorcery was this?

He quickly continued, "I don't mean like you have to be my permanent roommate or anything. Just until you get on your feet. It can be a place for you to stay in the interim. Or longer, you know, if you wanted to."

I looked away from him, my eyes widening, heartrate speeding up. This was all kinds of right and wrong. Especially wrong. So much wrong.

"Perry?"

I shook my head and struggled for words. "I don't know what to say."

"Saying yes would be a start."

"I need to think about this…"

"Please, don't think long." His voice had dropped

another register and was laced with a kind of urgency that made my skin feel tight.

He reached over and grabbed my hand and I let him. I looked down at it, at his long, strong fingers wrapping around mine, feeling like his hand was different in some way. But that was crazy. It wasn't. He was still cocky, self-assured Dex...asking me something I never, ever dreamed possible.

I knew my choices but I didn't have to like them. If I went with Dex, I knew I'd be safe. But would my heart? How could I ever trust him again? How could I think that living with him, even as his roommate, even for a short while, wouldn't be emotionally damaging in some way? After everything that had happened to me, I was sick of my heart being stomped on and would do whatever I could to prevent that situation from happening again.

But then there was Maximus. He was less messy for my emotional well-being. But let's face it, it's not like there was nothing between us. I had sex with the man. Several times. And no, I wasn't really in my right mind when I did it, but it still happened. It still made things awkward. It still put another well-hung elephant in the room. Not to mention that I didn't really trust Maximus. Sure he bailed out Dex, but that only made me question *why?* At times he seemed to be my greatest supporter yet he could rat me out to my parents in a heartbeat. I just didn't know where I stood – with either of them.

Dex squeezed my hand hard, bringing me back to earth.

"Don't you dare move in with Maximus," he warned, his eyes shining dangerously.

"What?" I exclaimed. Could he hear me thinking? "Why did you say that?"

"Because that's your only other option, unless you have a million bucks hidden in your barista tip-jar."

"I could go with Rebecca," I told him, not knowing if that would work either.

He shook his head. "She and Em are having some problems. Otherwise I'd suggest it."

I narrowed my eyes thoughtfully. "Would you really?"

He sighed and let go of my hand. "Look, I know things are kind of awkward right now."

I scoffed.

"OK, fine, really fucking awkward. I know that. And I know we have a lot to talk about-"

"We have nothing to talk about," I shot in.

His nostrils flared and he was trying hard to compose himself. "Fine. I guess we have nothing to talk about either. But for one second can you just accept the fact that despite what has happened between us, I still care about you. More than you'd probably want me to care about you. And that I'm going to do everything in my power to make sure you're going to be OK. I know I failed many times before…but you just have to believe me when I tell you I'm going to do everything I can now to make things right."

I studied him carefully, trying to ignore the sincerity in his words. He was buzzing with a sort of energy that I associated with our sexual encounters. I didn't know what it was, there was nothing really sexual about what he was saying or the way he was acting toward me. But it was there all the same. It was a buzzing, vibrant aura that represented sex and power and something else I couldn't put my finger on.

"There's something different about you," I said, squinting at him.

If he seemed annoyed at my avoidance of the topic, he didn't show it.

"There's something different about you," he replied. "But you're a woman and you change every five minutes."

I frowned. "Is that it?"

He returned the look. "I don't know, is it?"

I threw my hands up and went to go open the door.

"Wait," he cried out softly, putting his hand on my arm. "Please, please don't go like this."

"Like what?"

"Like not making a decision," he explained. "Can't you see the urgency?"

"Dex, you're asking me to move in with you. You. You of all people in this world."

He looked away, tugging at his hair again.

"I'm sorry," I went on, "I know it's urgent. I can feel that too. But this choice for me might end up being just as dangerous as staying here with my parents. I'm sorry."

Dex continued to look away but I saw the wince. I saw the strange cloud of despair over his eyes. I took in a deep breath, steadying my nerves, and opened the car door. Outside, the street was quiet and cold and my feet echoed loudly when they hit the ground.

"I'll let you know, OK?" I told him. He wouldn't even look at me.

I shut the door and walked away feeling like I had shut a window on a lifeline I was going to need desperately. Every step away from the Highlander felt like I was walking knee-deep through mud. And the closer I got to my house, all cheerily lit up against the darkness, the more I felt like I was heading into a dark hole. My pride was soaring inevitably high but as much as I enjoyed saying no to Dex, I knew it would crash-land later in a smoldering wreckage.

I stopped near the driveway and looked up at my bedroom window. It was hard to believe how close I had been to losing my life, to losing my very soul. If it hadn't been for Dex...I wouldn't have been burdened with the choice I currently had.

I exhaled, wiggled my fingers anxiously, then turned and jogged back to the Highlander that was still waiting at the roadside.

I rapped on the glass and Dex quickly undid the window.

"Hey," I said uneasily, peering into the car. "I was wondering if you could stop by here before you leave tomorrow."

He nodded coolly. "OK. What for?"

I could see the walls going up around him as well. They sure weren't there before.

I smiled shyly. "I don't want to be alone when I tell my parents I'm moving to Seattle."

There was a pause as he took it all in.

Then his grin filled the whole car.

3

Even though it was late by the time Dex left, I was on such an adrenaline high that I couldn't get to sleep even if I tried. And I did try. But after lying there for an hour, my mind going over everything that was suddenly *happening*, I threw off the covers and started packing up my room.

I knew I wasn't able to take everything I had with me to Seattle. I'd probably need a moving van for that. And who knew what was going to happen to my poor little Put-Put. I guess one day I was going to have to come back and get the motorbike but I knew that day wouldn't be a fun one. I really felt like if I left with Dex, I wasn't going to be allowed back in the house for an awful long time.

And that was another reason why I had to be sure I was making the right decision. I still wasn't 100% about it either, but the more I started gathering my clothes into an empty suitcase and piling shoes and purses and books together, I knew it didn't have to be forever. The important thing was I was getting away from my parents' prying eyes and though it was a long time coming, it was better late than never. And who knew, maybe within a week I'd luck out with a new job and be set to move out on my own. Maybe I'd find a house to share with a couple of young people. A whole new world of possibilities awaited me.

It still had me scared shitless though. When I finally fell asleep in the middle of the night it was only for a few hours and then I was up with the dawn, anxious and raring to go. I hadn't felt so cagey since I was teen coming down from a long and ill-advised coke session.

By the time Ada came knocking on my door, I had packed up as much stuff as I could into my suitcase and some boxes I quietly snuck out of the garage.

"Holy crap," she said from the doorway and I grabbed her skinny arm before she could say any more, pulling her inside, and closed the door behind her.

I shushed her, then said, "I don't want mom and dad to know yet. Not until Dex gets here."

Ada gave me a smile that was half-sad, half-proud. "You made your choice?"

I nodded. "It's not the best choice but it's really the only one I have."

She kept that smile pasted on her face and sat down on the bed with a sigh. "So you're really going?"

"Unless you can give me a reason not to..." I said and took a seat beside her.

She scooched closer to me, beanpole legs sticking out from plaid boxers. "I'm going to miss you."

I felt a pinch of emptiness in my chest at that. I put my arm around her and lay my head on her shoulder. I tried really hard not to cry but I'd be lying if I said a few tears hadn't leaked out.

"I'm going to miss you too," I told her. Then I pulled

away and put on my brave face. "But you're going to do great without me."

"I know but...oh my God, are you crying?" she admonished but I could see her eyes were glistening too.

"No." I sniffed and hit her lightly on the arm. "And neither are you."

I looked around the room. It looked strange with half the stuff packed away. It felt right though. Even the right things can be scary.

"What did Dex say?" she asked.

"Actually he asked if I'd move in with him."

Ada beamed. "That's my boy."

I laughed and gave her a funny look. "Your boy? I have to be honest; I'm not used to Little Fifteen being on Team Dex. I'm not even sure if I like it."

"Get used to it," she said. "He saved my sister. I owe him a lot. Hey, did you know Little Fifteen is actually a Depeche Mode song?"

"I'm surprised you know who Depeche Mode are," I said wryly.

"I know, I always thought it was a type of dessert. Anyway, I think he's coming around. Just give him time."

I bristled. "I don't have to give him anything. Not time, not friendship, not anything. This is just a temporary arrangement. Once I find a job, I'm out of there."

"And what, you'll never speak to him again? Yeah right."

I shrugged and looked down at my ratty nail polish job. "Things are too messed up right now. I know he saved my life. I know he nearly gave up his own for mine. I know that. But...it doesn't make the feelings go away. The hurt. What he did. I just can't trust him. I don't know if I even want to bother trusting him. What's the point? Why do I need him in my life anyway?"

She stared at me with her big eyes like I was some odd creature at the zoo, something she'd never seen before and wasn't sure what I was.

"What?" I snapped.

"You need him in your life to get out of your current one, Perry," she said softly. "Let's just start with that, m'kay?"

She gave me a quick pat on the shoulder and got up. "I better get ready for school. Don't you dare leave before I'm back or I'll be super pissed."

I told her I wouldn't dream of it, but then again, I had no idea what was in store. Dex was coming by at 2pm, that's the only thing I could count on.

She left the room and I set about getting ready myself and putting most of the boxes and suitcase in the closet and under the bed, just in case my parents decided to pop in. Now came the hardest part: waiting until the afternoon, pretending like my life wasn't about to undergo a humungous change that could potentially damage the already fragile relationship I had with my parents.

I thought about avoiding them for most of the day. And I tried, I really did, but around lunchtime my stomach was rumbling and I knew I'd have to eat or fall flat on my face. My panic attacks always worsened when I had low blood sugar.

My mom was in the kitchen puttering around as usual, putting things away that had already been put away, tidying dishcloths that were already hanging pin straight. She looked up at me in surprise, wringing her hands together.

"Oh, you're up! I didn't know if we should wake you or not," she said. Her voice sounded taut, forced.

I took a seat at the stool beside the island, the soles of my shoes bouncing on the rungs. "I've been up for a while."

"Oh. Can I get you something? I just made lunch for your father before he left."

"Sure, if you managed to save something for me," I said under my breath. She didn't seem to notice my tone and quickly pulled out a small portion of pasta from the fridge, popping it in the microwave.

"It's only a little bit," she said and couldn't help but let her eyes drift to my chest and arms. I knew what she was thinking, that I could afford to eat less. But instead of letting myself get enraged over it like I normally would have, I turned my thoughts off and looked out the window at the dreary day. If my weird telepathic thing was real and was magnified by my emotional state, I didn't want her to find out. Not yet, when I was so close to leaving.

"Such a bad winter," my mother said, following my absent gaze. We hadn't even seen much snow this year, so I didn't even know what she was talking about. I guess my mother had relegated herself to making small talk with me. It was better than, "so a medicine man helped cure your fever, huh?"

I made a grunt that didn't mean anything and at the microwave's loud beep, she bustled over to it and put the steaming bowl of marinara in front of me.

"Thanks," I said, poking at it with my fork.

"Eat slowly." She smiled cheerily and I wondered if she had recently gotten her teeth whitened. "It takes up to twenty-minutes for your brain to know it's full. That way you'll eat much less."

I put fake gratitude in my eyes and was about to take a deliberately slow bite when the doorbell rang. I jumped in my seat and the pasta almost went flying off the fork.

My mother didn't seem too concerned about the door and went out into the hall. I was praying it wasn't Dex. It was too early and I wasn't ready yet. Oh, I was nowhere near ready for this.

I sat rigidly, waiting to hear who it was, the air held in my lungs.

The sound of the door closing was followed by two pairs of footsteps coming down the hall.

A tall, red head poked around the doorway and smiled at me.

"Good afternoon, little lady," Maximus said. He leaned against the doorframe and folded his arms. Like usual, he was wearing plaid, purple this time, and was giving off an air of comfort which annoyed me. It was like he belonged in my house or something.

Ex-house, I reminded myself. *Ex-house or so help me God.*

Mom scuttled past him, her cheeks flush as if his company made her all girlish or something. "Come on in Max. Are you hungry? I could make you something?"

I pretended that didn't bother me and kept my eyes on Maximus like he was going to shapeshift if I looked the other way. I couldn't believe that it wasn't long ago that we were standing in the kitchen, doing a cleansing ritual. I couldn't believe I had been naked in his shower, getting off on his big fingers, having him come in my mouth. That didn't seem like me.

It wasn't me.

Was it?

"I'm fine, Mrs. Palomino. But thank you," he drawled. God damn stupid accent.

She clapped her hands together lightly. "All right then. I'll leave you two to it."

She left the kitchen. I wished he would have gone with her so I could have breathed a bit easier, but instead he sauntered his giant frame over to me and pulled out the stool.

"How are you?" he asked. It was innocent enough but I couldn't help but give him attitude.

"How do you think I am?"

His eyes drifted down to my chest. I tried to not look down. That was the last time I wore a tank top around the house. His eyes came up to mine before it became awkward. "You're looking mighty fine."

I wasn't buying it. "Why are you here?"

He rubbed at his broad chin, still grinning. "I'm here to see how you're doing."

Was he? I couldn't help but think back to the car the other day when it seemed like he could hear my thoughts. Did I want to try it out on him now? He definitely wasn't a normal man, I knew that much. But just how different was he? Was he really a ghost-sensitive type like Dex and I were, or was he something else? And was it only certain types of people that could potentially hear my thoughts, or was it everyone?

I decided it wasn't safe. I had a hard enough time trusting anyone already.

Though the expression on his face was gentle and somewhat cheeky, I could pick up a vibe of something else. Beneath the laissez faire façade, he was studying me.

I cleared my throat, suddenly feeling on the spot, and pushed my bowl of pasta toward him. "Do you want this? I lost my appetite."

"You sure?"

I nodded and looked back at the window, the grey sky my failsafe.

I saw him start to eat out of the corner of my eye, happy that the mouthfuls were keeping his giant mouth occupied.

I decided to take the nice route out of all of this.

"Thanks for bailing Dex out of jail."

He made an amused sound as he slurped up a noodle. "No problem."

"Did you do it because you like the guy or did you do it for me?"

I realized right then I was being a tad presumptuous with his feelings toward me but I pushed through it and looked him straight on.

He eyed his next bite of pasta like it was a question. "Well, I guess you could reckon I did both. Dex didn't deserve to be in jail. And I knew you'd be distraught without him."

"I wouldn't go that far," I said automatically.

His eyes narrowed into brief green slivers. "Interesting."

"What?"

"I thought you would have gotten over your little problems by now."

I leaned away from him. "Little problems? Need I remind you what those little problems did to me? Fuck, you men are all the same."

"I'm just saying," he said slowly, "that you seemed to have gotten over them when you were with me. That's all."

"I wasn't me. I was possessed."

He turned back to his pasta. "Darling, if you want to tell yourself that..."

Without meaning to, I punched him hard on his arm and the fork and pasta were finally set free across the kitchen, clattering to a stop on the floor.

He sighed and put his head in his hands.

"Sorry," he said, even though I was the one who should have apologized. "I shouldn't have...I should have known it wasn't you."

I breathed out in a huff and got off the stool. I threw the fork into the sink with a clatter and fished out a new one from the cutlery drawer.

"I'm sorry," I said, handing him the new fork. "You don't even know me. It's not your fault."

He gave me a sheepish look between his parted fingers. "You have to understand that when a gorgeous gal is throwing herself at you, it's really hard to say no. I knew you weren't quite yourself. I just reckoned it was a revenge thing...not a possessed thing."

I allowed myself a small smile. "It was both. Sometimes I think you can't separate the two."

"I know what you mean," he admitted. He held out his hand. "Friends?"

I hesitated, then shook it quickly. To his credit, he didn't try to hang on any longer than he needed to.

"So," I began. "You've checked up on me and eaten my lunch. Anything else you need?"

He grinned. "You're not getting rid of me that easily. I promised your mother I'd spend some time with you."

My face wrinkled with disgust, the feeling spreading through my veins. "Why? I don't need a babysitter."

He twirled pasta around his fork, watching the turns. "I know. But it makes your mother feel better."

"So?"

"So...so I can tell her you're doing great. And then she can relax and maybe not watch you 24/7, worrying that you're not well."

My hands suddenly felt cold.

"Is she really worried?"

"You have no idea," he said, then took a pointed mouthful.

I rubbed at my arms. He eyed me.

"Are you feeling chilly?"

I ignored him. The clock on the wall read twenty to one. What were the chances of getting Maximus to leave before Dex showed up? What were the chances I'd be able to keep the whole thing a secret with him staring me down like some test subject?

I started to loathe myself for getting involved with Maximus in the first place. I should have known better than to get with the guy who was always showing up at the most opportunistic times, including right now.

"Well," I said, pushing away from the counter, "you'll have to amuse yourself for the next while."

He cocked a brow.

"I've got womanly stuff to attend to," I finished.

He nodded, perhaps buying it. Or at least getting that I didn't want him anywhere near me.

"I'll be right here, little lady," he said, the hope inside me deflating like the tomato he speared with his fork.

I quickly ran up the stairs before he had the chance to say anything else.

I saw the Highlander out on the street, a black metal beast waiting in the low fog, and booked it down the stairs before Dex could ring the doorbell. The last hour had been the longest of my life and the stored up energy insured I got to the door in seconds flat.

I opened it to see Dex coming up the stairs. He looked different in the daylight, his nose a bit swollen and tinged with a purple bruise that had spread to his eye. It had been courtesy of my father and I only then realized how brave he was for coming back to the scene of the crime.

If he was nervous in any way, he didn't show it and his confidence gave some strength to my fluttering heart. His eyes were brown and clear, brow set in a determined fashion. He was wearing his black cargo jacket, hands thrust deep in his pockets and collar turned up against the cold. The newsboy cap perched on his head gave him an air of unique distinction though his face remained scruffy with a day's old stubble.

He didn't say anything but as usual with us, he didn't need to. His look said it all: *Are you ready?*

I nodded grimly and opened the door a bit wider, my heart thumping wildly in my chest. He walked past me into the foyer and I pretended the smell of his skin and shampoo didn't cause butterflies in my stomach.

"Perry?" I heard Maximus say from the living room.

I stood my ground and Dex stood beside me. His hands remained in his pockets though I was scared enough that I wished they were holding me instead.

Maximus appeared a few moments later, staring at us from down the hall. He didn't look surprised at all, if anything he just looked disappointed and maybe embarrassed.

He strode down to us and I could feel Dex stiffening up beside me. That strange energy I sensed in the car was back and it was doing funny things to the hairs on the back of my neck.

To his credit, Maximus stopped a few feet away and wiggled his lips in thought.

"Well, I figured this would have happened," he remarked casually. Everything was always so laid back with him, wasn't it?

"Because you know everything," Dex countered.

Maximus looked behind him for a second and lowered

his voice. "Look, I knew Perry was itching to get out of this joint."

"How did you know that?" I whispered, my voice sounding hoarse.

He chuckled. "Why else would Dex dare show his face here after what happened?" He gave Dex a pointed look. "You do realize that this can't end well."

Dex took a step toward him and looked him dead in the eye, brimming with intensity. "I realize that. That's why we're getting out of here. Perry's better off in Seattle than she is here. Even if she did move in with you, you're still too close to...this place."

Maximus rubbed at his jaw and for once looked a bit put-out. He looked up at the ceiling and the spaces around our heads without really looking at us. "If you would just give me some more time with them, they'll back off."

Dex and I exchanged a glance out of the corner of our eyes.

"Are you talking to us?" I asked Maximus.

"Max, who is it?" my mother's voice rang out.

"Fuck," I swore under my breath. I think a part of me thought I could get moved out of there without anyone noticing and I could just leave them a note or something. It felt an awful like I was running away from home and, you know what, I was OK with that.

"Perry, what-" she said then stopped dead as she saw Dex. Her face went from impassive Swede to full-on IKEA rage. "What the hell is he doing here?"

Impulsively, I grabbed Dex's arm and said, "Mom, we need to tell you something."

"We?" she questioned, her voice turning up into an ugly sneer. She marched toward us and suddenly I was afraid of her throwing a punch at him. I had deliberately picked 2pm knowing that my dad wouldn't be back from his classes until at least 4pm but maybe my mom had always been an equal threat in the abuse department.

"Mrs. Palomino, it's all right," Maximus said, putting his arm out to catch her. She shrugged away from his grasp and continued until she was straight up in Dex's face.

"You get the fuck out of this house and stay the hell away from my daughter."

My jaw nearly plummeted to the ground. I had almost never heard my mother swear before and on top of that, she was acting like she actually gave a shit about me.

Dex managed a small smile and without faltering said, "I'm afraid that's impossible Mrs. Palomino. I'm here for your daughter. I'm going to be doing the opposite of staying away from her. She's moving in with me. She's coming to Seattle."

My mom cackled like a witch, her face fighting between belief and disbelief. "You really think I would believe that?"

She looked at me with incredulous eyes. "Why is he here, Perry? Did you invite him?"

I looked at Dex who was keeping his eye on my mom and then I turned to Maximus. He gave me a sympathetic smile and I knew I had no choice but to bite the bullet.

I met her blue-eyed gaze with what little reserves of strength I had left. "Dex is telling the truth. I...I don't think I should live here anymore. I think it's time for me to move out."

She blinked at me a few times, her brain trying to fight the sincerity she heard in my voice. "But...pumpkin. That's OK. We can work through this. Just don't move in with him."

"I can't wait. There is nothing to work out. I need...I want to get out of here. Now. I'm going with him. I love you but it's time for me to go."

Her face fell into quiet lines. A flash of bitterness swept across her brow.

"You don't know anything about love," she said in a low voice, her accent heavy.

I hadn't prepared for that remark. That stung. That felt like a blow to the chest and a kick to the guts and I tried oh so hard to not let that all show up on my face. There were so many things I could launch into if I had the chance, but this wasn't that argument.

"I'm sorry," I said, trying to keep my voice steady. I noticed Dex had inched closer to me until his hard arm was flush against my shoulder. "I've made my choice."

I tried to brush past her and go for the stairs but to my utter surprise, she pushed at my collarbones until I stumbled back a foot or two.

I felt Dex's hands grab my arms and hold me with a vice-like grip while my mother came up to me, her once pretty face now boiling red with anger, her eyes sparking like a defensive animal.

"You'd choose to go with him over your own family?" she sneered. "You'd give us all up over a man? A good for nothing man who left you pregnant and on your own with only your family to look after you!"

Earlier, I had started to think that Dex was breaking some new record for not lashing out but that was gone in an instant.

He pulled the back of me closer to his chest and shot over my head, "Hey, for your information, ABBA, I had no fucking clue that she was pregnant and if I had, I can assure you things would have been a hell of a lot different."

"Right," my mother muttered, shaking her head in disgust.

"Exactly fucking right," Dex yelled. "And don't you dare

start throwing this love shit into this mix because if you actually knew a damn thing about that, your daughter wouldn't literally be dying to get out of your house of horrors. That should say something about your fucked up righteousness, the fact that she is moving in with the good for nothing man who left her, instead of rotting here with you!"

"Whoa now," Maximus interjected, raising his hands in a sign of peace. "Let's all calm down here."

"Fuck you, ginger balls," Dex sniped and pulled me toward the stairs. I let him lead me up them and usher me into my room. He shut the door, clapped his hands together and said, "Well that went well! Let's say we get your shit out of here before your dad comes home and I have to take both of them on."

I could only stand on the spot and look around me like a dumb cow. The fear and hurt and words and everything was swarming over me like a tidal wave and my brain was struggling to process what had just happened.

Next thing I knew, Dex was crouching in front of me and holding my shoulders, his eyes searching mine and just inches away.

"Focus, Perry. We have to get out of here while we can. It's only going to get worse."

Tears threatened my eyes as I fought for the words. "I...I can't leave like this."

He shook me slightly. "You have to. You have to now, right now, because this is the only time you are ever going to get the upper hand."

"But my mom doesn't think I love her," I whimpered.

"Well, my mom never loved me, so we all have our demons. But yours, yours have the potential to get much worse if you stay here a second longer. When people are angry, they do strange things, and I feel like this whole situation is more than personal to your mother. You hear me, kiddo?"

I nodded, my mind dwelling a bit on what relationship Dex must have had with his mother while he flung open my closet and let out a satisfied sigh when he saw my suitcase. "All right, this is a start. But this can't be all of it. I know you...you must have a caravan out back full of ugly concert tees or something."

I was about to tell him I had some boxes underneath the bed when the door opened and Maximus stepped in.

"Am I interrupting something?" he asked, shutting the door behind him.

"My God, you just can't keep away can you?" Dex mumbled, tossing the heavy suitcase onto the bed like it was a magazine.

Huh.

"Perry," Maximus said, looking to me with imploring green eyes, "you can't leave like this now. Your mother is downstairs crying her eyes out."

Gee, that was just what I needed to hear.

"You know what," I said, crossing my arms, pretending I wasn't crumbling inside, "I don't really give a flying fuck what you have to say. You should be happy that you get to take over my room when I'm gone, though you may have to fight Ada for it."

"So you're that eager to go that you're not even going to stick around to say goodbye to your sister?"

"Are you trying to make me feel guilty?" I came at him with my finger poised, ready for eye-gouging.

He didn't back off. "I'm just trying to bring you the truth. I'm trying to help you. Both of you."

He eyed Dex who was watching him like a big cat ready

to pounce. He turned back to me. "But I can't help you if you won't listen to reason. You're both hopeless. And, I'm sorry, right now you're acting a bit crazy."

The minute that word left Maximus's mouth, I knew there would be hell to pay. *I* didn't appreciate being called crazy. Dex hated it.

Dex was on him in a second, the cat finally pouncing. He grabbed Maximus around his throat and lifted him up, throwing his back against the wall, causing the window panes to rattle. I heard my mom utter a cry from somewhere downstairs.

"The only crazy person here," Dex growled as he brought his face right up to Maximus's, "is you, if you can't see the bigger picture. Go on sucking the Palomino family dick if it makes you feel better. I'll feel better knowing Perry is safe."

While Dex was spurting these things into Maximus's reddening face, my eyes drifted down to the floor. The room spun around me as I clued in to what I was seeing. Dex was actually holding him up around his neck with one hand. Maximus's toes were dangling several inches above the ground and considering the height and weight difference between David and Goliath, that feat was nearly impossible.

"Uh, Dex," I said softly.

He pried his eyes off of Maximus and followed my gaze. A wave of shock rolled over him when he realized what he was doing. He let go and Maximus's feet landed with a loud thump.

"Oh, sorry," he said, clearly flustered. He went over to the suitcase, pretending to be busy, but from the tense way he held his back, I could see he was bothered.

Maximus was rubbing at his throat lightly, faint pink

fingermarks running across it. He didn't seem upset but he was watching Dex and thinking hard about something.

"Where's the rest of your stuff?" Dex asked and I told him to look under the bed, my eyes never leaving Maximus's pensive face.

"Not used to being beat up on, are you?" I asked him carefully, wanting to talk about it. But maybe I was just overreacting. Dex was on an adrenaline high and your body can do some pretty freaky stuff.

Maximus slowly brought his face toward mine and smiled. "I don't know, I reckon you did a pretty good job." He tapped the spot on his face where I'd scratched him mid-sex, back when I was all demonic. He knew exactly what buttons to push with us and he was pushing the same ones again.

If Dex wasn't tense before, he was now. I was ready for him to flip around and go after Maximus again, but he didn't bite. He just kept his mouth shut and picked up the first box. He turned around and I could see the temper swirling around in his eyes, the killer grip on the box's edge. He gave Maximus a forced smile that looked completely menacing.

"Please move," he said, gesturing to the way he was blocking the door. "I'd like to get out of here before I break your nose."

"I'd like to see you do it," Maximus answered, not moving.

"Oh, come on," I chided them. "You can measure penises after I move out."

"You don't think I can do it?" Dex continued, ignoring me.

"I know you can do it. I just want to see it."

"I've done it before."

"I want to see you do it...now," Maximus replied. I didn't

like the squirrely way he sounded, like he was attempting to do Dex a favor or something.

"Dex," I said loudly. He and Maximus were locked in some internal showdown, brown eyes against green, short against tall, caveman against caveman.

"Dex!"

With great reluctance, he broke the staring contest and looked my way.

"Please. Let's go."

He nodded and readjusted his hold on the box.

I glared at Maximus. "And you, please get out of the way. I, personally, have no problems with breaking your nose."

Maximus sighed and moved over, opening the door for us. Dex pushed past him and Maximus whispered in a voice so low, I could barely pick it out. "You watch yourself."

Dex didn't even pay attention. I quickly scooped up a box of books and went after him.

The minute I hit the top of the stairs, I could hear my mom on the phone, crying to my dad. I knew if we didn't act fast, we'd be majorly hooped. For all I knew, he could be calling the cops and making up a whole bunch of shit to get Dex in trouble again.

Our footfalls were quick and silent and when we reached the ground floor, he gave me a steady look, making sure I wasn't about to run into the kitchen where my mom was and plead insanity. I swallowed hard, as tempted as I was to totally cave in, and together we scampered over to the car and started piling the stuff in the trunk.

"I'm going to go get the rest," he told me, putting his hand on my arm. "Will you be OK here?"

I nodded, though I knew I was on the verge of crying or panicking or something.

He gave me one last deep look and when he was satisfied

that I was going to be OK, he patted me lightly on the shoulder. "I'll be back."

I whimpered something and leaned against the car, the trunk door open. It was hard to believe that in a few moments it would contain most of my life.

It didn't feel right to leave this way. I wanted nothing more than to go back inside and plead with my mother and try to get her to understand. I wasn't doing any of this to hurt her, I was doing this so that she wouldn't hurt me. But what did it matter in the end. In the end I would be seen as the villain and nothing else. They were so damn ignorant they'd never ever see the truth, even if it was crying in front of their face.

But then there was my dad, who I knew had a smidge more respect for me than mom had. I knew he'd be absolutely livid and confused as to why his daughter would leave in such a harried, disrespectful manner.

And Ada...she was on the inside but the way things were going, we'd be safe and gone before she returned from school. Sometimes it was hard to believe she was in high school and lately I'd been relying on her more and more. Maybe as sisters we had a backward relationship, but it was one that worked and one that I would miss dearly. I owed it to Ada to stick around. But if there was anyone who would understand, it would be her.

Even though she'd be pissed.

Dex was back in an instant, hauling the luggage behind him with one hand and carrying three heavy boxes with the other.

I raised a brow. "So, have you traded in cigarettes for steroids, or what?"

He threw the suitcase in the back, not caring at all if I

had valuables in there and plunked the boxes down. "Oh you know, chicks dig men with muscles."

I narrowed my eyes at him. "Another Dex Foray mystery?"

He wiped his hands and gave me a charming smile. "Will you ever run out?"

"I guess not," I replied absently. I looked at the house like I'd never see it again. It might as well be true. Maximus came to the doorway with his arm around my mother who was sobbing into her sleeve. I'd always imagined the day I'd leave home, but I've got to say it never looked like this.

I cleared my throat and stood up tall as Dex slammed the back shut.

"I'll call you when I get to Seattle," I told them. My mom wasn't looking at me, so I unfortunately had to say it to Maximus.

He nodded solemnly and gave my mother a squeeze, like he was playing the part in a play. It left a film of bad taste in my mouth but I could only ignore it and turn around. I took the slow steps toward the front door, conflicted by the need to get the hell out of there while I could and the need to stay behind and tell my mother that everything was going to be OK.

If it wasn't for the energy I felt from Dex on the other side of the car, the reality, the reason for leaving, I wouldn't have been able to do it. But I pushed through and went by on that instinctive need to protect myself.

I got in the car, shut the door, and we roared off down that fog-shrouded road I grew up on.

4

The drive to Seattle was as pensive as the grey, low clouds that flew past the windows as we made our way up the I-5. In a few areas there were patches of snow that piqued my interest, but most of the time I just sat as close to the door as possible, as if it was my only escape route.

I watched the scenery with forced attention, a distraction from reality, until reality bit me in the form of Ada. Her texts came through in a frantic succession and though I knew she understood deep down, I could imagine how hurt she was that I left without saying goodbye. Then the phone calls from my parents came and I quickly turned off my phone before they had a chance to really get to me. I needed to know I was making the right choice and in that car, packed to the brim with my belongings, with my life, I still didn't know.

We were just outside of Olympia when Dex asked, "Can we talk about it?"

I had this cold feeling, like someone deposited a chunk

of ice in my gut. I didn't want to clarify what he meant, but my mouth was faster than my heart.

"Talk about what?"

A heady silence filled the car, heavy like a sandbag. I picked at my nails and waited. I knew this wasn't going to be some random question. Wasn't there a theory about the size of a pause after someone asks you a question or a favor? The greater the pause, the greater the favor. Maybe that was all Jerry Seinfeld.

He sighed softly and steadied his grip on the wheel.

"I don't even know where to start."

"Well if there's more than one thing, I'd rather we didn't talk about it," I mumbled, watching the pavement roll past. Lord knows I had a million things I wanted to ask him: How come you look better after everything I'd gone through? Why did I have to suffer after you left me, and you're looking and acting like a modern day Adonis? When am I going to stop being mad at you?

He tugged the front of his cap down, so that his eyes were covered in shadow.

The pause amplified. If anticipation was a breathing, living thing, it would have popped out the windows and made a run for it.

He kept his gaze locked on the cars in front of us and said in a low voice, "Why didn't you tell me you were pregnant?"

I had a feeling that was the question. Ever since my mom brought it up earlier, pointed like a spear, I knew Dex had been stuck on it.

But I still wasn't ready for it.

I took in a deep breath. "I didn't know until it was too late."

"Perry..."

"It's true," I said angrily.

He bit his lip, keeping his eyes hidden. "Would you have told me anyway?"

I shook my head. "No."

"That's not fair-"

"That's not fair?!" I exploded. He winced and tightened his grip on the wheel. "Don't you dare tell me what's not fair! Do you think I wanted to be fucking pregnant! If I had found out earlier, I would have gotten rid of it. I would have gotten rid of anything that had something to do with you!"

Dex lifted his head up, like I had just slapped him in the face. His eyes prickled with clarity. He was stunned.

I felt bad but it didn't stop me from continuing, my feelings rumbling out like an overdue avalanche. "You ended things. You fucked up and you ruined me and I owe you nothing! You have no right to know what was going on in my life. You have no business in it. You have nothing!"

"I had a right," he protested, words gravely and barely above a whisper.

"You had no -"

"That was my baby too!" he yelled, his body shaking with the force. He yelled it with such acute pain and intensity that I jumped in my seat. I shut my mouth, feeling stupid and embarrassed and very small.

A few moments passed as his words sank into the atmosphere, making the air even heavier than before. I squirmed, wondering if I had made a huge mistake by going with him. Apparently I wasn't the only one who was mad about things, but I still felt I was the only one who had a reason.

I could feel his head turn toward me, watching me.

"You're not the only one with a reason to be mad, Perry," he said, struggling to keep his voice calm.

I shivered and eyed him incredulously. "What?"

"Nevermind," he said with a shake of his head. "It doesn't matter anymore."

It did matter and it would matter for a long time. But that wasn't the issue now.

"Did you just hear me thinking that?" I asked. I watched him carefully, searching for a lie.

He frowned. "What does that mean?"

"I was just thinking that. Did you read my thoughts?"

"I knew what you were thinking, if that's what you're getting at."

He looked a little confused but didn't add anything else to it. He relaxed a bit in his shoulders and I decided not to press it. Things were already weird and strained without going down this road. If he couldn't read my thoughts, then I didn't want to bring it to his attention.

I wanted to keep everything to myself.

SEATTLE WELCOMED me with lashings of bone-chilling rain and heavy grey arms. It did little to comfort me and the moment I saw his Parisian-style apartment building just beside the monorail, I felt even colder.

In a surreal state, we parked the car in the underground garage and I pretended the last time I was there, I wasn't picking up my shattered heart and jumping on my bike for a snowy escape. We went up the elevator with my suitcase and the first of the boxes, and when we got to his front door, I pretended I hadn't slammed it in his face, telling him I quit the show. And when we walked into the apartment, I looked away from the kitchen island, pretending that it wasn't there where we had made love.

We hadn't made love, anyway. We had made hate.

And now I had to live in it.

"Well," Dex said, clearing his throat. "Let's show you to your new room."

I followed him toward the den where I had slept in last. It was a mess, with the bed missing all its linen and shoved into the corner. His desk was piled with papers and heavy books. I wondered if he still kept his pills in that hollowed out novel.

He rubbed anxiously at his forehead. "Obviously I wasn't planning for you to come here. Sorry, I'll clean it up. Things have been a mess since Jenn left. She was the neat one."

And a bitch, I couldn't help but think. Not that it was fair to think that way anymore. She had been cheating on Dex, but Dex cheated on her with me and that wasn't cool either. I wasn't innocent in all of this and it tugged at my conscience from time to time. She was still a bitch, though, and Dex was better off without her. That was a fact.

"Don't worry about it," I told him, putting the boxes down on the chair. "And don't worry about getting the rest of the stuff. I think I need to be alone for a while."

He looked surprised. "Are you sure? It'll just take a second. I've got spare linen in the closet, I think. Or I'm sure I can borrow some from Rebecca when I go to pick up Fat Rabbit."

"It's fine." I turned away from him and choked back the tears that were just sneaking up on me. It was too much. Being here. Leaving home. Having no future to count on. Even though I wasn't alone, I felt more alone than ever.

"Perry," he whispered behind me. I felt him come closer to me, his energy radiating at my back. My skin prickled and I fought the urge to turn around and bury my head in his chest and cry until there was nothing left. I knew he would hold me for as long as I needed. I knew his touch would put my fears away.

But that fact was scary in itself.

I shook my head and looked up at the lights, blinking hard.

He placed his hand on my shoulder and my nerves instantly calmed, like they were coated with wine. I closed my eyes and a warm tear ran slowly down my cheek.

"Perry," he said again, softer. His fingers tightened. "Baby, please."

That word was like a nail into my chest. My reaction was instinctive.

I whirled around at him, my eyes aflame and throwing as much venom as possible.

"You don't get to call me that anymore," I spat at him. "I am not that to you. I never was."

He took a step back, a wash of fright in his eyes. Maybe it was hurt. I didn't know. I didn't care.

"I'm sorry," he said, sucking back his breath. And for what, it didn't matter.

"Get out," I said, trying to steady my voice. "Please. Go."

He hesitated, then nodded and went for the door.

"I'll go and get Fat Rabbit in a bit," he told me, pausing in the doorway. I could feel the tension in his body, his muscles unsure whether to move or not. I felt just as torn. As much as I wanted to be alone, I still wanted him to be there too. I just wanted things to go back to the way it was. When he could touch me and it didn't feel wrong. When I could like the things he said or the way he looked without hating myself for it.

I don't know if my face betrayed any of that. But his head

dropped slightly and his eyes softened with sincerity. "If you need me, you'll know where I am. The room next door."

And with that he left, closing the door behind him.

I stood there for at least a few minutes, an empty feeling spreading inside of me. Then I collapsed into the bed with silent tears that led to sleep.

WHEN I WOKE UP, my eyes were sticking together with dried and clumpy mascara and there was a snuffling sound outside the door. A light spilled in from underneath it, a shadow moving back and forth.

I frowned, momentarily forgetting where I was, and pressed at my forehead, trying to rub out the exhaustion and sleepiness that resided there. I was utterly exhausted from crying myself to sleep, from everything that happened earlier. But it was the good kind of exhausted, where your eyes are puffy and your heart is hard and you don't feel anything anymore because you've already felt it too much. You're spent. Somehow, mercifully, you just don't care. Tears and a nap can be the best therapy.

I sat up slowly and took in a deep breath. I needed to hold it together. If I kept dwelling on things, I'd never get out of bed. I made the choice to come to Seattle. I made the choice to leave home. And, I made the original choice to leave Dex back in December. Those had all been in my control and I needed to own those choices.

I listened for signs of Dex outside and heard faint music and cupboards closing in the kitchen. The snuffling outside the door continued. For once, I wasn't concerned that some ghost or supernatural being was outside. This was no demon. This was Fat Rabbit. And that dog's face was a sure pick-me-up.

I reached for the door in the darkness and pulled it open to see the pudgy French bulldog's face turned up at me in a sloppy, tongue-hanging out smile. He came in the room along with the light from the apartment, and immediately started jumping up on my legs and giving me doggy kisses.

"Hey fatty," I heard Dex call out from the kitchen in a sing-song voice.

I poked my head out and looked at him. I had to blink twice to get my sight right. Dex was dancing in front of the stove to Depeche Mode's "Personal Jesus", a too-tiny apron wrapped around him, looking utterly ridiculous as he ground pepper into a steaming pot. The minute he saw me, he froze, pepper mill in mid-grind, then calmly turned down the volume on the music player.

I tried to stifle my amusement. "Were you talking to me?"

He gave me a wry look and went back to grinding. "No. Naturally Fat Rabbit's name is just Fatty now. Fatty Rab, if I'm being more formal."

"Naturally," I mused, looking down at the adoring dog who *was* looking a bit plumper. He obviously wasn't on the same diet as Dex.

I walked tentatively toward him, peering at his apron.

"Kiss the cook," I read it out loud. "Classic."

He looked down at himself and grinned. "It's more of a suggestion than a command."

"That's insinuating you can cook," I told him as I looked into the pot.

"It's mac and cheese with cut up hotdogs," he said, wagging his eyebrow. "Another classic."

"Huh," I said and sat down at the barstool. "Is that your dinner?"

"This is *our* dinner, kiddo," he said, flicking a pinch of salt into the pot and grabbing for a bottle of hot sauce. "I know you're used to gourmet grub every night, but at Chez Derry, this is what you get."

I raised my brow at the presumptuous "Chez Derry" comment but ignored it. "So, tell me, is this what you've been feeding yourself because judging from the way your chest is trying to break free of your apron, I'd say you're used to eating raw eggs and power shakes."

There was a hint of satisfaction as he smiled, as if he was waiting for me to comment on his newly buff body. I looked away, wishing I hadn't brought it up. Still, I was far too curious and his shirt was far too tight.

"I mean," I continued, studying the lines on the counter, pretending my ass hadn't once been rammed up against it in a fit of passion, "what the hell have you been doing?"

He took a hard swallow and averted his eyes to the food. "Shall we eat first?"

I raised my chin. "Seriously, Dex. You never did explain any of this."

He sighed and plopped the wooden spoon back in the pot, flicking off the burner. He leaned with his hands on the counter and looked me straight on.

"When you left," he started, pausing to lick his lips, "I wasn't in the best of circumstances. That's sort of putting it mildly. To top it off, I hated myself for what I did to you. I mean, I really fucking loathed myself. Do you know what it's like, to really loathe yourself? So that you can't even look in the mirror?"

I kept my face impassive, but I knew exactly what he meant.

"And, after some time," he continued, "I decided I didn't want to be that person anymore. That person never got me anything but a fuckload of pain and did the same for a lot of other people. So I started with what was easiest first – my health. I started going to the gym. I started running. I quit smoking, re-did my whole diet...for the most part, anyway. I'll never give up Mr. Daniels or the occasional mac, cheese and hotdog night."

I sat there in silence, watching his face carefully. His eyes were darker than normal, and there was a grim twist to his mouth.

He lowered his head. "I was trying to be a better man, Perry. For you."

I shifted in my seat. "Dex..."

"And I'll keep trying," he quickly said, voice low and somber. "Until I get it right."

Oh God, it felt like my heart was shrinking. I tightened my hands into fists and quickly loosened them.

"Please don't try," I told him, even though saying those words made my stomach roll. "That's in the past. It's over. It's done."

He rubbed the heel of his palm against his chest. "But it's not over. It's not done. I can see it in your eyes."

I let out a deep breath, nausea prickling at my core, and started focusing on my cuticles. He came around the counter and stood right beside me. I felt warm and heavy at the same time and fought with myself to stay strong.

"It's not over until you forgive me," he said, voice low and rough, causing the hair on the back of my neck to stiffen. "I know you need time..."

I avoided the eyes that were boring into the side of my head. "I don't need time. I do...I do forgive you."

Suddenly both his hands were on the sides of my face, a

hot and firm grip. He brought my face towards his and forced me to look at him.

His eyes roamed deeply in mine, searching every crevice. "No you don't. You say it, but you don't mean it. I want you to mean it. I *need* you to mean it."

Is that why I'm here? I thought. *Is that why you asked me to move in with you? To win me over?*

But I couldn't say it. My mouth opened and closed and I was just so lost in his eyes, trapped in his hold.

"You're losing your touch at lying, Perry," he said.

Then he kissed me. The shock of his parted lips on mine rendered me helpless for a moment. The only thing I could do was kiss him back, because my brain wasn't working and that's what my body wanted. That's what my body always wanted. Him.

He let out a low moan that was more felt than heard and one of his hands disappeared into the back of my hair, pressing me closer to him. He tasted like I remembered and the memory caused my legs to part, my muscles to go slack. Shivers passed over the small of my back. I wanted to run my fingers over his arms and chest, feel how hard he was, then go south and feel him even harder. Even though, just kissing him, feeling his tongue against mine, made me crave him like a junkie craved their next high.

And I was terrified of coming down.

I pulled back, maybe too hard. Dex flinched, but dropped his hands away from my face. He was so still, so close and breathing hard, his eyes glistening and pupils larger than life.

"I'm sorry," I said, having difficulty forming the words. "This isn't...this..."

He nodded and straightened up. "No, I'm sorry. You're right...this isn't..."

He couldn't finish the sentence either. It wasn't wrong and it wasn't right either. God, we were fucked up.

I gave him a small smile and smoothed down my hair. "If we're going to be roommates for the next while, we should probably avoid doing...*that*. You know, make some house rules."

He breathed sharply out of his nose but I saw the acceptance in his face.

"Sort of like, you do the dishes on certain days, I do laundry on others, no smoking, no kissing, no sex?"

I felt my ears burn. "Yeah. Something like that."

"That doesn't sound like a lot of fun."

I shot him a killer look and he showed me his palms.

"Kidding," he said. He cleared his throat and went back around to the stove. "So, hungry now?"

Actually, I wasn't. All I could think about was how cold and empty my mouth felt without him there and food wouldn't cut it. But I told him I was famished and we soon settled down on the couch to eat and watch mindless television. He sat in the middle, and I shrank up in the corner with the vague fear that if I touched him, I'd be straddling him in seconds.

I turned in early with bedding he had found. After texting back and forth with Ada, failing to ignore the huge mess I left behind, I was left in the dark room with only my thoughts.

Somehow, despite the fact that I had just left home for the first time, that I just hurt every member of my family, and that I had no clue what the hell I was doing, I could only think of Dex. Sleeping in the next room. Alone.

My insides swirled as I replayed the kiss in my mind. Moving out wasn't a mistake. But moving in with Dex might have been. I didn't know how long I could go with someone like him around me all the time. Scratch that, not someone *like* him. Him, period. No matter what happened, he was Dex and I was Perry and that combination only led to trouble.

With a sleepy head, I started plotting out my next plan: get a job, fast, and move out, even faster.

5

"Shut your piehole, Fatty Rab!" Dex bellowed from the bathroom where I could hear his electric razor running.

There had just been a knock at the door, which got the mutt all excited and yappy, even though it was just Rebecca coming by to take me out for lunch.

"I'll get it," I told Dex, and wiped my hands on my jeans. I was a tiny bit nervous about seeing Rebecca again. The last time I had seen her, I wasn't very cordial. She had come to Portland to try and convince me to give Dex another chance and I pretty much told her to fuck off. I cringed a bit, remembering my behavior. Perhaps I was already not in the right frame of mind at the time.

I took a quick breath and opened the door. Rebecca looked immaculate as always, dressed in a red shift dress under a grey tweed, funnel-necked coat, with spiderweb tights and platform booties. Her hair was still a shiny, raven bob and her face was bare except for red lipstick. Next to me in my ponytail, mutt-slobbered jeans and black-and-white striped sweater, she looked positively Hollywood.

She gently pushed away Fat Rabbit who was attempting to claw up her tights, and with a wide smile, embraced me in a hug. Whatever nerves I felt quickly dissolved.

She pulled away and held me in place, eyes warm and shining.

"I'm so sorry to be last minute. I know you only got here last night and I was texting you like a twit, forgetting that I don't have your new number."

"Yeah, thanks for phoning me at 7:00 AM," Dex yelled from the bathroom. "It wasn't like I planned on sleeping or anything."

She rolled her eyes and then gave one quick last hug.

"So, how are you settling in here?" she asked.

I looked at the stack of boxes right beside us that still hadn't made their way into the den.

"Well, I'm not quite there yet."

She smiled sympathetically, taking note of my eyes that I knew were still puffy from yesterday. "You'll get there. This must be all so overwhelming for you."

I raised my brows wryly and lowered my voice. "You don't even know."

She patted my arm gently and yelled past me. "Hey, Dex, I'm going to be taking her out now. Will you be here later?"

"I'm taking the car to the shop," he said and I felt a pang of guilt in my chest from the memory of trying to take his car off the road, the horror of the crash. I know it wasn't me doing the actions, but still.

"But you can just give Perry your spare keys," he continued and he stepped out of the bathroom. "They belong to her now anyway."

I tried to not let my jaw hit the ground as he walked toward us. He had shaven, so he was less beardy and more stubbly, which showed off the strong lines of his jaw, the twinkle in his brown eyes. But that wasn't what had me in lustful awe.

With only a white towel wrapped around his waist, Dex was looking...unbelievable. While he always had a nice and rather firm body, now he was definitely packing some serious muscle. His chest was hard and sculpted and I wouldn't have recognized it had the words *And with madness comes the light* not been tattooed across it. Now, it was a lethal combination.

Below his chest, there was a genuine six-pack, precise squares etched on his tight stomach and his hips had those lines of perpendicular muscles leading in a V down into his towel. For a second, I was caught up in a whirl of desire and I mentally kicked myself for instigating a no kissing, no sex house rule.

"Oh, Dex," Rebecca chided from beside me, bringing me back to reality. "Put your shirt back on. Are you trying to turn me straight or something?"

He grinned cheekily, dimples cutting in, and I then noticed he had his eyebrow ring back on. That, his smile, and his tattoo were the only things that reminded me that this was still Dex and he couldn't be trusted. Especially now, especially with that body.

I was starting to be distracted by the round girth of his shoulders and upper arms, when I felt Rebecca tug at my arm.

"Come on, let's let this show pony get back to his grooming," she said. I let her lead me away to the door, walking backward.

Dex smiled at me, a smile I was unable to return, and he turned around to head back into the bathroom. I caught a glimpse of his smooth, wide back and something else. A new tattoo, words written across the back of his left shoulder. Before I had a chance to read it properly, he was gone.

"He got a new tattoo," I commented to no one in particular as Rebecca pushed the dog away and opened the door.

She nodded. "Come on, we want to hit Icon before it gets too busy."

I snatched up my purse and jacket and we left the apartment, Dex's tattoo on my mind. I couldn't even imagine what it could have said.

It turned out that the Icon restaurant was just down the street from the apartment, which was super handy, considering it was my new home, something I needed to keep reminding myself of. It was a weird feeling. The walk also gave me time to pepper Rebecca with questions. Surely, she knew this was coming.

"Thank you for taking me out for lunch," I told her.

"No worries."

"When did Dex get that tattoo?"

She smiled quickly to herself before answering. "A couple of weeks ago. I went with him."

"What does it say?"

This time her smile was for me. "You'll have to ask him that, Perry. It's fairly personal to him."

Personal? This was going to drive me nuts. What on earth could be personal to Dex?

The restaurant was a popular place for lunch thanks to an extensive unique menu and a detailed décor of pink walls, candy-shaped glass objects, marble-cracked tables and a million lamps. I was so tempted to launch into a discussion about Dex but I did that the last time Rebecca took me out for lunch. So I feigned ignorance and asked her how she and Emily were doing.

She pressed her lips together and looked down at her tea. "Not too well, actually."

"I'm sorry."

She nodded then raised her chin. "Thank you. It's fine. It's just a rough patch. We all get those."

"I suppose so," I mused, trying to remember the last time I was in a relationship. The whole thing with Mason in college was one giant rough patch.

"Em is just younger and that's always been our problem. She's…hard to keep down. Not that I demand anything of her." She sighed and smoothed her hair back behind her ears. "But you know, I love her. I would like to make this official."

"Official, like marriage? Can you get married in Washington State?"

"There are legal unions here, like you have in Oregon. But I want the real deal. We'd just go up to British Columbia and make a honeymoon out of it at the same time. Well, that's what I proposed."

"You proposed?" I tried to picture Rebecca on one knee in her designer goods.

She let out a little laugh even though I could hear the pain in it. "No, I guess I'm not very romantic. I think I just blurted out, 'hey let's get married in Canada" and that's when all the problems really started. I scared her. And to be honest, she scared me. I thought we were more serious than that."

I fiddled with my napkin. "It's just a bump in the road. You guys seem meant to be together. You'll pull through."

She took a slow sip of her tea, her lipstick leaving neat prints.

"As will you," she replied knowingly.

"Me?"

"Yes. You. Moving here and everything. This can't be easy, especially after what happened to you. Dex told me a few things this morning, about going to Idaho...I was there when Ada called him, you know. He nearly collapsed on the street. I'd never seen him look so worried."

He wasn't worried enough, I thought angrily, the rage sneaking up on me and making my head feel hot.

She went on, "You don't have to tell me, but I'd like to hear what happened. The whole story. I'll believe you."

And from the earnest expression on her brow, I knew she would. I took in a deep breath and told her the entire story of my possession, starting with when I saw her in Portland and ending with Dex being tossed into jail.

It was no surprise then that by the end, Rebecca was speechless and I was breathless. The waitress delivered the artisan pizza we were sharing and Rebecca stared at it dumbly.

"So...wow...Perry, I don't know what to say." She delicately shook her head as if that would move some sense into it.

"You don't have to say anything. But that's how I ended up here, with Dex."

"I can't believe you survived all that...I'm just amazed."

I examined my pizza, ignoring a pinch near my heart.

"I'm just so sorry...I'm so sorry."

I looked up at her. "Why are you sorry?"

She shrugged. "I don't know. I saw you. I should have helped. I should have done something."

"How could you have known? I was fine at the time."

"Were you really? You were pregnant Perry. With Dex's child."

I felt like I just got a cold punch to the gut. My hand involuntarily rubbed at my stomach.

"I'm sorry," she said again.

"Quit saying you're sorry," I snapped. "I'm fine. It's over and done with."

"Does he know?"

I licked my lips, unsure of what to say. "Yes. He knows. He found out, though, from Ada. And not in the best way."

"How is he taking it?" she asked in a hush, her delicate face crunched in concern.

I flinched. "He? I don't know. Ask him about it."

"You haven't talked about it?"

I put my pizza down and gave her a steady look. "Rebecca, I don't know which way is up. One minute Dex breaks my heart, the next I have a miscarriage. Then I'm fucking possessed and being dragged to a shaman to exorcise the demon. During that time, I go to another freaking dimension with my dead grandmother, where Dex shows up and saves my ass. We're spit out, he's arrested and I realize that moving in with him is my only option of staying safe and sane in this world. And so far, I don't think it's doing my sanity any good. Have we talked about it? Sort of. He seems strangely upset. But I just…I can't deal with anything right now, let alone that. I just want to eat my pizza without adding tears as an extra topping. OK?"

"OK," she agreed and began nibbling at a slice. We ate in silence and I tried hard to concentrate on the wonderful goat cheese in the pizza. I failed.

"Oh and I'm telepathic now," I spoke up between chews. "People can hear my thoughts."

She didn't miss a beat. "Anything else?"

"Don't tell me you can hear what I'm thinking."

She shook her head and smiled. "No, I can't. I just don't think you can surprise me anymore, Perry Palomino."

I took in a deep breath. "Can you recommend a gynecologist? I'd like to get an IUD put in."

She coughed on her food and quickly gulped down some water. "All right, that was surprising. What brought that up?"

I shrugged. "Considering I have no desire to get pregnant again, I think it's the smart thing to do. I never did well on birth control pills anyway."

"Makes sense," she said slowly, her eyes glinting suspiciously. "You're not thinking of, er, shagging anyone in particular, are you?"

I frowned for a second before my slow brain caught on. "What? You mean Dex?"

She bit her lip, trying to suppress a smile. "Don't get so defensive."

"How could you think that after everything I just told you?"

"Look, darling, we all have our rough patches. I told you, you'd pull through."

"With life," I said adamantly. "Not with Dex."

"Dex is part of your life, whether you like it or not. You had the chance to cut him out."

"I did cut him out! I cut everyone out!"

"And yet here you are, having lunch with me, down the street from your new roommate."

My muscles tensed along my back. "That's not fair. I had no choice."

"You always have a choice. Besides, I almost had to wipe up the pile of drool you left on the floor earlier."

Oh God. Was I that obvious?

"He's looking good Perry. And I think he'd be good for you."

"You're singing a different tune now," I said thinking back to our last lunch together.

"You're different people now. He's changed. Quite a bit. And so have you. Maybe the new you will give him a second chance."

"The new me will give him nothing," I retorted, pushing the rest of my food away. "I owe him nothing."

She snorted and a subtle flash of malice crossed over her eyes. It made me sink a little inside.

"He only risked his own life to save yours, he only brought you back here so you could be safe, and live free of charge," she said in a flinty voice.

I didn't want to back down. "Well too little, too late. Where was he then when I was dying inside? Huh? You came and saw me. Where was he? Where was he when I needed him?"

She exhaled slowly through her nose and leaned back in her chair, folding the napkin in her lap. "He was scared. And he was in no position to be anywhere, let alone trying to win you back. He wouldn't have survived that."

"Bullshit."

"It's true, Perry. He's not this strong, invincible asshole that you think he is. He has issues."

"We all have issues."

"And sometimes those issues hold us back. You practically threw me out of your house. What would you have done to him?"

"Much worse."

"Exactly. Of course he knew that. Should he have tried anyway? Maybe. But at least he did try and when you needed him the most."

"I needed him when my heart was breaking," I cried softly, jabbing a finger at my chest.

"But maybe you needed to put those pieces back together by yourself."

She reached over and grabbed my hand.

"Look, I'm not here to argue with you. I know you're angry and you're hurt and confused and a whole mess of shite. But that funny man is one of my best friends. You're not the only one who is hurt and angry and confused. I just want you both to be happy. And if you think you can shag your way there, I am not judging. It might be good for you."

I rolled my eyes as my heart rate began to calm down. "If I remember correctly, it was sex with Dex that started this whole mess to begin with."

Her eyes narrowed thoughtfully and I swallowed hard, ready for the rebuttal I knew I deserved. But she didn't say that. She didn't bring up my lie. Instead she said, "Life has a funny way of drawing a circle. Well, I do happen to have a good gynecologist. I can't give you advice on IUD's or pills or anything like that, another bonus of being a lesbian, but I'm sure I could get you in right away."

After our rather volatile lunch was over, I thanked her profusely, feeling bad for once again turning the conversation onto myself. She didn't mind at all, saying she needed the distraction and that my problems looked a lot easier to solve than her own.

Obviously I didn't agree.

She ended up walking me back to the apartment. Outside the lobby, she placed the spare keys in my hand.

"These are yours now," she said, closing my hand over them. "Try and hold onto them for a while. Give this a chance."

"Being his roommate?"

"Being his everything."

Well, that was never going to happen. I glanced around

me at the cold, grey street. "I was thinking of getting a job, like, now. And moving out as soon as I got that."

"I know."

I frowned. "So you can hear my thoughts?"

"No, you twit. You're just very easy to read sometimes."

She gave me a quick hug, said goodbye and walked elegantly back to her car. I hoped she and Em would work things out. She deserved to be happy.

As for me, well, I thought I deserved to happy too. I just didn't know what that meant.

I looked up at the apartment building, steadied myself, and stepped inside.

6

When I walked into the apartment, Fat Rabbit came bounding toward me on chubby little legs and I could hear Dex in his bedroom talking on the phone to someone. It reminded me that I needed to face the music and call my parents at some point. I'd rather get teeth pulled.

I decided to make myself busy and settle in, in case I ended up staying here for a little while. Deep down, I did appreciate what Dex was doing for me, even if this was a way to ease his guilty conscience. But I didn't trust my increasingly raging hormones and the way they clouded my logic from time to time. I knew moving out would help immensely with salvaging whatever was left of our relationship. Staying would only complicate it.

Still, I lifted the boxes into my den and started unpacking things and tidying up the place so it was less like Dex's messy office and more like Perry temporary hidey hole.

While I was doing so, I kept hearing snippets of Dex's conversation. He sounded passionately engaged with someone and as his voice kept rising, I kept easing myself closer and closer to my open door, hoping to hear more and not get caught while I was at it. Eavesdropping wasn't cool, but hey, it's what roommates do.

"Jimmy, forget it. She's not doing it!" he yelled, voice muffled by his door.

If they could, my ears would have perked up. I stepped out into the hall, trying to hear better. Jimmy? Were they talking about me?

I held my breath and strained my head.

"No, I told you," Dex growled on the other side. "You get me, you don't get her. No. She's not going through that again. The whole Riverside deal almost killed her. Get someone else on the show, I don't really care. But I'm not putting Perry in danger again. And there's no way she'd want to do it anyway. She quit, remember. And she still hates my guts. I'm just waiting for her to chop my head off in my sleep." Pause. "Yeah, or my balls. She probably would go for those first."

My mouth dropped open. That kind of hurt, even though it was partly true.

"I know you need the money. Just get someone else, that's all. No, she won't do it for more money. She can't be bought like that."

That did it. I straightened up and knocked rapidly on his door.

"Oh fuck," I heard him say. "Listen, can you hold for a second."

The door opened and Dex poked his head out, smiling nervously when he saw my determined face on the other side.

"Hi roomie," he said with forced cheer. "How was lunch?"

Into the Hollow

"Why are you talking to Jimmy about me?"

His smile fell. "You heard all that?"

"Yeah, it's easy when you're eavesdropping," I said unapologetically.

He rubbed at his chin. "I think we're going to have to add a no eavesdropping clause to the house rules. We might have to take out the no sex thing though."

"Dex," I cried out and pushed his door open. Thank God he was fully clothed in grey t-shirt and black jeans, otherwise I wouldn't have protested so loudly.

He backed away from me, clutching the phone to his chest. "What?"

"Gimme the phone," I commanded, holding out my hand.

His head dropped solemnly. "I am on a very important call."

"Yes, about me," I said, reaching for it. "Now give it."

He shrank away and eyed the room anxiously. "Damn, I knew I should have kept a spare roll of duct tape somewhere."

I could hear Jimmy squawking on the other line.

Dex sighed and put the phone to his ear. "Sorry, sir, a rabid animal burst into my room. No, she's not taking questions right now."

With a final attempt, I lunged at him, but not to take the phone outright. Judging from the taut tendons on his forearms, I would have lost that battle.

Instead I played dirty and a hunch. I went for the sides of his stomach and tickled him.

"Holy shit!" he yelped, staggering backward and dropping the phone. I kept my fingers going until he was pinned against his wall. I should have picked up the phone but the feeling of his rigid stomach and soft, thin shirt underneath my hands was addicting. So was the fact that I was making him double over from unwanted laughter.

"Stop it!" he tried to plead during giggles. "You evil genius!"

I reluctantly stopped, our bodies up against each other, breathing and smiling hard. He raised his head, face pink and eyes pinched and I backed off before I started up again. I quickly snatched up the phone from the carpet.

"Hi, is this Jimmy?" I asked into it, keeping my eyes on Dex. He made a move to come forward but I wiggled my fingers as a threat. He frowned but stayed put.

"Well, well, well," came Jimmy Kwan's voice through the line. "Perry Palomino. You know, you have to learn how to write a better resignation letter than just, fuck you Dex, I quit. Though, I've heard that one quite a bit."

I smiled despite myself. "Well, he didn't leave me much choice."

Dex quickly looked up at the ceiling then made his way over to his bed, plunking down on it in defeat.

"I understand. I was just talking to Dex about bringing you back on the show, if you were interested, and he was quite adamant that you wouldn't be interested. He's quite concerned for your safety."

Dex was watching me as curiously as I was watching him. For once, he wasn't going to push me into anymore compromising situations. That was quite the change.

"What else did he say?"

"That was about it. You know, the show ended the moment you left. He thinks I can just pair him up with someone else but to be honest Perry, people watched that show because of your dynamic. Your ghost hunting skills are terrible."

Yeah, that's because they're the ones hunting us, I thought.

"Did the show really do well enough to warrant running again?"

"You'd be surprised. Anyway, the point is, I want to add you back to the lineup. He says no. What do you say?"

I wasn't really sure what I thought about that. Dex was right in that I shouldn't be putting myself in those situations again. I couldn't bear the idea of being frightened to death on camera, especially if it had anything to do with ghosts and demons. But a job was a job. And a job would get me out of Dex's apartment…even if it only put me back into his work.

"I heard him say something about money. Would you pay me more?" I asked, keeping my voice hard.

He sighed. "Yes, I'd pay both of you more. I was going to anyway, before you up and left."

Dex's face looked pained so I turned away and looked out the sliding door to the balcony. The Monorail roared past, making the walls shudder.

"I'm not particularly fond of ghosts right now. Or being on camera. But I need a job."

"I can give you a job. Your job back. You wouldn't have to deal with ghosts right away if you don't want. I was discussing a particular phenomenon with Dex. It's…well, it's ridiculous and nothing more than an urban legend, but I still think it's worth checking out."

"What is it?"

"Have you heard of Sasquatch?"

I burst out laughing, clutching the phone before I dropped it.

"Bigfoot?" I cried out when I could.

I looked incredulously at Dex who shrugged, a giant smirk on his face.

"Wait, wait, wait," I said to Jimmy, struggling to compose myself. "You want us to go Bigfoot hunting?"

"Sasquatch. He's different."

"He's still Harry and the Hendersons. Don't tell me you believe this?"

"Of course I don't," Jimmy sniped, sounding tired. "But this is very in right now. There's a llama outfitters up in BC, in the Rockies, and they've been dealing with something that sounds a lot like Sasquatch. Plus, you've seen the television shows about it. There's even an erotic novel about sex with Bigfoot, self-published of course."

"Ah, well if Bigfoot erotica is catching on, we better get to it," I joked, shaking my head.

"You and Dex will go up to the mountains, spending a few days there chasing around some llamas and maybe you'll get footage of a bear or something. I don't know. But it's something and I want it to happen. And it's a job. And, last time I looked, Bigfoot wasn't a ghost."

"Sasquatch," I corrected him with a sigh. "Look, I'll have to think about it. I don't think I could even keep a straight face if I was on camera."

"So don't be on camera," he said. "Put Dex on camera. You do the filming."

My heart slowed and I raised my brows at Dex who was leaning on his thighs and tapping his foot. He probably had no idea of what was just suggested.

"Um, what?"

"Dex is a better editor than he is a cameraman. Sometimes, anyway. Point and shoot. Film him. Interact with him. Just try it out anyway, if it makes you feel better. If it doesn't work, we can go back to what does. Point is, I want you."

"I know *you* do…"

"He does too, he's just trying to man up. I know, it doesn't suit him. Let me talk to him, please?"

"OK," I said, nodding and holding the phone out for Dex.

He got up and took it and I took that time to leave the bedroom. I went straight into the kitchen and poured myself a giant glass of water. I had never felt so thirsty and gulped it down quickly.

I leaned back against the fridge, Fat Rabbit sitting expectantly at my feet, and waited to hear Dex's reaction. I could already hear a yelp or two from the bedroom.

I knew I was probably crazy for even considering rejoining the show, but given how I now had the chance to hide behind a camera and go chasing after a creature that emphatically did not exist, and therefore, couldn't hurt me, it was hard to turn that down. Plus the pay would be more. And more pay would mean less living with Dex. Maybe after a few episodes I would be out. And yeah, it seemed redundant to then work with him, but whatever. I'd make myself deal. I was doing fine so far. Wasn't I?

A text came into my phone, distracting me. Rebecca finally had my right number and she texted: Got you an appointment tomorrow at 3:45pm. I can come with you.

I texted her back, telling her thank you. I felt like a total dick the way I had glossed over her problems over lunch, as if what I was going through was more important than what she was going through with Em. I knew I needed to apologize in person. She was much nicer to me than she needed to be, especially considering Dex was her friend first and foremost.

After a few nail-chewing moments, Dex came out of his room, tucking his phone into his pocket and walking straight up to me in determined strides. I stiffened.

He put his arms on either side of me and leaned against the fridge, trapping me in between them, and lowered his face to mine. "Listen, kiddo, we might need to add one more clause to the house rules. Something about not negotiating someone else's job behind their back."

I held my ground and looked right back into his eyes, refusing to be intimidated. "It was right in front of your face. And Jimmy suggested it. I don't recall saying yes."

"But you wanted to," he said huskily. He didn't sound angry, just serious.

"How do you know that?"

"There are reasons why I told Jimmy no, Perry. The last time we went ghost-hunting, you ended up with a demon in your soul."

"That demon started out as your ex-girlfriend," I said quietly, hating that I had to bring her up. "And she came from here, this apartment, not from the mental institute."

He winced, realizing what I had said. His eyes dropped away from mine and found my shoulder very interesting. "That may be true. But I never want to put you in danger again, intentional or not."

I took my hand and placed it on the crook of his elbow. He tensed for a second at my touch. "I appreciate that. But this should be my choice. It's a job, it's money, and we'll just take it one day at a time. I don't see how I could be in any danger from something that doesn't exist."

He smiled softly and I wished his face wasn't just inches from mine. "You can't be too sure about that."

I crossed my arms. "You don't actually believe in that shit."

"All I know is we've seen a hell of a lot of things that we can't explain. So I've learned to not discount the unexplainable."

"All right, Agent Mulder, say there is a Sasquatch, or Bigfoot, or just some really mangy bear out there. If I'm behind the camera, I'll be safer."

He took his arms off the sides of me and laughed, running a hand through his thick black hair. "Yeah, that's the other thing I wanted to talk to you about. Do you seriously want to do the filming?"

"Sure I do," I answered. Well, I guess I decided that one pretty fast.

"And you think that not only am I going to put you in potential danger with a mangy bear, but I'm going to hand over my precious equipment to you."

"Point and shoot."

"It's more than point and shoot."

"I know how to film, Dex. I think you're just afraid of being on camera."

He waved at me dismissively. "Please, this face was born to be on film."

"From Agent Mulder to Norma Desmond," I muttered. "Fine, I get that this might be odd but just do it for me."

"Do it for you? Perry...you know I'd do anything for you," he said softly. "I just didn't think returning to Experiment in Terror would be one of them."

I exhaled sharply, feeling I was very slowly wearing him down. "I guess it is. You know, this might be good for me. Look at this."

I raised my arms and glanced around the apartment. "I'm in another state. I left my family in an outright mess. I don't know how to explain to them why I left, I don't know how long I'm going to be living here, I don't know what the next step is. Being on the show is the only I do know right now. I just need this."

It was surprising how much I really did need it. In that instance, I knew I needed something solid to stand on.

He nodded. "You got it, kiddo. If this is what you want, this is what we'll do. But if at any point you want to pack it up and head back home, then that's the end of it. I am not going to risk anything happening to you."

"Aw, I'm pretty sure you could take on the big bad Bigfoot," I teased and without thinking, I reached out and grabbed his bicep, squeezing it. It was hard. Damn hard.

Dex watched me closely, a smirk slowly spreading across his lips.

I let go and cleared my throat. "I, uh, better go finish unpacking."

I hurried over to the den with Dex calling over my shoulder, "Hey I never saw a no-touching clause in the rules. Come back here."

I closed the door and felt my legs turn to jelly. We were definitely going to need to add a no-touching clause, for my sake as well as his.

AFTER A NIGHT of sharing sodium-soaked Chinese food with Dex and watching old seasons of The Simpsons together in semi-awkwardness, I felt bloated and gross the next day. I took Fat Rabbit for a walk and brought my phone along, knowing I had an important phone call to get out of the way.

I really didn't want to talk to my parents. Call me scared and selfish and I won't argue with you. The thought of having to face that mess terrified me but there was no way around it. I could procrastinate all I wanted, but the longer I left it, the more damaging it would be. For them, and probably for me.

I walked around the neighborhood several times as I made that call, past the pink elephant car wash and the duck buses, around brick apartment buildings and tourists heading to the Space Needle, even though the view would be stunted on this low clouded day. Fat Rabbit was looking seriously annoyed and dragging his lazy butt behind but the exercise would do him good and I was too anxious to care.

I talked to my dad first. Most of the conversation revolved around him yelling at me, while I tried to get a word in edgewise. The rest of it was a full-on guilt trip. I can't say I didn't understand where he was coming from. I know it didn't make a whole lot of sense to my family for me to just leave so abruptly, especially when I was in such a mentally fragile state. And maybe they were right, too, to be concerned about me.

But I'd gone too far to turn back now. Earlier I had told Jimmy that Dex and I would do the "Sasquatch Special." A new contract was faxed over to which we both signed, and it included the new pay raise. It was barely enough to survive on but it was a lot more than it was before. Even though I made sure the contract was on a show-by-show basis, so I wouldn't get roped into something I'd regret, I was still committed. And it felt good. My head and heart were all over the place and that one sense of stability is what I needed to keep going and not turn back.

Talking to Ada was the hardest. She called me back after I hung up with my parents and she sounded almost weepy over the phone. She missed me and dealing with my parents alone was harder than she thought.

"Can you hear my thoughts?" I asked her, looking into

the warm interior of Top Pot Doughnuts and debating a sweet treat.

"No," she said. "Nothing. You're probably too far away. What were you thinking about?"

"Donuts," I told her.

"You're probably not passionate enough about donuts," she said.

"Well I used to be."

"Can Dex hear you?" she asked.

"I don't think so."

"Maybe it's just a family thing."

"Yeah. Though I thought Maximus heard me that one time. Speaking of the douchecanoe, has he been around?"

She sighed. "Of course. Like, just this morning. But good news is that dad is like totally bored of him or something so he just told him to go."

"Good." Maximus now seemed like the ultimate meddler.

"So you're going back to the Experiment in Terror show now? Seriously, are you sure that's a wise idea?" I could hear the disapproval across the line.

I rolled my eyes even though she couldn't see it. "You sound just like Dex."

"Why? He doesn't want you to do it?"

"No, not really. He agreed now, but originally he told Jimmy that I wouldn't be a part of it. It didn't matter though, Jimmy wanted me and we both managed to convince Dex."

"Are you sure you convinced Dex? Maybe this was his backward way of convincing you."

I paused, my stomach heavy. "No, I don't think so. He was pretty determined to not let me do it. I think I believe him. He's pretty worried about me."

"Well I'm glad someone there is. It's hard to worry all the way down here."

"You're three hours away, Ada," I told her. "And I'll be back soon. I need to get the rest of my stuff and my bike. We're heading to BC to film in a couple of days, so I might come down in like a week or so."

"Here's hoping they've calmed down by then. They're being so spazzy and so unfair."

"That sounds like mom and dad."

"Well, stay in touch, all righty?" she pleaded. "And if all else fails, use the shining."

I giggled. "Yes, and I will expect you to show up with an axe and a snowmobile."

Pause. "What's that from?"

"The...Shining. Haven't you...oh nevermind. Love you."

"Love you too."

I hung up the phone and decided to skip the doughnut. But while I got closer the apartment, I ducked into the convenience store across the street. They didn't have donuts but they did have a sign that said "Fresh Beer" and a cute sandy-haired guy behind the counter who was filling large jugs from the tap for "to go" beer.

"Need some beer?" the cute guy asked. He looked to be maybe around 25-years old, of average height and nice build, very cute smile and a funny Battlestar Gallactica t-shirt.

I smiled shyly, glad I put some effort into my appearance that morning and looked at the clock on the wall. "It's after noon, is that allowed?"

He grinned and grabbed a jug. "You seem like a girl who makes her own rules, so sure why not. What will it be?"

I picked an amber ale, even though I really hadn't planned on drinking half a liter of beer before my gynecologist appointment. Oh well, it felt good to be out and meeting the neighbors.

"I haven't seen you around before," he said as he pulled back on the tap, keeping his eyes on me yet somehow not spilling a drop.

"I just moved to the city," I told him, fidgeting with my plaid scarf.

"Where did you move from?"

"Portland."

"Well, welcome to Seattle." He put down the jug and wiped his hand on a dishtowel. He held it out for me with a big, dimple-inducing smile. "I'm Paul."

I shook his hand. "Perry."

"Pretty name for a pretty girl," he said, and cranked a cap on the beer bottle. "Hope you enjoy the beer. If you do, come back here and let me know. I could take you to the brewery where they make these puppies."

"Speaking of puppies," a voice called out from behind us.

I whirled around to see Dex had strolled in the store. My palms immediately felt sweaty.

"Hey Dex," Paul greeted him casually.

"Hey," he said, his eyes narrowing on him for a split second. Then he brought them to me. "I was just going to get the car from the shop when I saw my poor dog tied outside, looking like he just ran a marathon."

"Sorry," I said, looking for my wallet. "I ended up talking to my parents. Took longer than I thought."

"And getting beer," he remarked. He smiled at Paul. "She's a troublemaker, this one."

Paul looked between us both as he placed the jug on the counter. "You know Perry?"

I could have sworn Dex winced. "Yes, I know Perry. And

it seems like you know Perry now too. She just moved in with me."

Paul's face reddened. "Oh, I'm sorry, I-"

"I'm his new roommate," I said quickly.

"She's my partner," said Dex.

"Work partner," I clarified to Paul with a smile.

"But we live together," Dex shot back.

I tried not to glare at him. "For now."

"Right," said Paul in that *I'm going to back away slowly* kind of voice. "Well, Dex. Here's your beer, uh, Perry. It's on the house. A welcome to Seattle thing."

"Thank you, that's mighty kind," Dex said with a slight bow and plucked the beer off the counter and headed out the door.

I shot Paul an apologetic look and ran after Dex, out of the store and onto the frigid street.

"Hey," I said, pulling on his coat for him to stop.

He turned and cocked his head. "Yes?"

"What was that about?"

"What? Oh right, here's your beer."

Dex shoved the cold jug into my hands. Then he undid Fat Rabbit's leash and handed that to me too.

"No," I said, trying to juggle the items. "The cock-blocking."

He burst out laughing, his brows raised as he looked at me. "Cockblocking? What? You have a cock now?"

I stamped my foot. "No, Paul. He was flirting with me and you totally shot him down."

His chin lowered and pulled back against his neck. "I don't even know what you're talking about. You were just chatting, from what I saw."

"He was flirting and you know it. You wanted to make it look like we were together."

"Why would I do a thing like that?"

"Because you're a jerk." I said the first thing that came to mind.

He looked around him, as if for backup. "Wow. Maybe we should add a no name-calling clause to the house rules."

"Enough with the damn rules already."

"Hey," he growled, coming right up to me, chest against mine. "If it weren't for those damn rules, we'd already be having dirty sex all over that apartment."

Whoa. *Whoa.*

Either it was the words "dirty sex" or the way he was looking down at me so intensely, or the fact that he might have been telling the truth or how damn confident he sounded, I was stunned and at a loss for words. My cheeks immediately flushed.

He kept his shining, dark eyes on mine until I had to look away, while my brain struggled to come up with something other than playing images of us having dirty sex together.

"That's right," he continued, voice low and velvet smooth. "*You* know it's true. I'm not saying I agree with the rules though, but you know, you started them."

I cleared my throat, finding my footing. "And I'm glad I did. Man, you are way too confident for someone who keeps getting shot down."

His eyes widened humorously. "Shot down? And who's doing the shooting, you?"

I opened my mouth then realized how egotistical I would have sounded.

"No, you're not shooting me down, kiddo," Dex went on. "Because I'm not really trying. When I do try, you'll know it. And then you'll throw the whole damn rulebook out the window."

He flashed me a smile and then turned and strolled down the street with wide, powerful strides. I watched him go, my brain still on the fritz, until Fat Rabbit started anxiously pulling at the collar. In a daze that made my heart feel like it was on spin cycle, I let the dog lead me across the street and back home.

7

The days leading up to our trip North went by quickly. Which was both a good and bad thing. Ever since our altercation and sexual threats outside the convenience store things were kind of strained between us. Well, they were to me. Dex seemed completely fine and at ease, despite dropping some suggestive comments here and there. They never went further than that, which meant Dex wasn't really trying and just teasing instead. I could live with that...for now.

Of course, I felt a lot better now that I had the IUD inside me. Not that I got it because of Dex, because really, I didn't, but it was nice knowing it was there for protection in case something happened. I couldn't go down that road again and I had to play it safe.

Rebecca was so sweet to take me and I apologized profusely to her, feeling bad for dismissing her problems and for ragging on Dex so much. She understood, cuz she's made of awesome, and I made a promise to myself not to put him down when I was around her. Besides, the longer I was living with him, the more I was warming up to him.

Maybe not my heart - I liked to keep that in the deep freezer - but definitely my body. Sleeping in the room next to him, hearing him in the shower, sneaking around for moments with his shirt off just so I could get a glimpse of what his tattoo was (regrettably, he's remained clothed around me) was making me a bit crazy and my libido was off the charts. I couldn't even masturbate without fearing I'd cry out his name and scare the damn dog.

Hence why the IUD seemed smarter with every waking second.

We had to rise early on the day we left for the shoot since the drive to the town of Snow Crest, BC, was at least eight hours away. We were still in Washington, just passing the snow-covered town of Ellensburg, when I noticed Dex's eyes weren't quite on the road but on my chest.

I sunk back into my seat a bit and lowered my scarf over my V-neck. "Can I help you?"

He grinned and popped a piece of gum in his mouth. For once, it wasn't Nicorette.

"Just wondering why your breasts are on display when we're heading up to the Canadian Rockies at the end of winter. That's all."

I grunted and pulled my cardigan around me. "I'm running out of clothes. This was the only clean shirt left."

"You know we could make a clothing optional rule around each other. That way we'd always be naked and never have to do laundry."

The way he said it made me shift in my seat uncomfortably.

"All right, Dex, quit it. You're beating a dead horse."

"I'm beating something horse-sized, that's for sure."

I shot him an unimpressed look. "Do you really think you'll win me over by having sex with me?"

He scratched at the side of his chin. "Well, they say the way to a woman's heart is through her vagina."

I almost laughed and stopped myself just in time. I shook my head instead and looked out the window at the rolling white, treeless hills. I thought that now that we were on our way to do the show, he would have simmered down a bit and gotten distracted by the Sasquatch project, but that didn't seem to be the case. It made me wonder if perhaps he needed to up his meds, perhaps down some Ritalin. Maybe I needed that too.

"I forget, are you going to get hassled for bringing your medication across the border?" I asked, having a hard time remembering if we got hassled the last time we went to BC.

"What medication?" he asked.

I had to look at him. He was looking back at me with an open expression.

"Your medication...you know. The..."

"The pills you switched on me without telling me?" he filled in. His voice had a flinty edge to it which made me cringe internally.

"Uh, yeah those."

"I'm not on medication anymore, kiddo. I quit the day you left. And I never looked back."

I was dumbstruck. And impressed. "But...the ghosts. Haven't they come back?"

He shrugged and sucked on his lip before speaking. "Sometimes they do. They did at first. The first month was the roughest. But things have been fine since. I think maybe all the working out has been helping too, somehow. Maybe it's a body-mind thing."

Shit. I had seen Dex on withdrawal from his meds. He was making it sound easy but I couldn't imagine how he must have been after I left, to go through all of that on his own, with only friends who didn't really understand the way I did. No wonder he never came after me right away. He was probably too afraid to leave the house.

I looked down at my hands, feeling small. The guilt over the pill-switching was swarming over me with hot flashes.

"I'm OK," he said after he shot me a reassuring look. "I feel great. If you can believe it, my sex drive is much higher now."

"What a surprise," I muttered softly. I raised my eyes to meet him. "Listen, I'm so sorry about the pill-switching, I didn't know what I was doing, I-"

"Perry, it's all right."

"No, it's not. That was a terrible thing for me to do. I totally broke your trust."

"Yeah, you did," he sniped, eyes flashing. A beat later he relaxed. "But I understand too. I know why you did it. It didn't mean I wasn't angry as all hell but I know why. I'm over it. Remember, like you said, it's in the past. It's done."

I squinted at him. "You're really not mad?"

He smiled, his eyes soft. "Do I look mad?"

I shook my head, hoping he'd always look like that to me. Open and trusting in ways I could never be.

We sat in silence for a few moments, lost in our thoughts.

"We are really fucked up," I finally remarked.

"Yeah, kiddo, we are. Now come on, let's go hunt Sasquatch."

∽

THE DRIVE to the small town of Snow Crest took most of the day, passing through the dry, arid landscapes of Eastern Washington and the panhandle of Idaho before we reached the winding, snow-capped peaks of the Canadian Rockies. By the time we got to our vintage motel with its antler-motif and mint-green coloring scheme, it was dark out and I was an unfortunate combination of feeling cagey and hungry.

Compared to all the other times Dex and I had gone "hunting" for our show, I was completely at ease. I wasn't nervous. I didn't feel any trepidation about our subject. This so-called Sasquatch would be the perfect way to sink back into Experiment in Terror and there was practically no research to be done. What could really be said about the beast that didn't exist?

Dex, on the other hand, seemed a bit more serious about the whole ordeal and was pensive for a lot of the car ride, making only the occasional small talk and changing songs on the mp3 player. Maybe it was because he was going to be on camera for once.

There just wasn't all that much to go on. A man called Rigby Adams ran an outfitters company out of the mountains surrounding Snow Crest, taking tourists out on weeklong hiking expeditions. Sometimes on horseback, but recently with llamas, who handled all the gear as people towed them along. He also ran hunting trips on the side. According to Jimmy, he'd always been seeing glimpses of this supposed creature in the woods and had evidence of the extra-large footprints it left behind. The reports had made the local news and attracted some explorers over the winter but nothing had turned up. That was until last week, when a member of his staff, a woman named Christina, was reportedly attacked by the creature and needed to get treatment for lacerations to her leg.

Christina was better now and would be meeting Dex and I for breakfast in the morning. The thought of it made my stomach rumble as we checked into the motel, the mountain air chilling me to my core. Even though we were in a bastion of civilization, the sky was black against the ghostly white peaks, looking faded in the darkness like old photographs.

Inside, the motel clerk was a smiling woman with a ton of turquoise jewelry around her neck and wild grey hair.

"Here are your keys." She passed them over the counter to Dex, who gave her a wink of thanks.

As we walked toward our rooms, my fingers growing numb from the cold, I had to remark, "I'm surprised you got me my own room."

"Well, you're right next door to me, as usual. Wouldn't want to break any of the rules, even on vacation."

My room was, in fact, right next to his and even had one of those locked doors that joined the rooms from the inside. I had just put my bag on the ground and tested the bed for firmness when there was an abrupt rap at the inner door, making my heart jump.

I got up and stood anxiously beside it.

"Who is it?" I asked teasingly.

"Bigfoot," Dex answered from his room.

"What do you want, Mr. Foot?"

"Please, just call me Big."

I snorted. "You wish."

"You *know*."

I really didn't need to picture his dick at that moment.

"Dex?" I prodded.

"I think I saw a pizza joint when we rolled into town," he said, voice muffled. "This is buttfuck Canada so I'm not sure we'll have much more selection than that. I'm going to try and order in, do you want some?"

Being with Dex was doing hell to my waistline. Unlike him and his daily gym sessions, I couldn't afford to keep eating junk. But we would be hiking for the next few days, so what the hell. I told him to get me whatever he wanted and in 30 minutes we were sitting cross-legged in his room, me on one bed and him on the other. We ate the thin pizza with its overdose of marinara sauce and flipped through the three crackly television channels until we were stuck watching a documentary on the CBC.

Despite the casual munchies and TV watching, sitting there with Dex wasn't as comfortable as I would have hoped. He seemed content just to relax and kept oddly quiet, though the constant drumming of his fingers on his thigh suggested he had something on his mind. His face was ashen from the long drive, which might have explained why the witty and suggestive comments had dwindled. It sounded funny, but I kind of missed them. Though, when you thought about it, being in a cheap motel room together probably wasn't the safest place for sexual sparring.

When the program was coming to an end, he gave a yawn, settling back into the stiff floral comforter.

I eyed the clock, which read 9pm.

"Hey, I think the hot tub is still open," I suggested, recalling the tiny tub outside surrounded by a tall metal gate. "The sign said it closed at 10."

The corner of his mouth lifted. "Did you bring a bathing suit with you?"

I hadn't thought of that. "Well, no. But I have matching bra and underwear."

He turned his attention back to the television. "So going commando was just a one-time thing, then."

My cheeks burned at the memory. "You sure you don't want to go?"

He frowned and glanced at me from the corner of his

eye. "You're being strangely insistent. I didn't know you wanted me with my shirt off that badly."

Bingo.

"What does your new tattoo say?" I pounced, unable to help myself.

His grin spread and he folded his hands behind his head, his black sweater lifting up slightly, showing off a tempting trail of hair and the dark waistband of his boxer briefs. "Oh, so you really *do* want to get my shirt off. I'm flattered, Perry. I thought it was just the other way around."

I leaned over so I was at the edge of my bed, my eyes imploring his. "What does it say?"

He gave his head one shake. "You'll find out in due time, kiddo."

"Why is it a secret?"

His eyes shone as he tilted his head at me. "It's not a secret. It's a tattoo. And now it's a bargaining chip."

"Bargaining chip?" I didn't like the sounds of this.

"Yes. I'll show you my back if you show me yours."

I straightened up. "Just my back?"

"Did I say back? I meant front." His eyebrows wagged. "No bra."

I crossed my arms and inched back. "You're a jerk."

He shrugged. "So I've heard."

Even though I had mastered the art of glaring thanks to being around him, Dex looked totally amused and unaffected.

I quickly had to remind myself that I didn't care.

"All right, well I'm going to go sleep," I told him, getting up.

"Don't let the bedbugs bite," he replied. "Knowing us, they'd probably be demonic."

"Right," I muttered and left Dex lying back on his bed,

eyes on the ancient television, still and blasé except for the tapping of his fingers on the quilt. The tattoo remained a mystery. And, in a way, so did Dex.

Even though it was quite early, the drive had taken a toll on me too and after I had taken a hot shower from a woefully low-pressure faucet, I crawled right into bed. The foreign, scratchy bedsheets and unfamiliar darkness of the room didn't even keep me up for more than a few minutes. This was a rarity, considering that ever since the possession, I hadn't been sleeping well. And who could blame me, really. When you've had actual monsters under your bed, nighttime becomes that much scarier.

My sleep was dreamless. At least, I didn't remember anything when I was awakened by an anguished cry from Dex's room followed by a deafening thud that shook my walls and caused a painting on the wall to fall to the ground.

"Dex!" I yelled, bolting straight out of bed. I stumbled over the blanket and made my way blindly to the door between our rooms. I quickly unlocked my door and thankfully found his unlocked.

I shoved it open and burst into his room.

It couldn't have been an eerier scene.

The room was dark except for a light coming from the bathroom vanity area. The light didn't do much to illuminate the room, however, because a bed, the same bed I had been sitting on earlier, was flipped entirely over and propped up against the bathroom door.

Dex was standing in front of it, back to me, an unmoving silhouette in a weary pose.

"Dex," I said cautiously, my heart in my throat. I walked carefully across the room, avoiding the bedding and pillows that had been scattered around.

I stopped right to the side of him. He was wearing a t-shirt and pajama pants and shaking lightly, from his loose fingers that hung down at his sides, all the way up to the flashing whites of his eyes. His gaze never left the flipped over mattress. He was staring at it like it was going to attack him any minute.

"Hey," I whispered. He didn't acknowledge me until I reached for him, touching his elbow. Then he jumped and spun around to face me, sucking in a giant rush of air. If he looked dazed before, now he was awake and aware.

And more afraid.

He shook harder, swallowing harder, as his eyes tried desperately to tell me something that his mouth couldn't.

It scared the living shit out of me, causing my skin to prickle down my back.

I quickly grabbed him and brought him close. The action was instinctive. I wrapped my arms around him and brought his head down into my neck. He was almost hyperventilating.

I had no idea what to do or what to say. I had no idea what happened. Had he flipped the bed over and thrown it against the vanity? The mirror behind it was cracked and glass had scattered on the ground. Why? Was he angry? How could he even flip the bed by himself? Why was he convulsing in my arms like a punished dog, making whimpering noises at my throat?

"It's going to be OK," I told him, holding him tighter. "Do you need help? A doctor?"

He shook his head violently and I squeezed him again.

"That's OK," I reassured him. "Let's go to my room. Come on."

I led him out of the room, keeping my grip steady on him, and ushered him through the doors. I closed his and as I did so, his head snapped up.

In the darkness of my room I could only see the glinting whites of his eyes.

"Lock it," he said in an ominous voice.

I nodded and quickly threw the lock over. I did the same to my door and led him over to my bed, sitting him down. I leaned over and flicked on the bedside light.

He propped his elbows up on his knees and held his head between his hands. I kneeled down in front of him and was suddenly reminded that I had in fact seen him like this before. In an alley in Seattle, when Abby had decided to pay him a visit.

That thought made my lungs constrict painfully, making it hard to breathe. Abby was gone. Abby had been destroyed. I couldn't deal with the alternative, I couldn't.

Now I was shaking. I took his hands off of his face and replaced them with mine. I got a good grip around his ears and hair and moved my head up until he had no choice but to look at me.

I didn't want to ask the question because I didn't want to hear the answer. But I had to know.

"Dex, please, what happened?" I asked, my voice cracking in its whisper.

His eyes, so close to mine, ebbed and flowed like a tumultuous tide.

"Please tell me." I brought my eyes off his and focused on his lips. Wanting him to talk. Wanting to kiss him. I blamed the adrenaline that was rushing through my body. I wasn't thinking clearly.

"I saw her," he said in a voice that seemed to float, delicate as air.

My heart pounded hard in my chest, as if it was just waking up. I struggled to breathe.

"Abby?" I squeaked.

His head shook, barely. "Not Abby."

"Who?"

He closed his eyes, brow furrowed in some internal pain. I stroked the side of his face with my fingers, feeling the solidness of his high cheekbones, the ever-present scratch of his facial hair, rough and hard under my touch. I hoped it was calming him as much as it was calming me.

"Who, Dex?" I repeated. I smoothed the skin under his eyes with my thumb until he finally looked back at me. They were wet with tears and my soul felt like it drained out of me and onto the floor. I didn't know if I wanted to know anymore, about someone worse than Abby. Someone that could reduce this strong man to this. I could feel his fragility in my hands, like I was holding eggshells.

His lips moved and a puff of air and words came out, words I couldn't understand. I moved my face closer to his and brushed his lips with mine. The room seemed to vibrate but maybe it was the beating of my heart.

"Please tell me," I whispered into his mouth.

His eyelids lowered as he gazed at me. "I don't want you to know. I can't..." he paused and licked his lips and his tongue invariably caught the inner rim of mine. It took everything I had inside to not go further with it. My chest heaved with the breath I was trying to control.

As scared, as curious as I was, I didn't want to upset him further. Not tonight.

"It's all right," I told him softly, my lips bumping against his as we spoke. "Just tell me how to help."

"Let me stay with you," he asked gently. "Let me sleep with you."

There was no hint of seductiveness in his voice, though his heavy eyes and parted lips suggested otherwise.

The question must have been on my face because he

continued, smooth and gentle, "Just like this. I need you tonight, just like this. Please."

I found myself nodding, not really knowing at all what he meant. When he said sleeping, did he mean actual sleeping or sex? And if it was sex, how come I wasn't pushing him away or coming up with excuses? Where was my rulebook now?

He got to his feet and I followed. He picked up the comforter and sheets from the floor and threw them on the bed. Then he climbed in, leaving an open, inviting spot in the bed for me. He nodded at the light for me to turn it off.

As if in slow motion, I clicked it off and the room went black. I was terrified of two things; whatever "she" was in the other room, if she'd come in here and find us. And getting into that bed with a man I used to love.

I gathered up my courage and climbed in with him. I was right up against his body, now warm from the covers, feeling the silkiness of his t-shirt rubbing against my arm. Thank goodness he was wearing clothes.

He shifted beside me so he was on his side and I leaned toward his chest. He put one arm around me, bringing his head down to mine. He put one hand into my hair and stroked it soothingly. I wished my nerves would follow suit, but his touch only excited them.

"Thank you," he whispered. My eyes adjusted to the dark of the room and I could see the outline of his face blocking everything else. "I just need you for a night. Just a night."

His lips met mine with a startling suppleness. I should have stopped him. I should have said no. But I didn't. I didn't want to.

I let him kiss me, let my tongue dance delicately with his, feeling a wave of hotness flush down from lips to lips.

Last time I had the strength to stop his kiss, this time I had none. I reached up with my hand and grabbed his bicep, getting excited at the firmness and strength he possessed. If he wanted me, he could have me and any way he wanted. And if he didn't start to devour me, I would devour him.

If that thought didn't surprise me, it was what Dex did next.

He gently pulled away and ran his thumb over my lip.

"Sorry," he said. "This isn't me trying. I just need to be with you."

I cocked my head from the pillow, thoughts jumbled and hormones raging. He was being completely sincere and it still confused the hell out of me.

"Come here," he whispered into my ear and pulled me in until he was spooning me. I could feel his rock hard erection now, pressed up against my ass, which only invigorated me more. He held me tight and I felt his lips at the back of my neck.

"Perry," he murmured through my hair.

I cleared my throat, trying to find my vocal chords. "Yeah?"

Silence. I listened, waiting in the black for his answer. Heavy breathing was my reply. He was asleep.

Minutes later I joined him, drifting off in his arms. It was one of the deepest sleeps I'd ever had.

8

When I woke up the next morning, I wasn't surprised to find Dex gone. At first I thought maybe the whole thing had been some crazy dream. I mean, I have had plenty of Dex dreams before, of course those all involved hot, uninhibited sex. Not purely kissing and spooning.

Then I heard a few muffled thumps from his room and I got up, feeling a chill as the morning mountain air seeped in through the thin windows. I pulled on a pair of jeans and slipped on a sweater and knocked lightly at his adjoining door.

"Dex?" I asked.

"Enter," was his formal response.

I opened the door and poked my head in. The bed was back in its place, covers and bedding looking freshly made. The only sign that something had gone wrong was the mirror. It was shattered in the middle, cracks seeping outward.

Oh, and Dex's wrist. He was standing at the sink, attempting to wrap a gauze bandage around it.

"Oh my God, what happened to you?" I asked and hustled toward him.

"Can you help me?" he inquired. I looked up at him, and seeing he looked fine, at least better than last night, I held up his wrist, the bandage falling away.

It wasn't too bad but the outer side of his wrist was bruised and bloody. At least the bleeding had stopped.

"What happened?" I asked again, grabbing for the bandage. "Seriously. Tell me."

He bit his lip momentarily and his eyes flitted to the mirror.

"I had an accident last night."

"I saw. You flipped over your bed."

He nodded. "Yeah, I guess I did."

"Why did you do that?"

And *how*?

He looked down at his wrist and the tendons around his neck stiffened. "I told you."

"You didn't. Last night you just said that you saw *her*."

"And that's the truth."

"Who is her?"

"She was in the mirror."

My mouth gaped and the grip on his wrist became loose. "You saw someone in the mirror?"

He nodded. "So, maybe I'm having a hard time adjusting to being drug-free after all. You think they have a drugstore around here?"

"Did you smash the mirror with your hand?"

He was silent. I took that as a yes.

I sighed. "And then you flipped over the bed. Why?"

He rubbed at his forehead with his spare hand and avoided my eyes. "Perry, I can't really say."

"You were trying to keep something out," I answered for him.

His breath hitched. For a moment I thought he was going to spill the beans. I was wrong.

"Please. I know you're worried-"

"Of course I'm worried, Dex!" I cried out. His eyes softened at my outburst.

"All right. It's all right."

"It's not."

"It was a ghost. It was just a ghost. And it's the first time I've ever seen her. It might not mean anything and I don't need this distraction right now. We have a mythical beast to shoot, I need to focus on that. Sasquatch and ghosts don't mix."

"Tell me who the ghost is."

"If I tell you, will you wrap up my wrist and promise not to ask any more questions about it? Ever?" he pushed.

I didn't want to promise that. I knew whatever he'd tell me would only bring a billion questions along with it. But I said, "Yes" and began to slowly rewrap his wrist.

"The ghost..." he said reluctantly, face turned away from mine. "The ghost was my mother."

I froze.

He jerked his attention back to me and gave a hard glance at my hands. "Keep wrapping."

I didn't know if I could. His mother. Dex had seen the ghost of his mother last night. In the mirror. And that sight was enough for him to smash it and make a dramatic barricade against it, flip over a fucking bed. It was enough to make him cower in fear and seek the comfort of my company. Normally I wouldn't put that past him, but last night Dex didn't want sex. He just didn't want to be alone. And that vulnerability, that was a side of him I rarely saw.

He rolled his eyes. "Here, do you want me to do it?"

I shook myself alert, feeling drugged and hazy. My fingers fumbled around the fabric. "Uh no. No I've got it."

"I hope you're packed, we gotta leave soon," he said. I looked up at him, so many questions begging to tumble from my lips. But his expression was a warning and I knew I made that promise. I couldn't push my luck. It would only annoy him and I didn't want to do that.

I nodded and quickly finished up his wrist, tucking the ends together.

He held it up to his face and examined it. "Nice work, Florence."

I pretended I wasn't examining the mirror, having a sick hope of seeing her myself, his infamous mother. Before he could catch me, I gave him a quick smile and took off to my room, throwing my clothes in the bag and remembering to put on a bra and do a quick application of makeup on my face. I wasn't on camera but I was still meeting people today and needed to look professional.

All the while my thoughts drifted back to Dex and his mother. He had never told me anything about her. I only knew a little bit about his father, that he left them when Dex was a teen and at some point during that whole thing, Pippa ended up being his nanny. He never told me how his mother died. Though, there was a strange feeling at the back of my head, like I was forgetting something. Like I knew something about her without ever knowing it, if that makes any sense.

Then it happened. My eyes filled with a flash of being in Roman's home, the demon fighting inside me during the exorcism. A feeling of utter hate rolling around in my guts. A French accent that had spoken through me: "Your little secret. You don't want anyone to know what happened to your dear old mother."

I nearly collapsed to the floor from that flashback. I could feel the evil slinking off of me like oil. If Dex's mother brought that kind of vileness and hatred with her in death, no wonder he was so afraid of her.

And no wonder I was suddenly so afraid for him.

A quick knock at the front door snapped me out of my morbid thoughts before I could dwell on them any longer.

"Kiddo?" he called from outside. "I'll meet you in the car. We were supposed to be at the diner two minutes ago."

I coughed. "Coming!"

I slipped on my coat, picked up my bag and ran out into the crisp morning.

The parking lot was coated with a thin layer of frost that sparkled underneath a sun that peeked between billowing clouds. My breath froze in the air and the chill nipped at my nose, but judging from how bare the streets and roofs were, winter was on its way out here. Only the mountains remained thick and white halfway up.

My Doc boots made a pleasing crunching sound on the frost as I carefully trotted toward the running Highlander and jumped in the passenger seat, flinging my bag in the back.

"Sorry," I apologized, eyeing Dex carefully now. But not too carefully. The last thing he'd want would be for me to treat him any differently because of who was haunting him.

Haunted, I corrected myself. *It only happened once. It might not happen again.*

Dex paid me no attention and brought the car out of the lot and down the main road. We could see the rotating sign for the diner loud and clear.

"I really hope this place is cheap," he remarked, "because I'm about $200 short now."

I stared at him, puzzled.

He shot me a sheepish grin. "Apparently motel mirrors are expensive."

Seconds later we were pulling up to an old-fashioned diner – The Raven's Nest - done up in log cabin style.

It was surprisingly dark inside, sticking to a whole "cabin in the woods" theme like the whole town seemed to adhere to, complete with walls of stuffed owls and wood carvings. It was also surprisingly busy, as if all of Snow Crest ate breakfast there on a daily basis. We stood at the entrance where the empty hostess stand was, surveying the room and its peculiar patrons.

Dex leaned down and whispered in my ear, hot breath tickling me, "I bet they make a fantastic cherry pie here."

I chuckled at the reference and shivered from his breath. I spotted a pretty teenage girl getting out of a booth and coming toward us with an expectant look on her face.

"Are you Dex and Perry?" the girl asked us. She was about Ada's age, with wide brown eyes and dark hair pulled back into a braid. She was wearing the latest distressed skinny jeans, but her feet were wrapped in worn hiking boots and a giant, ill-fitting flannel shirt graced her lithe upper body.

Dex and I exchanged a look.

"That we are," he said warily. "And you are?"

She stuck out her hand with a wide grin that showed a pleasing gap between her teeth.

"I'm Christina."

I scrunched up my forehead. "I thought Christina was one of the staff?"

She nodded, still smiling. "I am. I'm Rigby's daughter. Come on, I'll explain."

She turned and it was only then when we followed her back to the table that I noticed she was walking with a very slight limp, favoring her right leg.

We took a seat at the dark wood booth, Dex and I pressed up together on one side and the teen on the other.

"I hope you don't mind me saying this," Dex said, "But we thought you were older. Aren't you a bit too young to be working for your dad?"

She shrugged and proceeded to pour an obscene amount of sugar into her coffee cup. "Probably, but he needs the help. I'm home schooled over the winter by my ma. She lives right in town. Otherwise I help Rigby."

"Is he not your real dad?" I asked, noting it was weird she didn't call him "dad."

"Oh he's real," she said eyeing her coffee. She slurped it up and wiped the coffee spillage off the top of her lip. "You guys should get the coffee, they are famous for it here."

Like the waitress had supersonic hearing, a plump lady with purple eyeshadow appeared at the table, hovering with a pot of coffee.

"Hi folks," she greeted. "Welcome to Snow Crest. Coffee?"

Dex sat back in his seat and beamed at her. "Yes please, Norma. I'd like a cup of coffee and a slice of cherry pie."

She gave him the stink eye. "I hope you're being serious because we do have cherry pie. But the name's Sally."

"I'm always serious, Sally." Another grin.

She looked at me and I gave her the *I don't know this guy* look. "I'll have coffee for now."

She poured the black, steaming liquid in our cups and stalked off.

Christina gave Dex a funny look. "Why did you call her Norma?"

"Ignore him," I told her. "He thinks we're in Twin Peaks."

Her frown continued so I went on, "So you work for your dad. Then you're the one who was hurt…"

She grimaced and tapped her right leg.

"Yeah. No one would believe me. They thought it was a mountain lion that attacked me, but that was no mountain lion."

Despite the strange subject matter, she was talking awfully loud, like she wanted everyone in the restaurant to know. I looked around and a few folks were glancing over with faint interest. Their faces said it all. They had heard it all before and they didn't believe her.

Dex folded his hands in front of him and leaned in across the table.

"Tell us what happened."

She tilted her head and reached for his face, giving his eyebrow ring a light tug.

"Did that hurt?" she asked, sitting back.

He was nonplussed, as if teenage girls tugged on his eyebrow ring all the time.

"I don't remember. I was around your age."

"Things hurt more when you're my age."

"You'd be surprised at how untrue that is," he said solemnly. "So, back to…well, what happened."

Norma (er, Sally) came by and plunked the pie down for Dex who clapped his hands together. I ordered scrambled eggs and bacon and when the waitress was gone, Christina launched into it.

"We're not, like, running at the moment, so it's just this weird in-between stage up at the cabin. I take care of the llamas and horses and stuff, getting them ready for the tourist season, while Rigby goes out and starts clearing trails. He was gone really late one night and there's still snow up where the cabins are so I was worried cuz you know, it's a bit sketchy, especially on horseback. I went after him. I knew where he went. We have two cabins, as you'll find out. There's the one that we live in, well, when I'm not living in Snow Crest. And the other one is for hunters. We have a guy, Mitch, he's kind of a weirdo, but helps us out and runs private hunting tours with Rigby. They use the other cabin for that. So I took my horse out along the trail all the way to the cabin. You can do it in less than an hour if you're really booking it, but there was still snow here and there and so I could only trot in places. Anyway."

She paused, taking a giant breath and a giant inhale of her coffee. I looked over at Dex who was watching her thoughtfully while shoving the remains of the pie in his mouth. I wondered how he ate it so fast and he gave me a look that said *you know how I feel about pie*. I did and found myself smirking at the nostalgia.

"Where was I?" Christina said, wiping her lip. "Oh right. I go to the other cabin and it looked like someone was inside, so I thought it was Rigby. I tied up Taffy to the post and the door to cabin was open and everything and there was a very small, dying fire in the fireplace. But, like, no one was there. Then I heard Taffy scream. Like, you know when a horse really whinnies but it's like a scream? I ran out of the cabin and she was rearing and she just snapped the reins off of the post and galloped off. I didn't know what to do or what had spooked her. There's no phone or electricity in there so I was totally stuck. The only thing I could do was make my way back home. I was only a few feet away from the cabin when..."

She trailed off and I realized I was hunched over in

suspense. Dex's hand was on my thigh, squeezing it lightly. I wasn't sure if he was trying to comfort me or what. I turned my attention back to Christina and prodded her with my eyes for her to continue.

Her gaze ping-ponged between us quizzically. "Are you guys a couple?"

I snorted, unprepared for that question. "What? No."

She didn't look convinced. I gave Dex a disgusted look, and shaking my head, brought the same look over to her. "No. We're just partners. Why?"

She shrugged. "I can tell he's touching you under the table."

"I guess he thinks I'm scared," I explained slowly and moved an inch away from him.

Meanwhile Dex was smiling openly. "I'm trying to win her over. It only works about half the time."

I lowered my head toward him. "Oh, this is you trying now?"

He matched my look. "Shall I remove my hand?"

The thing was, I didn't want him to. I loved the feeling of his hands on me, and would love it more if he moved his hand to my inner thigh and slid it up. But I said, "Yes please."

"Hand has been removed," he said in a robotic voice. He took it off and my thigh was left feeling cold.

I tugged down at my sweater sleeves and swallowed. "You should probably ignore us for the time being. Please go on with your story."

She looked lost in her head for a moment. Man, this girl had the shortest attention span.

"So...yeah," she started up, finally. "I decided to go back home, you know, my other home. On foot. I could jog it. Anyway, I wasn't far when I heard branches breaking in the forest. I thought it was Rigby or maybe Bandy, so I stopped. I listened, cuz I wasn't sure. I mean, there are bears and mountain lions around, even though I swear it wasn't ether of those. I heard this weird low growl, not like a dog but kind of like if someone was trying to clear their throat hardcore. But it wasn't my dad. It sounded like bad news. I didn't want to find out what it was and I was totally about to go when I saw something shift coming around the corner of the cabin. It was so dark but it was low and hunched over like this."

She got out of her seat and stood in the restaurant, demonstrating. Her knees were bent, her back hunched over, her hands poised beneath her, ready to claw. She looked like a cross between a zombie and a velociraptor.

And considering how much *Jurassic Park* scared me, that was probably the worst combination on earth.

By now, everyone in the diner was staring at the teen and some were even giving a little laugh. She shot them all haughty looks and sat back down.

"Well that was demented looking," Dex remarked.

"It was demented looking!" she reiterated. "Jeez. And it was dark, covered in hair, and its eyes were crazy black, like holes. Obviously nothing I should stick around for. So I ran and I made it only a few steps before it knocked me down and clawed at my leg, dragging me backward. I tried to turn around to fight, to get a look at it but before I could, Taffy came screeching out of the woods, like she finally remembered she galloped off without me. The Sasquatch let go of me and took off. Here. Look at what it did."

Christina stuck her leg out of the booth and was trying to roll up her jeans when the waitress came by with our food and interrupted her.

Even though her story hadn't really scared me (because

how could you be scared of something that wasn't real), I had lost my appetite. I stuck the bacon in my mouth and pushed my eggs over to Dex, who snatched them up and added a helping of hot sauce.

"So, you called this thing Sasquatch," I said. "No offense, but this doesn't sound like Sasquatch. Isn't he, it, whatever, supposed to be tall and big? I mean, Bigfoot...he has big feet...means that it's tall."

"I don't know, do I look like a monster expert? I'm just saying what I saw."

"Then you went on the news and told everyone about it, that it was a Sasquatch," Dex said between chews. "But the doctors said your leg looked like you were scratched up by a mountain lion. Those kind of claws."

She narrowed her eyes. "Of course I went on the news. People should know it's out there! And yeah, I'll show you, they definitely were claws."

She reached down for her pant leg again but I patted her arm, stopping her.

"That's OK. We believe you. We're just trying to get our facts straight before we start filming."

She blew a loose strand of hair out of her face and crossed her arms in a huff. "Well those are my facts. If you want more, you have to talk to Rigby. He's the one who has seen this beast thing a bunch of times, and has molds of the footprints. And guess what, what I saw exactly matches what I saw. So explain that."

Dex put his fork down on the empty plate. "We will explain it. That's why we're here."

Ten minutes went past as Christina went off of the topic of Sasquatch and onto how much she wanted to get out of Snow Crest. Apparently her parents had been saving up for university when she finished her schooling but because of the economy and the rising Canadian dollar, the town and the tourism industry were hit really hard over the last few years. The business was dwindling, but she had no choice but to help out her dad. Despite her headstrong personality, I felt sorry for the girl. She might not have to go to school half the year, but it didn't sound like she should be working up in the mountains either.

After we paid the bill, we went outside and waited for Rigby to show up. My body still wasn't used to the cold, and I rubbed my hands together fast, wishing I had brought my gloves out of the duffel bag.

"He should be here," Christina said absently, looking around. "He'll be in a green truck. I'm just going to call my mom and see if he's left the house yet."

She ran back into the diner to use their phone.

"No cell phone," I noted, thinking it was odd for a teen.

"No service," said Dex, showing me his iPhone. He was right. I took my phone out of the pocket and it read the same.

"There was some reception at the motel."

"Maybe it comes and goes." He looked around him, at the majestic peaks that soared high above the main street. "So what do you think, kiddo?"

"About?"

He kept his hands in his pockets and gestured at the diner with his shoulder. "About all that. Christina. What do you think? Is she full of shit or is she telling the truth?"

I wiggled my lips. "Well, I don't think it's either, to be honest. I believe something attacked her but the creature she described isn't a Sasquatch. Even if she said it was 7 feet tall and as hairy as Robin Williams, I still wouldn't believe it's a Sasquatch. There's obviously some animal out there. I mean, look where we are. And it's the end of winter, times are tough, food is hard to come by. Maybe a mangy bear went after her because it was desperate."

"Ah, always blame the mangy bear," he said, amused.

"You believe her?"

"Not really," he admitted. "Just playing devil's advocate. I think we need that whole dynamic now if I'm going to be in front of the camera."

"Are you nervous about that?"

"Do I look nervous?"

No. I thought. *You look ridiculously handsome.*

He grinned and nodded to himself. "Are *you* nervous? First time handling the camera and all?"

"Oh, I'll be fine. I like a challenge."

"Is that why you like me?"

"Who said I liked you?"

His eyes shone playfully, turning his irises a deep cocoa. "That's why *I* like you, you're a challenge."

I folded my arms and leaned back on one leg. "Oh, so that's why…"

"Well, that and your ass."

My cheeks flamed. "Thanks."

"And your breasts."

"Got it."

"And what's between your-"

"Dex," I warned, cutting him off.

He grinned and stepped toward me. He took his hand out of his pocket and ran his finger down the length of my nose. "What's between your gorgeous eyes…your cute little nose."

I tried not to flinch, knowing I had powdered my nose that morning.

"I have a vague recollection of you comparing me to a sexy bunny once," I mumbled, scrunching it up.

He raised his brows in mock surprise. "Did I say that? Boy, I sure am a charmer sometimes, it's a wonder I even used to get laid. Must have been the big dick."

I glared at him. "You think way too much of your dick."

"So do you," he replied with a smile. And God damn it, I wished I hadn't been staring at his crotch right then.

"Dex!" I barked at him, noting that Christina was running back toward us. "There are children here."

He opened his mouth to retort something back but thankfully shut it as Christina joined our side.

"There he is," she said and we turned to see a rusted green cab with black exhaust fumes rumbling around the corner. The truck pulled up next to us and a middle-aged man stuck his head out the window. His cheeks were dusted with pock-marks and a red knit cap was pulled down until it met his bushy brown eyebrows. He had an impressive handlebar mustache which I hoped wouldn't inspire Dex. His mustache had been barely there lately and I liked it that way. It tickled less when I kissed him.

"I'm Rigby," the man said in a voice that sounded like his throat was filled with rocks. "Do you guys want to hop in your car and follow us? It's about an hour drive to the cabin. Do you have chains?"

Dex looked back at the Highlander. "I have snow tires on."

"That'll do," he said. He tapped the side of the door. "Hurry up Christina, we don't have all day."

She ran around and popped in the passenger side. Then the truck began to pull away.

"Uh, Dex!" I exclaimed. We exchanged a look and both started running for the Highlander before Rigby's truck was gone and out of our sight.

9

We were right about the cell reception being spotty. As our car climbed up the rough mountain roads, ¾ of a mile behind the dusty cloud of Rigby's truck, the bars on my phone would go from zero to barely anything from one curve to the next.

When it seemed like I had the last chance to do so, I texted Ada telling her the situation. I never heard back and after twenty minutes, as we got further from the town, I knew I wouldn't get a response until our time hunting Sasquatch was over and we were back in "civilization."

I spent the car ride getting to know Dex's camera properly. We were going to be shooting with a hand-held one just because it was easier to manage and not worth a fortune if it accidently got destroyed. That seemed to happen a lot in our expeditions. Even if that did happen, I had a plan. I was sick and tired of losing our footage because our camera had drowned or something. I had found a super tiny Ziploc bag that some earrings had come in and placed the empty case for the SD card in there. If anything dicey were to happen, I'd try and pop out the memory card at the last minute and stick it in the case and bag and shove in my mouth or bra or something.

I felt quite secure about that and decided not to tell Dex. I hoped nothing bad would happen to our equipment but I wanted to prove to him that I was more than just a pretty face. I wanted to show that I could handle both sides of the operation.

I could tell he was a bit wary of me being the camera person, too. He kept sneaking glances at me as I filmed the tall, towering trees with their powdered sugar toppings, ready to give advice on the simplest things. Then it occurred to me that he actually was nervous. The way his eyes were darting about. The way he popped gum in his mouth, chewing fast. The way he scratched at his sideburns and chewed on his lip. These were all classic neurotic Dex maneuvers. I'd seen them from day one.

Then again, he had a lot to be neurotic about. The whole incident in the night, his mother. It would drift into my head from time to time and jar me with fright. I could only imagine it did the same to him but he was so damn good at hiding things. Of course, it didn't help that it was all probably because I fucked with his meds to begin with. Though I liked to pretend it wasn't that big of a deal at the time, I knew it was wrong. I knew it was very wrong. I had just spent months blaming Dex for everything, I didn't feel the need to focus on anything I did. I was amazed and a little ashamed that he seemed to forgive me so easily after I broke his trust like that. I wished I had that ability.

We were extremely happy to finally reach the cabin and my boobs were grateful to not bounce over anymore massive bumps and potholes. Later Rigby would tell us it was a logging road, used to hell during the summer, then navigated only by snowmobiles in the winter. It was a long way to town from where we were and we weren't even in the backcountry yet, where we'd be shooting. I remembered what I had told Ada about The Shining and hoped I hadn't jinxed myself.

"Welcome to my humble abode," Rigby said, walking toward us as we got out of the car, his arms outstretched and boots crunching on the snow.

It really was humble. His cabin was two stories with small windows. There was some frost on the sloping, shingled roof and a few patches of melting snow, giving it a quaint ski-chalet look. Beside it were several woodsheds, all of them half-full with stacks of wood. The landscaping was rough and consisted of dark rocky ground poking through a thin layer of hard snow, with a small gravel path leading from the cabin to the woodsheds and toward a small barn. I could see the shape of a horse in its stall, waiting in the darkness. Beyond that was a tiny hut labeled "office" and next to that a large paddock that disappeared down the hill, holding a few curious llamas.

Rigby caught my gaze. "Those are the llamas," he said. "They are the star attractions here. Llama trekking is the biggest trend in eco-adventures. We started out with twenty of them, but now we just have eight. Times are tough. Good news for you both is that you get to take two llamas with you on your expedition."

"Um," I said. "What?"

I looked at Dex for an explanation. He raised his shoulders though I swore I saw a knowing smile teasing on his lips.

"Of course you'll have the llamas to assist you," Rigby boomed as if I was a total idiot. "You can't go camping without the llamas. They carry everything for you and don't damage the environment."

I was hit with the sudden realization that I had no idea what this Sasquatch shoot entailed. "I thought we were staying in a cabin in the woods somewhere?"

He nodded vigorously. "You are, you are. But just because Christina says she was attacked by the cabin, it doesn't mean that's where you'll find the beast. You're going to have to go exploring. But it's OK, I've drawn on a detailed map for you all the areas where I've spotted it."

"About that," Dex spoke up, fingers under his chin. "We'd like to interview you on camera and get some inside information on exactly what you've seen."

He waved at us haphazardly. "Sure, sure, there's plenty of time for that later. For now, I want to see what you guys have packed. We're going to need to outfit it all for these guys. You get one llama each, you know, but we don't like to load them with more than 50 pounds during the winter when they aren't as in shape and the terrain is rough."

My mind was going back to camping. I hadn't agreed to that. It was still winter. In Canada. In the mountains. How would camping here, now, work? We'd freeze our asses off.

Rigby answered my next question. "Here, let's go inside for some tea. Christina will put it on. Bring your stuff and we'll go through it, taking only what you need for the next few days. I'll be lending you some winter-ready camping equipment and it can weigh quite a bit."

We followed him down the path toward the cabin. As we went up the short steps, Dex leaned over and murmured, "Feel like sharing a sleeping bag again?"

I looked him dead-on. "Yes, actually I will be sharing a damn sleeping bag with you. I'll use your body as a blanket if I have to."

He pursed his lips, looking impressed.

Inside, Christina was doing the brunt of the work. She

ran around getting the tea ready and putting out store-bought shortbread cookies and was in and out with various packs, sleeping bags and tents from a storage closet. She didn't complain once about the work but I could see the sheen of resentment on her forehead.

I decided to only take the jeans I was wearing, warm tights, pajamas, a few layer tops, two hoodies, my coat and a waterproof jacket. A bunch of thick socks, gloves, scarves and a knit hunting cap topped it off. I contemplated bringing my Kindle but knew there wouldn't be a place to charge it, and when I thought about it, whenever Dex and I were together, no matter what we were doing, there was rarely any downtime between us. If we weren't being harassed and terrorized, we were pretty good at entertaining each other.

And a warming part of me thought we could entertain each other a lot better now.

Anyway, aside from me feeling uneasy about camping in the cold, I was also unsure of our traveling companions: The llamas. I loved pretty much all animals but I had a bad experience with a camel when I was younger and llamas seemed to be nothing more than shorter, ornery cousins with a greater capacity for spitting.

Thankfully for Dex and I, we weren't heading out alone, at least not to the hunting cabin. Rigby and Christina were going to come with us on horseback, accompanied by another guide, Mitch, whom Christina had declared a weirdo earlier on.

While we waited for Mitch to show up, we got the llamas packed up. They were much bigger than I had thought and actually a lot cuter too. My llama was the size of a hefty pony and had brown and white patches. His name was Tonto and he seemed to be a real sweetie, with a mouth that was held in a permanent smile and eyes that were framed by heavy lashes.

Dex, on the other hand, got a real bastard of a llama.

His name was Apricot, even though he was purely white in color, and within minutes Dex has christened him "Twatwaffle." Seemed appropriate for an animal that was constantly trying to spit on him and butt heads.

"Tell me, why did I get the Twatwaffle here?" Dex asked as we pulled our llamas out of the pen and onto the logging road, his being stubborn and yanking the lead back.

Rigby looked hurt at the name-calling. "*Apricot* is a good guy. He's been raised by hand since birth so he just thinks humans are llamas. Take it as a compliment."

Dex and Twatwaffle gave each other the eye.

"Here Rigby," Christina said, giving her father the reins to a brown horse named Bandy. She quickly mounted her giant coal-colored horse, Taffy, a draft horse mix judging by the faint feathering by its hocks. I felt really small and a bit silly standing by the horses with a curious llama at my side, loaded up with packs like a mule.

The sound of crunching tires and a roaring engine filled the trees around us and Rigby announced, "Ah, and here is Mitch. Late as always."

A rugged-looking jeep with hefty wheels came climbing around the corner and came to an abrupt stop beside the Highlander. I watched the scene curiously, wondering about the "weirdo" and I soon saw why Christina called him that.

Mitch was a 6'2" behemoth of a man, and because he was dressed head to toe in camo gear, he had this look of just escaping from a military compound. It didn't help that he was wild-eyed, with an ugly scar down the side of his face and that his head was shaved down to a sharp crew cut with an extreme widow's peak. The more I looked at him as he came closer and his eyes fixed on my body like a falcon, the more I thought he wasn't a "weirdo" and just a "scary ass motherfucker."

"Where's mine?" he commanded to Christina, not paying the rest of us any attention.

"She's tied up," she said, nodding to the gate where the third llama was waiting, packed and ready. Christina's voice grew noticeably smaller when she talked to Mitch and I couldn't blame her. I felt myself shrinking as he hulked past, his startling blue eyes flitting to mine now and again. He gave me a ghost of a smile. I didn't know whether to take that as a friendly thing or to be creeped out.

Even Dex was watching him curiously, brow furrowed in thought.

"At least I didn't get Jackass over there," Mitch said, nodding at Twatwaffle and Dex while untying his llama and leading it over to us.

"Jackass is a good name too," Dex conceded.

Rigby cleared his throat. "Perry and Dex, this is Mitch. He leads the hunting tours out here. He'll be accompanying you on your expeditions."

My eyes widened and flew to Dex. His expression was blank but I knew this was also news to him to.

Rigby caught our exchange. "Obviously I'm not going to let you take my precious llamas out into the wilderness by yourselves. You'll need someone who knows the land. Mitch knows these mountains like the back of his hand."

"Damn right," Mitch agreed, giving us both a stony glance. "You're in good hands with me. Either of you know how to shoot?"

I swallowed hard, feeling Dex's eyes on me. "I do. But just a handgun."

"Just a handgun?" Mitch repeated. "I'll teach you more

than that. It's a great time to bag some bears. The more hunters, the merrier."

"We're really only interested in bagging Sasquatch," Dex spoke up.

Mitch laughed. I never thought a laugh could be frightening. "Oh right. Fucking Bigfoot."

"He's a skeptic," Rigby explained. "Now come on, we oughta head out before it gets too dark. That's when the beasts show up and we don't want to be unprepared."

Rigby led the way with Mitch behind him, snorting his disbelief. I let out a deep breath, feeling strangely on edge about the next couple of days, and followed behind them. Dex struggled with Twatwaffle/Jackass/Apricot behind me while Christina brought up the rear, taking it extra slow with her horse so she wasn't riding up the llama's asses.

The walk to the cabin was long but peaceful. We started out along the road for a bit, heading down the mountain and then cutting across a high ridge. The path was fairly wide but the sharp drop to the one side made my insides curdle. The view was gorgeous, a fairy-tale image of splintered peaks and waves of undulating trees but my stomach wouldn't let me enjoy it. Tonto was a big help though and when I was walking too slow, she'd take the outer side of me, shielding me from the drop.

It wasn't as cold as I first thought, but after about 45 minutes of walking, I couldn't feel my fingers through the gloves and kept dropping Tonto's lead. Then a light snow began to fall, covering the crunchy snow in a dusting of powder. Occasionally there would be a thump of falling snow from the heavy fir trees, or a bird might have flown out from a nearby bush, but other than that it was totally silent. Our talking was down to minimum since it was hard to converse when we were traveling single file, and the llamas barely made any sound as they glided through the white.

As nice – but cold – as the journey was, the cabin was a sight for sore, snow-blinded eyes. Though it was smaller than Rigby and Christina's cabin, I thought it was better. It was just so classic, a one-level with snow-covered flower-boxes beneath the windows and shiny icicles hanging from the roof above the porch. It immediately reminded me of the cabin my family and I used to stay in when I was a little girl. The memory of cross-country skiing with my mother and coming home to my father stoking a roaring fire made my heart split open.

"You all right, kiddo?" Dex asked softly, placing his hand on my shoulder and squeezing it.

I sucked in a breath at the memory and flashed him a quick smile. "I'm fine. Just…reminds me of something."

He nodded, eyes kind and knowing.

"So this is your new home base," Rigby said. He and Christina were tying their horses to the nearby hitching post.

"It's lovely," I told him honestly.

Christina came over and took the llamas from us. "There's no TV though. Kinda sucks if you ask me."

"I've got porn on my phone, I'm fine," Dex answered.

I elbowed him while Christina giggled at his remark.

"No reception," Mitch countered with his hard face trying to suss Dex out. He didn't realize Dex was joking. Then again, I wasn't sure either.

I gave Dex a sharp look making sure he didn't say anything else controversial. It was fine when he was acting like this around me, I was used to it, but Mitch looked like he'd pound his head in over nothing.

"Where do the llamas stay?" I asked, trying to change

the subject. Christina and Rigby were quickly removing the packs from the animals.

"I've got a little paddock set up for them around the bend. Actually I could let them roam free, they're so well trained they'd never leave," Rigby boasted, looking proud of himself. "That's why they're called the dolphins of the land."

"More like assholes of the land," Dex muttered, showing me his sleeve which was covered in gobs of llama spit.

I grimaced which melted into a laugh. "I thought you were the asshole of the land?"

He didn't find it as amusing.

Christina handed us our stuff and took the llamas down the path a few feet and around the corner of the cabin. I noticed Mitch was removing a formidable looking shotgun from his belongings, looking it over like it could have gotten damaged during the journey.

His eyes caught mine for a second and they narrowed faintly. I looked away quickly and picked up my pack, heading into the cabin.

It was just as cold inside as it was outside but Rigby was quick to get the fireplace going. He also threw some kindling in the wood stove that was located in the teeny tiny kitchen. The cabin was sparsely furnished and bit cramped but I guess that added to its charm. The living room was small, consisting of a leather couch and a rocking chair, the walls covered with landscape paintings and stuffed animal heads. There was a small hand-carved table in the corner with two ancient looking chairs and the floor was hardwood, covered in several animal hide rugs that spread from the couch to the fireplace. I had a wicked image of having sex on one of those rugs, the fireplace warming my ass. It was no surprise that I was picturing being on top of Dex.

I felt ashamed at the thought and turned my head away

from him, making sure to keep my eyes on the rest of the room. This was one of the many times I really hoped he couldn't hear my thoughts.

Unfortunately, all that remained were the bedrooms. There were two small ones, one with two twin beds and the other with a full. Old-fashioned wash basins sat in one corner and a Swiss-style wardrobe sat in the other. And when Rigby told us he and Christina would be taking the room with the double beds and Mitch was taking the couch, Dex shot me a cheeky grin.

Yeah. This trip was making my heart race in more ways than one.

"We'll just be staying the night," Rigby explained. "We'll be off in the morning. After that you're welcome to use the double beds and Mitch can take the other room."

"Oh, it's not a problem," Dex replied quickly.

"You sure?" Mitch questioned, those steely eyes focused on me. He looked like he was waiting for me to make a fuss.

"No, it's cool," I said firmly. I tugged off my jacket. "I should get unpacked."

I went into the room with Dex trailing behind me.

"Make sure you hang your wet things in front of the fire after," Rigby called out.

I smiled and quickly shut the door. The room had a single window that was letting in the late afternoon light. Soon it would be totally dark and there was no electricity.

Dex walked past me to the bedside table where a kerosene lamp sat. He picked it up and started playing with it. "Looks like this will be it for tonight."

I put my pack down on the bed, pressing my hands down on the cold duvet.

"How are you feeling about all of this?" he asked, putting the lamp back down and coming up to me.

"Weird," I admitted.

"I promise I won't snore anymore," he said.

I tilted my head and looked at him dryly. "I don't feel weird about sleeping with you. I survived last night."

His eyes flinched for a second as if he were reliving the bad part of the night. He recovered fast though.

"You might not survive tonight," he teased.

Again, that image of me riding him in front of the fireplace entered my mind. I quickly buried it away, deep inside, and ignored the flushed feeling between my legs.

"I feel weird about…the whole set-up," I told him.

He chewed on his lip and eyed the closed door. He lowered his voice. "I do too. Not like in a dangerous way or anything but, fuck, who invited a member of the Westboro Baptist Church on our camping trip?"

Especially when I don't like the way he looks at me, I thought briefly.

He continued, "Not to mention that I'm beginning to think this whole Sasquatch thing is a hoax."

I was surprised to hear him say that. "Really?"

He stepped closer to me. I could feel the chill of his coat.

"We've got to get Rigby to explain what he's seen. He's not been very forthcoming so far and I'm starting to think that Christina really was attacked by a mountain lion."

"Of course she was," I whispered. "Her description makes total sense. How the hell did she get Sasquatch out of that? And did you notice how she craves the attention about the whole thing? She was speaking loudly in the diner, wanting everyone to hear."

"Oh, right. I thought that was just a woman thing."

I punched him lightly in the arm, careful to avoid the goopy llama spit.

"No, dumbass. I feel like she made it all up for attention."

"Which means we're really going to be spending the next few days camping, helping Colonel Kurtz hunt down bears."

I shrugged. "Looks like."

He let out a long breath of air then shook his head and rolled back his shoulders. "Well, we're here, we might as well make the most of it. I'm getting Rigby to talk on camera, tonight. Christina too. If they're both bullshitting, well at least we can air their bullshit."

He started for the door but I held him back.

"You mean, I'm getting them to talk on camera. I'm the camera person here, remember? You're the host."

"Ah, fuck."

I smiled gleefully. "Don't worry, you're looking very pretty right now. Perhaps take off the llama goo though."

"You sure? I heard llama goo was an aphrodisiac." He winked at me and headed into the living room.

Like I need an aphrodisiac, I thought and followed him into the cabin.

10

The evening passed by pleasantly, as pleasantly as possible when you were sitting in a room surrounded by bear rugs and animal heads and a fire that cast dark slinking shadows on the wooden walls. There was an elaborate camping stove in the kitchen nook, where Christina prepared some hearty chili that made our mouths burn from an overdose of chilies.

Dex and I were sitting on the couch with Christina, our stomachs full and mouths still hot, when Mitch brought out a massive bottle of orange-labeled bourbon from the bag beside his rocking chair. He began to pour us all a glass, Christina included, when the cabin was filled with a stark white light.

I gasped and squinted at the light coming from outside. "What the hell?"

Dex stood up. "Aliens!"

"Sit down, Mulder," I said, tugging him back to his seat.

"Don't worry," Rigby said, getting up from his chair and going to the window. "'It's the motion detector light."

"How do you have a motion detector light?" Dex asked. "And why?"

Rigby surveyed the window and nodded, spotting something. "It's just a deer."

Mitch's head snapped up and his eyes immediately went to his gun, which was propped up on a gun rack in the corner.

Noticing that, Rigby said, "No Mitch, no shooting tonight. Tonight we relax and have fun." He took his seat back at one of the chairs and gave Dex and I an open look. "After what happened to Christina, I wanted to see if this was in fact The Beast, or maybe just a mountain lion. I wanted people to be safer here, either way. So I set it up over the weekend. Runs fairly well and on solar panels. I've got one at the back of the roof. It gets just enough light to power these babies. Though, if I can afford it, I might do more solar panels here in the summer. Get the whole cabin running. People don't like the rustic stuff as much anymore."

"Such a shame," Dex said, shaking his head and taking a glass of bourbon from Mitch. "There's nothing like shitting in the woods."

Rigby laughed. "Speaking of, the lights should make going to the outhouse much easier. I can't tell you how many times I've gone off course in the middle of the night. Not the place you want to be caught with your pants down."

I shivered at the thought of having to use the outhouse in the night. It wasn't pleasant during the day and using it at night brought back bad memories of D'Arcy Island. I'd take Sasquatch over creepy Mary and the lepers any day.

Dex nudged me then said to Rigby, "If you don't mind doing this over a glass of bourbon, Perry here would love to get an interview of us on film."

"Ah, sure what the hell," he said and leaned back in the

chair, propping one boot on top of the other one. "I'll tell you anything you want to know."

Dex smiled and went to the room to rummage for the gear. Suddenly I felt nervous. The lighting in the cabin was creepy and dark, which would be great for atmosphere but I didn't know as much about lighting as Dex did. And I wasn't about to ask him either.

I took a big gulp of the drink and it went down smoother and sweeter than expected.

"Take it easy, gorgeous," Mitch whispered from beside me. My eyes snapped to his and my shoulders automatically hunched in from the look in his eyes. Talk about feral.

I shot him an uneasy smile, then looked at Christina. She had the same look on her face and brought her knees up to her chin, hugging them.

"All righty," Dex said, coming out of the room with the camera and a mic which he pinned onto Rigby's flannel shirt. He attached another wireless mic to his dark fishermen's sweater. I got up and joined him and he placed the camera in my hands.

"Just try to get us both in the shot for a few questions," he told me, "then just a close-up of Rigby for the rest of it. I'll be able to edit with that."

I nodded, my swallow clicking in my throat.

He leaned into my ear and whispered, "You'll do fine, kiddo. Just remember to take the lens cap off."

His words warmed me from inside and I gave him a grateful smile. I took the cap off the camera, flipped the camera on and framed up a shot of the two of them. Dex sat on the edge of the coffee table, while Rigby sat forward in his chair, both of them sipping the bourbon. I fiddled with the ISO settings on the camera, hoping to get their faces light enough but still keep the creepy, shadowy aspect of the room. As it turned out, it didn't look too bad. I angled myself so I was more behind Dex's left shoulder and that way I could see the hint of the fireplace in the background, the flames making the dark eyes of the animal heads dance.

OK, so maybe that was a little too creepy. The animals looked like they were watching me. I brushed off the feeling and concentrated on the job at hand.

Dex started with the basic questions about Rigby's life and his business, totally at ease in this position. I hated to admit it, but he was much better at being the host than I was. I took a silent sip of my drink, being careful not to jostle the camera too much.

"Tell us about the first time you saw Sasquatch," Dex prompted.

Rigby took in a deep breath and exhaled until his handlebar mustache wiggled up and down. "Well, that takes me back a few years to be honest. That's when I first saw the beast. That's what I tend to call it. Unlike my daughter, I cannot be sure what the creature is. But it is a beast. Oh yes, a terrible beast."

He paused to have a sip of his drink and I found myself leaning forward in anticipation. I adjusted my grip and kept the camera focused on his face.

"The first time I saw the beast was right here in this cabin. It was in the fall and the first snows had come. The first snows here always come like a feather. Very light, very beautiful. And damn cold. I didn't have enough wood in the shed out back to keep the fireplace going at full blast, so I spent the night in front of the fire, wrapped in my sleeping bag."

My eyes went to the fireplace and I imagined the scene. There was no way I could stay in this cabin alone.

"I must have drifted off," he went on, his eyes becoming

wide at the recollection. "Because I was suddenly aware of a sound. It started off far away, like my ears were blocked. Then I heard it more clearly. It was the sound of the door handle going up and down. Up. And down."

The skin at the back of my neck tightened and I resisted the urge to turn around and look at the door. I needed to keep filming them, even though it felt like this dark, heavy subject was looming behind me.

"I was facing the fire at the time and it had died down to the point where it wasn't as bright. I turned around and looked. I wasn't really afraid, just curious as all hell. What was there to be afraid of? Bears don't usually try the door handle when they're trying to break in."

"Then what happened?" Dex asked, placing his empty glass of bourbon on the table behind him. Like magic, Christina had Mitch's bottle and refilled his glass in seconds.

Rigby stroked at his mustache, his eyes on the door, lost in the moment. "Something I can't forget, that's for sure. Even now, I remember this as well as the day Christina was born. I saw the door handle go up and down, like someone was standing outside, trying to get in. But get in as silently as possible. But, you see, I had locked the door. It was windy that night and the latch back then was rotted, so I put the deadbolt on it. And I was glad I did. I only had that deadbolt so that guests would feel secure during their stay, even though there are no wild mountain men roaming the woods. But at that moment I thought maybe there *were* crazy mountain men out there, looking for a warm place to hide."

He paused, taking a deep breath. "Thinking that, my first instinct was to go for my rifle. So I got to my feet, and believe me I was careful not to make a sound. It was freezing in this cabin with the fire so low and I remember how cold the gun felt in my fingers. But in the moment I grabbed the gun, the noise stopped. I looked and the handle was still. I may have shit my pants, because I'm telling ya, I was sure that if the person wasn't at the door, they were at the window. And watching me. Just look around now. Can you see out with the glare of the fireplace bouncing back at you?"

Dex turned his head and looked behind him. As he did so, he gave me a nod. I took the camera off of them and aimed it at the window behind Christina and Mitch. Rigby was right. All you could see at the window was the hazy, flickering reflection of everything inside. Someone could have been looking at us right then and there was no way we could have seen them.

"So," Rigby started and I brought the camera back to his face, "I froze and tried to figure out what to do next. They couldn't get in and I had a gun, so I figured I was at an advantage. Then I remembered the windows in the bedroom. They aren't that high above the ground and are easy to break."

Oh great. He was basically explaining how fucked we were in the cabin if anything were to happen to us.

"I went back there to check. It was easier to see out since the light didn't reach in the bedrooms. I looked outside. I didn't see anything. At first. Then the moon came out of a cloud and illuminated the snow. I saw prints out in it. Very large prints that hadn't been snowed in. Fresh. Then..."

I could feel the heaviness in the air, like everyone in the room was anticipating his next words.

"Then I heard another noise. A scratching sound. A sound that made me feel like losing my guts right there. It was worse than nails on a chalkboard. I can't even describe it but it made me sick. I gripped my gun tighter and I went back out here. The doorhandle wasn't moving. But something beneath it was. There's a space between the floor and the door. I've got rubber lining there to keep out the cold but that night, the rubber had been pushed up. There was a set of four claws sliding their way underneath the door."

I gasped, my heart thudding in my chest. I couldn't help it. Christina made a similar whimper.

Rigby nodded and wiped at his brow. "They were there for a second and they quickly withdrew like it knew I was watching. Ah, I don't even want to think about what would have happened if...well, anyway, those weren't normal claws. They were much longer and straighter than a mountain lion's and black like they were carved from black rock. The first claw was the longest...it was sharper, thinner, and twice as long as the other ones. It looked a lot like...fingers."

He finished off the rest of his drink, wiped his mouth and held it out for Christina to fill. I took that moment to nudge my now empty glass toward her too. Fuck this shit, I was getting drunk tonight. There's no way I was going to sleep if I didn't. Even though I didn't really believe what Rigby was saying, my imagination was overactive and I'd be thinking about it anyway. I was so, so glad that I was sleeping with Dex. I had a feeling I literally would be using him as a blanket. No, make that a shield.

"And that was that," Rigby said, leaning back in his chair.

"That was it?" Dex questioned.

"Yup. The claws disappeared. I spent the night awake, huddled in the corner, wrapped in a sleeping bag with the rifle in my hands. Like some damned fool. Next day I went outside and the tracks were gone. Snow had buried them so deep."

"But you said you had tracks, a mold of them made, right?"

"I do. That was from another time. Actually last year. And I'll show them to you tomorrow morning before we take off and tell you a bit more. But, I think I've talked enough for tonight. Time for drinking and talking about other things, don't you think?'

Dex agreed and I turned the camera off and put it down. I wobbled slightly from the bourbon and smiled at my light-headedness. Dex got up, stretching and came over to me. He patted me on the arm.

"Don't put that camera away," he warned. "We should go shoot some scenes outside."

Ha. Funny. "Uh, how about no?"

He grinned. "But you're the camera gal now. You don't get to be scared."

"I'm not scared," I mumbled. "I'm cold."

"You should be scared!" Christina exclaimed suddenly, getting off the couch. I jumped a bit, forgetting she was there for a second. She shot her dad the evil eye as she passed him by. "Thanks Rigby, now I'll be up all night. You weren't the one attacked, remember."

He smiled sympathetically at her as she took off to their room and slammed the door. He looked to us. "I didn't want to bring Christina here, but she insisted. She's hard to say no to."

I tried to look like I understood, though inside I was kind of judging him for the way he treated her. They had a whacked out father and daughter relationship, though I suppose it was no better than my own.

"Come on," Dex insisted, bringing me my coat and holding it out.

I sighed and let him put it on me.

Moments later we were all bundled up and heading out the door. I studied it, wondering how the claws - or God forbid - fingers, could fit under the door. They must have been quite thin. *If* it actually happened.

Now that Dex and I were outside with the camera and staring at the cabin from there, our surroundings lit up by the motion detector lights, I felt further removed from the story. And the bourbon was swirling nicely in my stomach, a pleasant distraction.

"Film the horses at the post," Dex suggested. I did, though they were just standing there, tails swishing, half in the dark and half in the light. I guess it was kind of atmospheric.

"That was quite something," I said about the interview, moving the camera's focus over to the cabin in a wide shot.

Dex rubbed his gloves together and held them up to his mouth, blowing hot air on them.

"He's quite the little storyteller, I was quite surprised," he admitted. "He seemed to believe it too. Maybe it's not a hoax."

I raised my brow at him. His eyes were dark and serious.

"You changed your mind fast," I noted.

"I think he's telling the truth. What can I say?"

"How about, what the hell has black claws? Bears do. You know, I've been camping in California and they have bear bins everywhere. Apparently those get broken into anyway because bears are damn smart when there's food around. I bet this was nothing more than a bear trying to get in the cabin. First by the handle and then underneath the door."

"Good explanation, Scully."

"Shut up."

"You're feisty when you've had something to drink," he noted with a sly grin.

Wasn't that the truth...

"Anyway, just because it freaked me out, doesn't mean it's true. And I'd like to go on believing it's not true. It would be better for both of us."

He walked up to me, his footsteps deliberate in the snow. "Are you planning on keeping me up all night?"

I lowered the camera and switched the subject. "So how did I do? I mean, with the filming."

He reached out and tucked a loose strand of hair underneath my hat. Even through his gloves, his fingers felt warm. "You did wonderful, Perry."

I closed my eyes and kept them closed until he took his fingers away.

"Let's go back in and relax," he said softly. "Deal with the beasty stuff in the morning."

That sounded like a good idea. I went straight for the bourbon.

11

"Crazy eights!" I yelled later that evening, throwing my hand of cards down on the table.

Dex put his palm to his face while Rigby put his finger to his mouth.

"Hey, Christina is trying to sleep," Rigby admonished me.

I grinned sheepishly. Sheepishly and sloppily.

I was drunk and we were all playing a game of Crazy Eights. I was kicking ass, naturally, since bourbon was like kryptonite. Or the opposite of that. I was awesome at cards when I was drunk.

We'd been playing for a couple of hours and the rustic clock on the wall, made of a shiny slab of wood with ducks painted on it, read 10pm. It wasn't late to me but I could tell the old farts were getting tired. Rigby kept yawning and Mitch looked like he was asleep with his eyes open. Only Dex and I were really playing though I was much more drunk than he was. That's probably because I drank more bourbon.

"Sorry," I said, trying to whisper. It came out hoarse. "I'm just really good at cards."

Dex gave Rigby a wry smile. "Just let her have this."

I reached across the table and smacked Dex's hand. "Hey! No patronizing me, remember!"

His eyes danced. "No, I don't remember. Was that one of our house rules?"

"Screw the rules," I said.

I swore his pupils suddenly expanded. "I can definitely screw the rules."

I smiled to myself and felt a wave of heat rush over me. It wasn't even all that warm in the cabin and the bourbon had me as hot as I was going to get. That wild look in Dex's eyes was supplying the rest.

Rigby eyed us both suspiciously and stood up. "I'm going to bed you two. Tomorrow will be a big day, I'm sure. For all of you."

There was an edge to his last words and I felt Mitch stir beside me. Oh right. I guess we were kind of hanging out where he was supposed to sleep. That wasn't very nice of us.

Dex picked up on it. He put his cards down, got up, and then reached down for me.

"Up you go, drunky," he said affectionately. He grabbed my arms and pulled me up. My feet failed – I don't know where they went – and I fell straight into his chest. Damn. I had forgotten how hard it was. He tightened his arms around me and damn, I had forgotten how hard they were too.

I was standing, no, leaning at an angle, unwilling to help myself. I raised up my head so that my face was peering up at his, inches away and smiled. "Thank you for catching me."

"Will you be OK?" Rigby asked Dex. Dex nodded without taking his amused eyes off of mine.

"I've got her," he said. I kept smiling.

He raised me up easily and plunked me properly on my feet like he was stacking a chair. Then he put his arm around me, holding me to him, and led me to our room.

"Good night," he told the guys over his shoulder.

They mumbled something I couldn't hear and soon I was in the pitch black bedroom. Dex let go of me to close the door and I began to sway to the side. Suddenly he was there, strong hands on me again, and leading me to the bed.

"Here, sit down," he said placing me on it. He began to take off my shoes.

My back didn't want to sit up so I leaned back until I was flat on the bed. The room began to spin a bit.

"It's dark in here and spinny," I muttered as he removed one boot. "Sorry if my feet stink."

"I've dealt with worse," he said and quickly removed the other. I was left alone for a few seconds while he did something in the corner. Then light glowed behind my closed lids. I opened them. He had gotten the kerosene lamp going.

His face appeared above me as he leaned over. "How are you feeling?"

"Good," I grinned. "Take off your shirt."

He laughed. "Whoa, OK. You're feeling fine, that's for sure."

"How about your pants?"

His smile twisted. "Oh Perry. You should be careful of what you ask of me."

I reached up and grabbed his head and pulled him down toward me. My body was being pumped full of alcohol and the adrenaline of being scared earlier and the charged concept of sleeping with him. Being naked with him. Of having sex in front of the fireplace. It swirled around in my veins, making me feel deliciously heavy inside and at the same time making me crave him, like I was a space that needed filling.

My fingers buried themselves in his hair, wrapping around the strands and holding on tight. I brought his anxious face down to mine and whispered, "You're going to have to take my clothes off then."

His eyes swept across my face in a lustful gaze before he blinked hard and tried to regain some control.

"I'll get you into your pajamas," he countered in a rough voice.

"I sleep naked now."

"Not tonight, you don't." He promptly began to undo my jeans. As I raised my hips to let him pull them off, I quickly took off my sweater and shirt. The neckline got caught on my face but when it was finally off, I lay there, languishing in the fact that I was wearing brand new undergarments: A lacy maroon bra and matching boy shorts that I had picked up when shopping with Rebecca the other day. It was a pricey purchase but it was worth it to see the expression on Dex's face as he looked over me. He was stunned.

"Oh Jesus," he murmured, his eyes lingering on every part of me like a man studying a most intoxicating puzzle. "Why are you doing this to me?"

I laughed and propped myself up on my elbows. The room spun a bit more and I tried to ignore the nausea. "Me? I'm not doing anything."

He stroked his chin. "Oh, yes you are. You are doing many things."

My eyes naturally fell to his groin but he quickly turned and was at my duffel bag, bringing out my Slayer shirt and flannel pajama pants. "Here we are. Aren't you cold?"

I shook my head even though my nipples were so hard they could have cut flesh. That wasn't just from being cold though.

Dex ignored that and ordered me to raise my hands in the air.

"I feel like I'm a disappointment to mankind," he remarked woefully as he placed the shirt through my arms and began to pull it down over my breasts. "Someone this gorgeous should be on display in a museum."

As he pulled it down, he let his hands drift softly over my breasts and my knees quivered from his hot touch. His mouth parted and he closed his eyes briefly, relishing the feeling of my breasts as much as I did from his fingers. He stroked them delicately, rubbing his thumb over my aching nipples. A pained whimper escaped from my mouth.

In a burst of passion, I leaned in and kissed him, using his wet mouth to bury my cries. All I wanted was him, now. I wanted to feel his cock in my hands, feel how hard I knew I made him. I wanted to taste him and make him moan. I wanted to be someone else, someone with no rules, no boundaries. No heart.

He tongued me back, eagerly at first, like I was a thirst he couldn't quench. A small groan escaped his lips. A sound of resigned annoyance. He reluctantly pulled his head back, leaving my lips wanting, my lungs breathless.

"Perry, this isn't you," he whispered. He placed his forehead on mine and closed his eyes. "Don't do this to yourself."

"What are you talking about?" I said and winced knowing I slurred the whole sentence.

"Let's go to bed," he said. He straightened up and pulled back the covers. He walked around the bed to his side and began to take off his cargo pants. I marveled at how sculpted his ass was in his boxer briefs before it was covered up by drawstring pants.

He turned and saw me gawking at him.

Pointing at the covers, he ordered, "Come on. Get in. Now."

I didn't move. I watched him get in, tossing off his shirt at the last minute. He lay flat on his back and pulled the covers up to obscure his ridiculously smooth and fit body.

"No," I told him. I flipped around until I was on all fours and slinked my way over to him until I was hovering above his body, the tips of my breasts grazing the covers.

"Perry," he warned. "You're drunk."

"You're chicken," I replied in my most seductive voice. "You can talk the talk but you can't walk the walk."

His eyes narrowed in challenge. "Oh, I can walk the walk. I can walk the walk so hard that you'll be sore for days."

"Put your money where your mouth is."

He angled his head and I noticed a twitch underneath the covers. His breathing was becoming more labored.

"Forget it," I said and, in one quick motion, pulled back the covers so he was exposed. "I'll put my mouth where your money is."

I didn't even know if that made any sense, but it sounded good. I dragged my fingernails down his chest and went straight for his pants, tugging the drawstring until it was loose, then I slipped the pants down.

I raised my head to look at Dex. He was watching me with a feverish intensity, confliction swarming his brow. I didn't understand why.

I ran my hand over his boxer briefs, sliding it over the massive rise of his erection. It was bigger than I remembered and harder than a brick. I was mesmerized by the feel of him pulsing beneath my touch, my brain clouding over with blood and alcohol.

Dex cleared his throat, sounding very far away. "Perry, please stop. I can't believe I'm saying this, but you have to stop."

I shook my head. The room spun faster. My grip on his dick grew tighter. "But you're so hard."

"Of course I'm hard," he sputtered out as if he were in pain. "I'm always hard when I'm around you. I'm thinking about investing in a jockstrap just to keep things in line."

I grinned and rolled back the band so just his shiny tip was exposed.

"Oh shit," Dex cried out and I glanced up to see him covering his face with his hands in anguish. "Oh no. Oh, please, I forbid you to go any further. Do not touch my cock."

There was a quick pounding at the wall at that and a muffled Mitch yelled, "Hey would you shut up in there? I'm trying to sleep!"

I giggled to myself, strangely unembarrassed. I fixed my attention back on Dex, who looked a bit mortified instead.

"You told me to throw out the rule book," I reminded him.

His eyes flashed. "You're drunk. You don't know what you're doing and I am *not* going to take advantage of you."

I laughed. "I think *I'm* taking advantage of *you*. Besides, when did you get so moral?"

"I don't know," he mumbled with eyes clenched shut, shaking his head back and forth on the pillow. "I don't know God damn it!"

"Shut up!" Mitch yelled again.

I ignored both of them. Then just before I lowered my lips on to the head of his cock, he reached forward, grabbed me hard and swiftly pulled me up with agile strength. Now my face was right up to his, my breasts, squished against his chest, his cock pressing into my pelvis.

"Please," he implored hoarsely. The lamp illuminated his eyes so they were wavering between desire and control. "You're not in your right mind. I know you're scared and confused – and my God, obviously horny as hell – but I can't let you do this. My balls are so blue they're black now, and I'm loathing myself for telling you to stop, but you *have* to. Please. I might not have the strength to make you."

I narrowed my eyes, feeling annoyed at the words that were coming out of his mouth and the firmness of his erection. Totally contradictory. Why couldn't I just get what I wanted?

"Perry," he said slowly, deliberately as he speared me with his gaze. "You'll regret this in the morning. You will hate yourself for doing this and you'll end up hating me. And you already hate me so much, that my heart can't take anymore of it. Please, let's just sleep and save the blow job for another day."

"There'll be no other day," I snarled, feeling mean and dizzy.

"Exactly," he whispered, giving me a small shake with his hands.

I watched him curiously. And more curiously. His face was growing darker. Blurrier.

I blinked hard and pulled out of his grasp a bit.

"You said you don't have the strength to stop me," I slurred, moving backward, wriggling my hips into him as I went. I put my arms underneath me until his dick was firmly in my hands again. He closed his eyes and let out a little moan.

I grinned as the world around me swirled. "You won't regret..."

My mouth decided forming words was too much effort and gave up. The room spun violently and the next thing I knew my head was face-planting into his chest and everything went silent and black.

12

"Good morning, sunshine," Dex's voice broke into my sleep like a jackhammer. My eyes sprung open from a dark, deep hole and I winced at the painful brightness.

I immediately shut my eyes and prayed for death. That didn't happen. I heard the door shut and Dex walk over, placing something on the table beside me. He sat down beside me and the bed lurched like stormy seas and my poor stomach and brains were the sinking ship.

He placed a hand on my forehead. "I'm sorry I couldn't let you sleep in but we have a big day ahead of us."

I groaned and slowly pried one eye open. He was dressed in grey jeans and black hoodie, newsboy cap on his head. His eyes looked a little dark and shadowy and I guess he must have been feeling mildly hungover. I would have given my right arm to only feel "mildly" hungover.

My God, why did I drink so much bourbon?

My God. What the fucking hell did I do last night?

My eyes widened at the sudden memory of groping Dex

in just my bra and underwear and I jumped in my bed, as if I could somehow escape it.

He smiled at my reaction. "Remembering something?"

"Oh my God," I groaned and lay my head back down on the pillow, covering my eyes with my palms. "Oh my God."

"I thought you'd say that," he said.

"Oh no," I mumbled rolling over. "I am just...oh God, bury me in a dark hole somewhere."

"Why are you so embarrassed?" he asked playfully. "So you passed out during an attempted blowjob. Who doesn't?"

My insides recoiled and my body went hot with shame. I let out a whimper as more images came back to me. "You were trying to stop me."

"Trying is the key word here," he said and he tapped the table where I saw a mug and a couple of painkillers. "Come now, sit up Miss Palomino. There's some tea here with hair of the dog. It'll make it better."

"It won't make everything better," I cried out softly and slowly brought myself to a sitting position. I eyed him, my eyes having trouble focusing. "You wouldn't let me do it."

"You sound amazed. No, I was trying to not let you. But had you not passed out, I don't know what would have happened. Let me tell you something though." He pointed at me and his eyes darkened. "As your friend, as your roommate, and I suppose your part-time lover, please don't do that to me again. I don't want to be in that position."

I snorted caustically, even though I felt like a few particles in my brain came loose. "You don't like saying no? I don't believe it."

He passed the mug to me and pressed the pills into my hand, hard. "Well believe it. I don't like saying no to you. Especially not like that. I've spent the morning gathering my balls from the floor and I'm sure the others aren't too happy with all the time I was spending in the outhouse."

A twinge of guilt tugged at my core but I ignored it. "Did it feel good to turn me down?"

He frowned. "I don't think you get it, Perry. It felt terrible. I still feel terrible. You presented yourself to me like a dinner before dying and I had to say no to that?"

I didn't know how to pose the next question delicately, so I just came out and said it.

"If asked you to," I said, my voice low so no one else in the cabin would hear my crudeness, "would you fuck me right now?"

He raised his brows, either in surprise at my vulgarity or at the question itself.

"I don't think you've ever asked a stupider question."

"Then why wouldn't you last night?" I felt so small asking it and buried my voice with a sip of the tea. It was sweet and strong and good and I felt sour and weak and bad.

"You still don't know?" He looked bewildered and tugged at his hair with annoyance. "Because you weren't sober. You were as drunk as I've ever seen you."

"So?"

"So? This might come as a shock but as I told you last night, I'm not about to take advantage of you."

"Even if I wanted you to?"

He leaned forward on his knees and clasped his hands together. He turned his head and looked me dead in the eye, mouth drawn in a tight line. "Perry, when I fuck you, you're going to want it. And you're going to be sober. I don't want just your body in all of this. I want everything. Your soul too."

"That's a pretty tall order," I said breathlessly. His words were causing butterflies to fly loose in my stomach.

"I know," he said determinedly. "And it's something I am willing to work for."

We elapsed into a somewhat awkward silence as I swallowed back the pills with the hot liquid. Everything about our relationship was so confusing now. But then again, when hadn't we been confusing, after everything we had been through. He was right when he called me his friend, his roommate and his part-time lover. I felt the same way about him, even though my brain screamed at me not to. I wanted sex from him and that was all. That *had* to be all. I had to remember that above all else. And I had to remind myself that it was OK to just want sex. Surely, he didn't really need my soul. He didn't deserve every part of me.

I sighed. "Well. Thank you for saying no."

He straightened up and looked away. "You're welcome. Thank you for passing out."

Then he got to his feet and left the room.

DEX HAD BEEN KIND ENOUGH to let me sleep through breakfast. When I emerged out of my room, fully-dressed and ready for my voyage to the outhouse, only the lingering smells of fried pork and eggs remained in the kitchen. Christina was busy doing the dishes and shot me a cheeky look.

"You've seen better days," she commented with her gap-toothed smile.

I nodded gently; any extra movement was making my veins press against my skull. I did my best to look presentable by soaking my face in the ice cold wash basin for a few minutes and wearing a load of blush and undereye concealer but this was one of those things I guess you couldn't hide.

"Where is everyone else?" I asked, carefully pulling on my boots.

She shrugged as she wiped down the cast iron pan. "I think they're outside looking over Mitch's guns."

I opened my mouth then shut it again, feeling uneasy.

She was watching me. "What?"

I looked around the cabin even though I knew no one was in earshot and came closer to her.

"Is Mitch all right? I mean he's a bit…"

"Intense?" she supplied.

"That, yes. He kind of creeps me out."

Christina looked grim. "That's Mitch. I stay away from his gross ass as much as possible."

"But are Dex and I going to be safe with him?"

She seemed to think that over. "Even though he doesn't believe it exists, if you're ever attacked by the Sasquatch, or any kind of wild animal, you couldn't do better than Mitch."

It sounded like she wasn't finishing her sentence.

"Otherwise?" I asked.

"You've got your boyfriend with you. You'll be fine."

"He's not my boyfriend," I said quickly.

She rolled her eyes. "Right."

I didn't have time to explain and I had a feeling she must have had some inkling about my drunken shenanigans last night – something I didn't feel like revisiting – so I grabbed my coat and stepped out into the cold morning.

They say everything always looks better in the light of day but the area around the cabin looked just as ominous and desolate as it did at night. The sky was a moody grey and the only brightness came from the few inches of snow that had fallen overnight. In the distance, beyond the tall, suffocating reach of the fir trees, were the jagged white peaks reaching into the sky, their sides marred by slashes of dark rock.

I shuffled my way through the white powder to the outhouse and got my business done as quickly as possible. The near freezing temperatures definitely kept the smell and grossness at bay, but my ass ended up almost getting frostbite.

I had just emerged and was washing my hands in a clump of snow when I heard the men emerge from around the cabin.

"Perry, you're awake," Rigby said as he and Dex came into view, Mitch behind them. Naturally he was holding a shotgun in his demented arms. "Thought we might not see you today."

I avoided Dex's eyes, knowing they were swimming with delight, and put on my best face. "I feel great. How about we get started?"

"You don't want breakfast?" Dex asked.

I kept smiling. Me hungover? Me positively mortified at my behavior last night? Get out of town. "I'm good."

Rigby nodded. "Then let's take a little walk, what do you think? I'd like to leave you with some idea of what to look for."

Dex folded his arms and looked at him sternly. "And fill us in on the rest of your story."

"Stories," Rigby corrected. "All true."

I didn't need to know that Dex was imploring me with his eyes to get the camera, so I quickly jumped back inside the cabin and got the equipment ready. Christina watched on with amusement as I clearly didn't know what I was doing, my hands cold and fumbling. She told me she wasn't coming with us though, and was going to stay behind at the cabin. It struck me as a little dangerous considering what had happened to her, but I guess going off with us as Rigby filled the lens with more horror stories wasn't the best either.

When I came back to the men, Mitch looked pumped and impatient, like he was jacked up on coke and ready to kill something. Even though that kind of attitude was probably preferable when you're seeking out a mythical beast like Sasquatch, it didn't make me feel any better.

We set out walking down a shale-strewn slope but my boots started sliding on the fresh snow. Before I fell to the jagged ground, Dex was at my side, grasping my arm and keeping me steady. I shot him a look of gratitude and was surprised to see a grave, strangely solemn, glint in his eyes. He kept his hand around my elbow, even though I was watching the terrain more carefully now. Still, I didn't feel like shrugging him off.

After we navigated the hill, we leveled out and came toward a rather ominous sight: A forest of soaring fir trees, their tops hunched over like they were huddling from the cold. In between the trees was a dark hollow, a path that led into the belly of the beast. It seemed like a rough and fathomless passage and a chilling breeze swept out from it, tossing back my hair and stinging my eyes.

"Are we going in there?" I asked quietly, knowing we were and not caring that it was a stupid question.

Rigby marched on, following behind Mitch, and raised his hand in the air dismissively.

"It was in the hollow that I first saw the footprint," he said.

I exchanged a look with Dex whose grip was tightening on my elbow.

"You scared?" I teased him in a whisper.

He rolled his eyes and let go of my arm, brushing past me to catch up with the others. I went after him, adjusting the camera in my hand, not too happy about being the last one.

Now that we were at a lower elevation than the cabin, the amount of snow was reduced to a thin trace and inside the hollow of trees the ground was frozen but bare. It crunched loudly under my feet and echoed despite the faint whistling from the wind that seemed to be born from blackness. With the overhanging trees blocking out all light from the sky, it felt like we were entering the dark Mines of Moria and looking ahead at the three men I was with, I knew none of them would make a good Gandalf substitute.

We walked cautiously through the forest for what seemed like forever, though was probably only a few minutes, until Rigby brought us to a stop. I looked around and saw nothing but the black shapes of trees – no way out and no way in. The light here was a dusky grey and I could barely make out the color of my red scarf.

Rigby kneeled down and swiped his gloved hands along the ground at the edge of the rugged trail.

"Here is where I took the cast of the footprint," he said and took his hands away. I squinted hard at the shape on the ground. It was just a few indents in hardened earth, marked by what looked to be remnants of dried plaster.

I felt a hard jab in my side and looked up to see Dex wielding his elbow like a weapon, motioning to my camera.

"All right, all right," I muttered and quickly turned it on. I fiddled with the settings to try and make the most of the low light until Dex's hand took over the buttons and in a few seconds, my screen glowed brighter.

I mumbled a defensive "thank you" and he stepped out to join Rigby at his side.

With the camera now recording their grainy images, Rigby told Dex the rest of his encounters with the Beast. After the incident outside the cabin, he had scoured the area looking for something that would explain what he saw. He too thought perhaps a black bear had been nosing around, but it didn't explain the tracks he saw, nor the shape and length of the claws. They were like fingers, he insisted, nothing that would ever be found on a bear.

It wasn't till the next spring, when he took out an American couple on a hunting trip, that something strange began happening. The couple had reported a feeling of being watched and hearing something walking behind them. When they had turned around, however, they never saw anything. Rigby said he stayed up late, waiting to see if he'd witness something similar. He never did until the last night, when he heard a low, gurgled breathing, like something was looking down his neck. He turned and saw nothing but a pair of red eyes in the distance. He grabbed his gun and followed it but didn't want to leave the camp out of his sight. It was then that he decided llamas would be a good animal to bring along on the trips – they made excellent watchdogs.

The next day they went back to the cabin, the couple spooked out and eager to go home. It was then that they walked through this very hollow and Rigby spotted the footprints. At the time there were a few of them, just across the path, like the creature crossed from woods to woods. They all took photos and the next day Rigby made his way back to take a cast of it. Unfortunately heavy rains fell in the night and only the one print remained.

"What did the American couple think?" Dex asked him.

Rigby smiled. "Well, actually they were excited. They

right away thought it was Sasquatch or Bigfoot. It didn't mean they wanted to stay and find out, but a few days later I got an email from them. The woman – Jill – had done some research on her own and found out that similar prints had been reported in the area with a connection to a red-eyed animal in the woods."

Chills slivered down my spine and I tried to keep the camera from shaking. It was getting colder in the woods and I was getting more spooked.

"Apparently," Rigby continued, "the local tribes here, the natives, believe in a creature called the Stiyaha. I contacted Ted Peppers, a native in Snow Crest who sells me great vegetables in the summer for my trips, and had a little talk with him. He said that a lot of natives in the Kootenays believe in two types of "monsters" in the area. One of them is a giant, hairy being that takes people and animals away. The other type is smaller and leads people astray. He personally believed they were probably one and the same. Then of course he went on to say he didn't believe in the nonsense anyway. Still, maybe he was onto something. The male kind of acts as a queen bee and stays deep in caves in the mountains, hibernating. Like a queen bee, he's much larger than the rest, in this case, the lady beasts, who are smaller. And like most ladies, more vicious."

I rolled my eyes while Dex nodded at Rigby in agreement.

"The females go out and find the prey and drag it back to the male, sometimes the prey is still alive or sometimes its dead."

"Like carrion," Dex commented.

"Right. Vultures in a way. Anyway, I poked around some more and I like to think that theory is true."

And at that he crossed his arms and hocked a disgusting loogy on the ground.

"So you think it's more than one beast?" I asked.

He shrugged. "It could be. I'll still call it the Beast until I have proof that there is more than one out there. But one is enough for me."

Dex looked down the dark path. "Should we continue down that way?"

Rigby shook his head. "I just wanted to show you this. Mitch will be taking you down here tomorrow and out to the other side. I've made a map and marked the spots where the Americans and I experienced a feeling of being watched, or where we camped. I also added some other areas where I've found strange hair caught on tree branches and crunched up animal bones. Mitch here will tell you it's all the work of a bear but I figured it couldn't hurt to include it."

I nodded, relieved that we wouldn't be going down the path just now but terrified that we'd have to be doing it tomorrow. And with Mitch, who was still eyeing me from time to time like he was the vulture and I was dead meat.

By the time we made it back to the cabin, my nose was cold as ice and my feet were frozen. I decided the next time I went on a hike, I'd wear all my socks at once.

Christina was all packed and ready to go and had the fire roaring to pleasurable levels. Rigby went straight to the bedroom and quickly emerged with a long box in his hands.

I raised my brows, not knowing what he was going to show us, until he told me I'd want to film this. I turned the camera on and he placed the box on the table for Dex and I to see.

When he pulled back the lid, I expected it to glow like

the briefcase in *Pulp Fiction*. Instead it was the plaster cast of the Beast's footprint.

It was like nothing I'd seen before and definitely not what I had built-up in my mind. For one thing, it was a weird shape. About a foot and a half long with three toe indents that were slightly bird like, complete with a touch of claw marks. The heel was very narrow and deep, like it pressed down hard, while the middle part of the foot was barely perceptible.

"Wow," I said in an exhale. "What the hell is this?"

Rigby raised his head, a twinkle in his eyes. "Not what you thought you'd see, is it?"

"I was expecting, you know, Bigfoot," Dex said, looking over my shoulder.

"You're expecting the hoax," Rigby explained. "Hoaxes come from somewhere, that's what I say."

He had a point there, which actually made the whole thing more believable. Of course, my mind was cycling through a list of things that could have made the print. It really could have been anything. Perhaps the toe area was caused by an eagle or a bear that was running and the rest was something else. It was found in a forest – albeit a creepy one – and I could imagine there was more than one animal walking around out there. To me, the print didn't say "weird beast creature" but a mix of a forest's inhabitants, much like the look of a freshly-cemented sidewalk on a busy street.

After I got enough footage of the print and Rigby prattled on about his theory and the unusualness of the shape, he snapped the case shut and gave us a wink. "So I saved the best for last."

I couldn't help but smile at his enthusiasm. No matter what lurked out in the woods, hoax or not, Rigby believed it fully and it was his belief that would fuel the episode. Even if nothing else were to happen to us during the trip, even if we never saw any other signs and it turned out to be nothing more than a scary hunting expedition with Mitch, it would still be entertaining.

Rigby put the case away in his pack and we went back outside into the cold as Christina was done readying their horses for the jaunt back home. I wanted nothing more than to stay inside with my ass parked by the fire, but I didn't want to be rude either and not see them off.

I was just leaving the cabin when Christina came up to me, thrusting a small vinyl bag into my hands.

"Here," she said, zipping it open. Inside was a folded piece of paper and two walkie talkies. "I know Rigby gave you his map but I thought you'd want my map. I don't want to tell him how often I've been out before and after the accident or he'd freak. But I circled some spots that I thought were kinda weird."

I eyed her carefully, seeing sincerity in her big eyes. "Kinda weird?"

She looked over her shoulder at her father who was getting on his horse, and took a step closer. "The other day I found a deer gutted from belly to neck. All its organs were gone."

I both frowned and grimaced. "The other day? You came back out here?"

"I had to know," she whispered harshly. "Dad was in town so I thought I'd explore. Nothing happened to me, obvs, and I was on Taffy. I didn't tell him cuz he'd be totally mad but I thought you might wanna know where it happened. It looked like it had been dragged a few feet too and then left behind. I don't know why. It was too gross to look closely and smelled raunchy, so I booked it home after that. Anyway, I circled it on my map for you."

"Oh," I said uneasily. "Thanks, I guess."

"And the walkie talkies are also for you guys. I know your phones don't work here and Rigby and I have a set back at the cabin. In case you get into danger. Mitch doesn't even carry one so, you know, thought it would make you feel safer."

Actually, it kind of did. I thanked her and she beamed in response before running back to Taffy.

"Well," Rigby said, leaning lazily on the horn on his western saddle. "I'll be leaving you guys for a few days. I probably should have packed some walkie talkies for you all…"

"I just gave them to Perry," Christina piped up as she swung up on Taffy.

He looked to me in surprise and I picked up one of the talkies out of the bag and waved it at him.

"Oh, good," he said, straightening up. "Glad I've got a daughter with bigger brains than I. Well, God forbid anything should go wrong, but if it does, just use those and I'll come a running. I'll leave it on all day and night, just in case, so don't you worry."

I swallowed hard at the thought but managed to look confident.

"Safe ride back," Dex said to them with a wave, before coming toward me.

I watched Rigby and Christina coax their horses into a walk and soon they were out of sight, leaving only me, Dex and Mitch. Alone. It took Dex standing in front of me and staring down at my hands to realize I had been gripping the bag until my knuckles had turned white.

13

Dinner that evening was stiff and awkward between the three of us. Dex decided to take over Christina's role of making dinner, which normally would have been quite sexy, but him being preoccupied meant that I was alone in the living room with Mitch, both of us staring at the fire.

Well, I was staring at the fire. Mitch was staring at me. And he hadn't stopped staring at me for the last fifteen minutes. It would have been creepy on its own, but it was made worse by the incident we had earlier.

After Rigby and Christina left, we all went inside to get warm and plot out the rest of the day. Mitch had toyed with the idea of going hunting, for what I didn't know, while the sky was still clear. He invited me to come and be his spotter and when I immediately declined, he decided he wasn't going to go after all. Just great.

So Dex took the initiative and began to plan out the next few days. Over bags of Rigby's homemade venison jerky and cups of coffee, the three of sat around the table figuring out our shooting schedule. Mitch wanted us to go camping the next day but Dex decided that it would be best to have the cabin as a home base for as long as possible and maybe ditch the whole camping idea all together. Mitch was used to the outdoors but we weren't and we didn't want to camp in this weather until we absolutely had to. There was still plenty of stuff to film around the cabin and we couldn't ignore the fact that Rigby mentioned it would snow for the next 48 hours.

Mitch relented, though he told us in order to reach some of the places on the map, we'd have to pack up the llamas and make a night of it. I didn't like that idea at all, but from the quick look I had at the map, I knew short journeys were out of the question. At least Dex and I had convinced him to be in the cabin for the next few days.

It was after this conversation when Dex excused himself to go to the bathroom. I watched him leave the cabin, feeling alone and nervous, and I quickly got up to busy myself by making another pot of coffee.

I had my back turned to Mitch and didn't even hear him until he breathed down my neck and said, "You making me one?"

I gasped and turned around, nearly spilling the instant coffee container. Mitch was nearly pressed up against me, way too close for comfort and way inside my personal space. I had to lean my head back to feel remotely comfortable and my hands gripped the edge of the counter.

"Sorry," I said, my voice heavy with annoyance. "I can make you one if you want."

He grinned and I hated that I was so close I could see his front teeth were all fake, their whiteness not matching the rest. He had obviously lost them all somewhere and I didn't care to know about it.

"Girly, you making one for him?"

I cocked a brow and adjusted myself. I wished I had more room to maneuver away from him.

"For Dex?"

"You his woman?"

I narrowed my eyes in thought. Did I tell him yes or no? I wasn't Dex's woman but this was the type of circumstance you were supposed to lie in.

"I'm his partner," I managed to say. It was the truth.

"You ever been with a real man?"

Had I not been in such a vulnerable position, I would have laughed. I felt a smiling coming on but I swallowed it with a click in my throat.

"Yes I have," I said, finding strength in my gut. I looked him right in his beady eyes. "And I don't need you to show me, if that's what you're getting at."

A flash of hatred washed across his eyes, the kind that made my breath hitch, then it was gone. He straightened up and took a step back.

"I'm not getting at anything girly," he said, looking suddenly nonchalant. "But I'd still like a coffee, if you wouldn't mind."

He turned and went back to the table. I watched him for a few beats, a weird knot in my stomach, until Dex came back into the cabin. A cold gust of wind followed him in and he quickly shut the door but I only felt relief. As he brushed a few flakes off his shoulders and hung up his jacket, he said, "It's really starting to come down out there."

I nodded and turned back to the coffee preparations. I wasn't sure if I should say anything to him about Mitch or not. If I did, I had a feeling Dex wouldn't take to it very well and it would probably mess up the whole shoot. If Dex didn't get his ass beaten by the giant bald monkey, he'd at least piss Mitch off and everything would be over. So I decided to keep my mouth shut.

For the time being.

Now it was dinner and while Mitch hadn't made any moves, his staring was driving into my core, making me feel weak from the inside out. I kept my eyes on the crackle of the flames, allowing myself to be hypnotized by them.

When Dex finally announced that dinner was served, I practically jumped to my feet and scampered over to the table. I would have eaten pig's brains if that's what he was serving, but it was just grilled cheese sandwiches with a bit of canned Irish stew. Not gourmet but good enough and I was starving.

Mitch brought the bottle of bourbon to the table, which Dex and I both promptly refused. No way in hell was I going down that road again, especially since I felt like shit for most of the day. In fact, by the time dinner was over, even though it was only 7pm, I was ready for bed.

I quickly did the dishes, then grabbed a bottle of water from the box of food supplies and headed to the room. Dex looked up at me from the couch where he was analyzing footage I had shot. Mitch looked at me too with glazed eyes, the bourbon bottle in his lap.

"I'm turning in early," I told them. Well, I told Dex. I didn't want to look at Mitch any longer than I had to.

Dex looked concerned and started to get up.

"Stay," I commanded him. "I'm just really exhausted. Long day."

Long hungover day.

He bit his lip briefly, then nodded. "All right, well let me know if you need anything. I won't be up too long either, just want to get an idea of what we need to shoot."

I smiled quickly and shut the door behind me.

I immediately ran into the wardrobe. I had forgotten how dark the room was when the lamp wasn't lit and the night sky was moonless as a steady stream of snow fell to the ground in waves.

I fished a flashlight out of my pants and then proceeded to get into my pajamas in record time. Though it was warm by the door, the closer to the bed – and the window – you got, the colder the room was. It was as iced as the air outside, the walls and window providing no insulation at all. By the time I had slipped on a hoodie and more socks, I jumped under the covers and bundled myself up in them until I stopped shivering.

Lying there alone gave me a chance to think unfettered. I wondered what to do about Mitch and if there would be any further weirdness from him. I figured I'd just stick as close to Dex as possible. Maybe I was overreacting and maybe Mitch would get the hint, but it didn't hurt to be careful.

Of course, it could hurt to be close to Dex. I still felt flushed at the thought of what I did last night and even more flushed when my mind began to pull up some of the drunken memories and dwell on them. The feeling of his smooth skin beneath my hands, the look in his eyes, the hardness of his cock beneath my pelvis. It was like watching a porn in my head, only I wasn't the star of it. Drunk Perry was and I winced a few times in disbelief at my actions. Though I was mildly insulted earlier when I found out that Dex had stopped me from going down on him, I was mainly grateful as hell. He was right. I would have hated myself and if he had let me do it, I would have hated him. This was one of the few times where rejection didn't completely suck and a warmness squeezed around my heart. I didn't know how I felt about that man half the time, but he earned my trust again last night. I just hoped he knew how to hold onto it.

I was half-asleep in these chaotic thoughts, my mind now focusing on the Beast and the stories Rigby had told us, when a light crept behind my eyelids and I felt someone else in the room with me.

I lifted up the covers and poked my head out into the frigid air. The kerosene lamp was lit and Dex was standing on the other side of the bed with his back to me, slipping on his drawstring pajama pants.

Then he took off his sweater and shirt and bent down to pick up another shirt. His back was bare, the tattoo on his shoulder hard to read but totally visible.

"What's that say?" I whispered, not finding my full voice in the cold.

He started at the sound of my voice and slowly pivoted at the waist, shooting me a sly look from over his shoulder.

"I thought you were sleeping."

"It's too cold for sleep."

He grinned and turned totally around. "That's what I'm here for."

He shoved his arms in the shirt and was about to raise it above his head when I stuck a hand out and pointed at him.

"Seriously, Dex, what does it say?"

He dipped his chin to chest and gave me a long look, his eyes wheeling and dealing. After a thick pause, he said, "All right. But I'm putting my shirt back on after cuz it is cold as balls in here."

I nodded, feeling a smile spreading inside my stomach and raised myself up on my elbows.

He came over and took back the covers and climbed on in. Then he turned so I could see his shoulder, bringing the covers up to his waist.

Written in the same italic font as the "And with madness comes the light" tattoo on his chest read the new tattoo.

It said: "Within your light, I lose the madness."

I didn't know what to think or say so I just took my hand and gently pressed my fingers against the words, tracing along it. He shivered from my touch but his skin was as cold as stone.

"You seen it?" he asked and gave me a backwards glance.

"Yeah," I whispered, my breath clouding in the air.

"Good," he said and twisted around, putting his shirt on. He shifted his body under the covers and rolled over to his side, as if he was going to sleep.

I wanted to talk about it. What did it mean? Did it mean what I thought it meant? Was I his light? Did Dex get a tattoo about me? Or was I so far out of touch that it wasn't about me at all? Maybe it wasn't about a person. Maybe it was a thing.

"Dex," I said gently.

He grunted in return.

"Dex, what does it mean?"

Silence.

"The tattoo," I proceeded. "Within your light I lose the madness. What or who is the light?"

"It's anything you want it to be," he mumbled, his voice heavy and obscured by the covers.

"But what is it to you?"

I watched him carefully in the lamplight. His body deflated with one long exhale and I knew he was having a debate in his head over what to tell me, if anything. He always gave you something, just not everything. At least, the old Dex was like that.

He said something so low and so muffled that I strained to hear him.

"What was that?" I asked, leaning forward until my chest was pressed up against his back.

I heard him pull the covers away from his face and the sharp exhale through his nose.

"You," he said, voice low enough to vibrate.

I felt frozen on the outside but inside my heart had vaulted.

It was about me.

"Me?" I repeated quietly, my throat thick.

He turned onto his back, and rolled his head to the side to look at me. I was blocking most of the light, so his eyes looked dark and fathomless. Unreadable.

"You," he said slowly. "You're the light. You're *my* light."

My chest pinched at his words and wave of warmth flooded me from head to toe. I was no longer cold. I was glowing from the inside out.

I breathed heavily, studying the darkness that was his face. I felt the unmistakable urge to crawl into the space between his chest and arm, to hold him. My eyes dropped to his chest, to the fine patches of hair there and I fought the need to trail my fingers through it.

"I know it doesn't matter to you anymore," he went on gently. "But you've always been my light. When I'm with you, I lose this darkness, this madness around me. The madness *inside* me. But I had to go mad to realize that. I had to lose you to know it."

Within your light, I lose the madness. Dex had gotten a tattoo about me. I was his light. I couldn't comprehend any of it. It just didn't make sense.

I looked away from his eyes and at the window that was laced with ice crystals and snow, a light sheen of condensation on the interior. I didn't know what I was feeling but it was something that made me feel extremely unbalanced, like I was navigating new territory.

He rolled back onto his side, facing away from me and tucking the blankets up around him. "You asked, I told."

He did. I wasn't expecting his honesty, for him to be so blunt. I thought he'd skirt the issue or make something up but there he was telling me he got something about me inked on his body. Something about me that would be there for life, regardless if I came back into it or not.

"It's a beautiful tattoo," I finally told him, my voice breaking slightly. I cleared my throat then settled back to my side of the bed. I waited, watching him for a few beats. He didn't say anything else, though I knew he was still awake.

I WOKE up to the eerie feeling that something wasn't quite right.

My eyes sprung open and focused on a greying point on the slanted ceiling. The room was a bit lighter now that it was dark and I guessed that the amount of snow from outside was throwing in light from the window.

The air wasn't as cold above the blankets as earlier and inside I was nice and toasty. Beside me I could hear Dex's breath going in and out in the easy depths of sleep. But that wasn't the only sound in the room.

A low, rough scratch came from the wall behind me, just right of the window and above Dex's head. I moved slightly to get a better look, my neck craning and ears straining.

There it was again. It wasn't coming from inside the room, but outside. It sounded an awful lot like nails being run down a chalkboard, only replace the chalk board with a wooden cabin. The sound didn't even flow smoothly; it stopped and started like a nail was getting caught on bits of wood. It was loud and deliberate and reverberated in my head.

I didn't dare breath, didn't dare make a sound, didn't even swallow. I just listened as the sound slowly repeated itself, starting up high and then making its way down. All my instincts told me that it was probably a tree – when I thought about the view out of the window, I couldn't remember what exactly was out there. If it wasn't a tree though, I didn't know what the hell it could be. And I didn't want to find out either.

In fact, all I wanted to do was bury my head back under the covers and pray for morning. I didn't believe in Sasquatch, Bigfoot or some Beast. But I'd seen enough shit to know that there was still plenty for me to be afraid of out there. What if it was a ghost or demon? I knew we were out in the middle of nowhere, but what if Dex's mom had followed him here and was standing outside the cabin, trailing her fingers down the side of the cabin? Though her fingers would have to be thick long claws to duplicate the sound I was hearing.

So I did the only thing that's ever worked in these situations.

"Dex?" I whispered harshly. "Are you awake?"

No answer. I poked him in the side. No movement. I contemplated tickling him awake but decided his laughter might scare off the thing making the noise. Not that I wanted it to stick around but I at least wanted him to hear what I had been hearing.

I poked him again. "Dex," I hissed.

Finally he stirred.

I placed my hand on his arm and whispered, "Be quiet."

"Be quiet?" he answered back and I had to shush him

right away. "I'm half-asleep and you're telling me to be quiet."

"There's a noise outside, listen."

He held in his breath and we both listened.

Nothing.

"What was it?" he asked.

I shushed him again and closed my eyes, thinking it would help.

Nothing. The scratching had stopped.

"Fuck," I muttered.

"What was it?" he asked again, his voice drowsy.

"Scratching," I told him. "Like nails on the side of the cabin."

He let out a low, short laugh. "Maybe it's deer. Remember on D'Arcy Island?"

"It wasn't deer. This was something worse than that."

"You're just spooked," he said with a yawn. "Go to sleep. Or at least let me go to sleep."

"I heard something," I said determinedly.

"Then go look out the window and check."

I really didn't want to do that. I was afraid that if I looked out the window, the face of a big ugly monster with red eyes would pop up and scare the shit out of me. Yeah, I know that sounds like something that only happens in the movies, but they were a common occurrence with me. And that didn't make them any less scary.

"Fine," I mumbled and slowly eased myself out of the covers. I placed my hands on the corners of the window sill and pulled myself up. I kept my eyes closed until the right moment and, after taking a breath of courage, opened them.

It was white outside. The snow had stopped falling with only a casual flake drifting slowly and the sky was lit up glowing grey. I could make out the white-dusted trees nearby and the edge of the outhouse farther off. To my disappointment, there were no trees next to the cabin, nothing that could have made the noise I had heard.

If I had even heard a noise at all.

I lowered myself down to the bed and snuggled under the covers until I was warm again, hugging my knees in the fetal position. Eventually Dex said, "See anything freaky?"

I bumped my butt against his back in response and soon I was asleep.

14
―――――

"Holy fuck."

Dex's voice rang out from behind the cabin just as I was heading outside to use the outhouse. Mitch was at the llama corral, feeding them their daily dose of hay and grains.

I quickly shut the door and stomped my way through the snow. It was about ten in the morning and the sun was high in the sky, making the snow that had fallen during the night sparkle like diamonds, and feel just as hard beneath my boots.

I rounded the corner, pulling my knit cap down over my forehead and stopped when I saw Dex standing beneath our bedroom window looking at the ground, then up at the window and back down again.

"What is it?" I asked, my pulse quickening.

"Tell me about the sound you heard last night," he said, his voice trailing off.

I bit my lip anxiously and came over to join him.

Dex was standing right in front of a set of footprints that lay right beneath the window. Footprints that looked eerily like the one Rigby had shown us. And on closer inspection, I realized that it wasn't just one set of prints but many. They were messy and blurry with snow having blown down their ridges, looking like they were left in a hurry.

Dex pointed off to the otherside of the cabin.

"They disappear into the forest over there," he said. He finally brought his eyes over to look at me and they looked startlingly brown and clear in the harsh, snow-blind white of morning.

I held his gaze for a minute, surprised at the sudden way my heart was tingling at the sight of him. Memories of what he said last night, his tattoo, that I was his light, surfaced in my head. Then I broke away. I crouched down to the snow and lightly touched the print. It wasn't quite as clear as the cast but it was definitely the same shape. About a foot and a half long with a deep, narrow indent at the heel. Whoever – or whatever – left these seemed to have stood in the one place for a long time, then perhaps circled the area before taking off for the woods. Considering the place was right below the window, it probably meant it was the source of the sound.

"I told you," I said, my eyes focusing and un-focusing on the glittering snow, "it was a scratching sound."

"Huh," Dex said. He had stepped forward and was running his hand down the side of the building. I got up and peered at it. There were five grooves made into the rough cabin wall, fresh splinters sticking out of it. They weren't that deep but they was there. And that was enough.

I suddenly felt sick to my stomach and turned away from the sight, walking a few feet away until I was at the base of a tree. I leaned against it and breathed in sharply through my nose, trying to keep the nausea at bay.

"Perry," Dex said in quiet alarm and came beside me. I felt his hand on my shoulder, giving me strength.

I closed my eyes. "There was something there last night. While we were *sleeping*."

"It could be anything," he said, though his voice wavered with lack of confidence.

"Anything is still something." I swallowed back the bitter taste in my mouth and stood up. I don't know why I was having such a physical reaction to the fear but I suppose fear wasn't something I handled very well anymore. This was the first time I was met with something terrifying since the whole possession game.

"Maybe this was a mistake," Dex whispered. His gloved hand went from my shoulder down to my hand and he squeezed it hard, hard enough that I had to look up at him. He couldn't have looked more worried. "I knew I shouldn't have brought you out here."

I cleared my throat. "Once again, it was my idea to do this. I didn't believe in a Sasquatch."

"Do you now?"

I shook my head in confusion. "I don't know what I believe. Something was here though. Something big with sharp claws and it was right beneath our window."

Dex looked over my shoulder at the cabin and his gaze trailed beyond that. "Maybe it's Rigby. Or Christina."

"Or Mitch," I supplied.

He fixed his eyes on mine. "Maybe."

"But why?"

"Publicity."

The wheels started turning in my head. "Publicity. But this would be bad publicity."

Dex took a step closer and lowered his voice in confidence. "But it's better than no publicity. And in this economy, it's worth as much as gold."

He scratched at his nose and looked around him again. "Look, Rigby and Christina could be telling the truth. Or they could all be big fat liars who brought us out here so their business would get featured on the show."

"What about Mitch?"

"I'm sure Mitch would benefit too. But I'm not too sure about him yet. He seems like the type who would go around bagging Labrador puppies, but he doesn't strike me as smart or someone who would keep his mouth shut about this kind of thing."

"So you think there is no Beast here at all?"

His eyes narrowed in thought. "I honestly don't know. But before we both start freaking out over this, maybe we need to take things with a grain of salt."

I nodded and eyed the prints again. "So what now? Do we tell Mitch what we found?"

He bit his lip for a few moments. "Tell you what, I'll go back inside and get the camera. We'll record it and then destroy the evidence. I don't think we need to say anything to him right now."

He took off and a minute later he was quickly filming the prints, whispering commentary into the camera. I felt momentarily ousted as cameraperson but decided to ignore it. And when he switched it off, checking around to see if Mitch had witnessed any of it, I went over and snatched it out of his hands.

The corner of his mouth lifted in amusement. "Worried I'm stepping on your toes?"

"A little bit," I admitted, cradling the camera in my arms like a baby.

He studied me for a beat before turning his attention to

the ground and quickly rubbing his black army boots through the snow, covering up the prints so all that was left was a messy disturbance.

He stepped back to admire his footwork and shook his head. "No. Doesn't look right. Too much snow."

With glinting eyes he turned to me and smiled. Then, as quick as a flash, he bent down, scooped up snow into his hand, balling it up.

I had no time to react. I saw white, then the snowball connected with my head with a thump, sending snow flying everywhere, including down into my eyes.

I blew the snow away from my face and tried to glare at him through watery eyes.

"I was wondering how long it would take you to-"

Whoomp.

Another snowball, this time it impacted on my shoulder.

I dusted the snow off my coat with my free hand and gave him the biggest stinkeye I could muster.

"How old are you again? Twelve?"

He grinned, teeth white as the snow he had freshly gathered.

"Old enough to make you come, young enough to make you hate me for it."

"Oh jeez," I muttered, shaking my head, and turned around.

Bam.

Snowball to the back of my head.

I didn't bother turning around and just walked straight to the outhouse, hearing him call behind me.

"Aww, spoilsport."

∼

THE REST of the day Dex and I stayed mum about the footprints, which was easy since Mitch took off after our lunch of dehydrated soup, mumbling something about spotting deer in the area. That gave Dex and I a whole lot of time to do nothing.

Well, *I* did nothing, except flip through about 20 old Reader's Digests that were left on the bookshelf. Dex took a nap in the bedroom. For a brief instant I wondered if us having time alone together would result in seduction of some sort. It was incredibly romantic, when you thought about it. Both of us were alone in a cabin in the woods, a light snow falling outside, a roaring fire with that God damn rug that I could not stop thinking about having sex on. I had a short fantasy of him inviting me to bed with him, or perhaps taking me right there on the floor. If we were together like *that*, there would be no downtime for us. We'd never be bored.

But we weren't together like that and we weren't together at all and that was a good thing. Whatever I had now with Dex was strained at times and weird at best, but we were managing. I'd probably manage better if I wasn't so horny, if I wasn't so tempted to just jump him half the time. And if I hadn't found out that his tattoo was about me. That definitely threw me for another loop, adding another layer of confusion to our relationship dip.

I have to admit, I was a bit worried about myself, afraid I would do something stupid again, like try and give him a blowjob. It was one thing to avoid getting drunk around him, but sometimes I feared I would just kiss him out of the blue. Then what would happen? We'd have sex, most definitely. But then what? What did that lead to between us except for douchecanoe maneuvers and heartache?

Well, and a tattoo.

That damn tattoo. Dex saw the light.

He saw me.

I shook my head of the thoughts, trying to ease away the slow squeezing of my chest and the warmth between my legs. Funny how part of you could be so emotionally confused, yet the other part just wanted to get the fuck off.

I flipped the pages of the musty-smelling digest, turning my thoughts to Ada and wondering how she was holding up with my parents. I missed them all to be honest with you. Ada the most, but I also missed my father's snide comments when he watched the news at night, or the way my mom prettied herself in the hall mirror before stepping outside. Silly, stupid things, but I missed them just the same. I had to remind myself that things wouldn't have stayed easy had I remained behind. They would have been watching me like crazy, waiting for me to go crazy. Like poor Pippa.

The thought of her also added an extra pang to my insides. I wondered where she was right now, if she was watching me. I wondered about the Thin Veil and how close it was to me. If I looked hard enough for it, could I see it? And if I could, would I go through it? I went in somewhat normal and came out with some weird ability for Ada – and maybe others – to hear my thoughts. What would happen if I went through again?

My eyes gazed around the cabin, growing a bit sleepy from the approaching twilight and the heat of the flames. Pippa no longer scared me and I hoped that one day she would show herself to me again. I still had questions and I knew none of this, the hardships she faced, was going to bypass me completely.

I must have fallen asleep in my chair because the next thing I knew I was waking up to hear Dex and Mitch laughing over the clatter of plates and cutlery.

I raised my head, a stream of drool latching onto my shoulder, and looked behind me at the kitchen area. The two of them were chopping up some small dead animal and they even seemed to be getting along. I didn't like that one bit.

I wiped my chin and got up, weak from the nap and not surprised to see it was pitch black outside.

Dex was the first to notice my presence.

"Sleeping beauty is awake," he said with a smirk.

I rested my elbow on the chair and watched them from a distance. "What are you guys doing?"

"Wow, you really were out like a light," Dex commented. "You sure you didn't get into Mitch's bourbon? I feel like I could take you on tonight, if you did."

He waggled his brows suggestively. I responded with a wry look and was pleased to see Mitch was eyeing Dex with careful disdain, like he never considered him a threat until that moment. Perhaps I shouldn't have felt smug over that, but I wanted Mitch to know his creepy game wouldn't go very far.

I nodded at the animal. "What is that?"

Mitch slowly pried his hawk eyes off of Dex and went back to slicing and dicing.

"Hare," he growled and whacked a cleaver down hard. "And grouse."

Oh, yum. I quickly thought about reverting to vegetarianism.

"We've got a grill going on outside," Dex said, washing his hands with a bottle of water and hand sanitizer. "I have no doubt it'll be tastier than it looks."

I nodded absently and made my way over to the door, getting my coat off the peg and piling on my scarf and hat. That was the most annoying thing about being where we were: every time I wanted to use the bathroom, I had to brave the elements. I felt like the younger brother in *A Christmas Story*.

When I came back, Mitch was standing over a grill he had set up by the door, turning over the grouse on the hot coals. The smell it gave off was delicious and the steam and heat formed thick clouds in the cold night air above.

"He seems to think you're his woman," he said under his breath. His tone made my back feel like snow had dribbled down it.

I clamped my mouth shut, trying not to say anything as I walked to the door but just as I closed my hand around the knob, I said in a haughty voice, "He can think any damn thing he wants."

I wondered how much of that I actually meant.

To my surprise, the packet of mashed potatoes and grilled grouse was actually tasty. Much better than the canned crap we had been eating. I begrudgingly told Mitch that. He just glared at me, which I preferred to his other look. Dex seemed to pick up on the strain between us but he was happily stuffing his face and didn't say anything.

The three of us retired to the living room after dinner – and by that, I mean we moved a couple of feet and plunked ourselves down, me on the rug, face to the fire, and Dex and Mitch on the armchairs. Mitch had finished off the old bottle of bourbon and had brought out another, albeit cheaper, version. This time Dex and I did partake in a glass each, both of which Dex iced with a clump of fresh snow. It was delicious and though I was keeping myself in check, I was grateful for the simple act of drinking. It gave us something to do instead of just staring at each other, and despite being sluggish from the heavy meal, I knew it would be quite a while before I was ready for bed. My mind was racing and that vague threat of the beast – or someone pretending to be the beast – was sitting at the back of my head.

I had taken my last sip of bourbon and was debating whether I should ask Mitch for another or not when the dim cabin was suddenly aglow with a blinding bright light.

"The motion detectors," Dex announced excitedly, quickly getting out of the chair and heading to the windows. Mitch did the same, while I rolled over and scooped the camera off of the table.

Even with a heavy sweater on, I could feel my hairs standing straight up on my arms. I was scared of being scared, as stupid as that sounded, and made sure I was right beside Dex, my shoulder rubbing against his.

"Turn it on," he hissed at me, not taking his eyes off of the scene outside.

I did as he said and kept the camera focused out the window. I held it still while my own eyes came off the viewfinder and scanned the scene. There was nothing outside that I could see. It had stopped snowing for the moment and the trees were still. We all stared until the fog from inside steamed up the glass and no amount of rubbing would clear the view.

Mitch slipped on his boots and a jacket and picked up his shotgun that was resting behind the door.

"Let me check this out," he barked, the crazy excitement showing in his eyes. He opened the door and bolted out into the night. I gave Dex the camera while I quickly got dressed for the elements and soon we were outside too, our boots making no noise on the fresh powder. It was colder than normal and when I looked up to the sky I saw only a few thick clouds hanging lazily near the moon. Everything was still and I couldn't hear much except the beating of my heart and Dex's ragged breath beside me, the air freezing in thin clouds near his face.

Everything was illuminated by the cold lights, bathing us in an otherworldly blue glow. Dex's face took on a sickly pallor against his dark hair and eyes.

"You still filming?" he whispered as he searched the darkness beyond the light.

"Yes sir," I answered, though I wasn't sure what I was supposed to be filming. What had tripped the lights?

"Maybe we should go check on the llamas?" Dex asked.

"Why?"

He cocked a brow at me. "Because we'd look like quite the idiots if we're freaking out because Twatwaffle got loose."

Fair enough. Still, I wanted to know where Mitch went.

"Mitch?" I called out softly. I didn't want to yell and attract attention to myself, even though it was pretty obvious that if there was something out there, it knew about us. It could have easily been watching us from the trees and we wouldn't have a clue. I hoped to God I wouldn't see glints of red in the darkness.

Dex tugged at my arm. "Come on. I'm sure he's finding something new to kill."

"I just hope it's not us," I said under my breath but I let Dex lead me around the other side of the cabin toward the corral where the llamas were kept.

We were halfway between the cabin and the pen, amongst a border of low bushes, when we were suddenly engulfed in darkness. The motion detectors went out and the cloud had settled over the moon.

"Shit," Dex swore. "I knew I should have brought a flashlight."

I turned and looked back at the cabin. The light from

inside was barely visible, this side of the cabin having no windows.

I chewed on my cold lip, feeling the moisture evaporate in the dry air.

"Do you have that light for the camera?" I asked.

"Inside," he said with sigh. "Well, fuck, let's just run back and-"

He was cut off by a blood-curdling scream. I don't use that phrase lightly. That scream was inhuman and made my insides shrink in terror.

"This isn't good," Dex said quickly and I felt his arm go around my waist, holding me against him. I appreciated it but it didn't make me feel any less terrified.

"What was that?" I squeaked. "Was that...Mitch?"

"Kiddo, I don't even think it was human."

Another scream punctuated the end of that sentence, followed by a few drooling rasps and growls. I pressed myself harder against Dex as the growling continued. It sounded like a pack of lions feasting on something. No, this wasn't good. This was a nightmare. And we were far, far from home.

A shotgun blast suddenly ripped through the air, making us both jump where we were standing. It sounded from the other side of the cabin and was followed by a "Jesus Christ."

It was Mitch. Dex grabbed my hand and began running toward the cabin. I kept the camera on though it was capturing nothing but our legs as we scampered through billows of soft snow.

When we came around the corner and were able to see a bit from the firelight of the cabin windows, we saw Mitch's silhouette near the outhouse. The motion detector lights hadn't come back on despite the commotion, which made me wonder if they were even working anymore.

"Mitch!" Dex yelled and we walked toward him cautiously. After all, he had just fired off a shotgun and we didn't want to surprise him.

As we got closer we could see a tiny light bobbing up and down, then fix its focus on us, blinding us for a second.

"It's us, lay off," I said through a shaking breath. Mitch lowered the flashlight so it was illuminating the ground again.

"I've never seen anything like this before," he replied blankly.

As we got closer, the color red jumped into my vision. The ground near Mitch's feet was smeared in it. My heartbeat intensified in my throat and I felt unsteady all over. Dex squeezed my hand again for comfort as we stopped just a couple of feet away.

At Mitch's feet lay a pool of spreading blood, an ugly dark blot on the pristine whiteness. In the middle of that dark, bloody smudge was a llama's head. One of them had been decapitated, and cleanly from the look of it.

Not that I was looking long. Upon the realization of what it was, and that this was all real, I turned away and buried my head into the crook of Dex's arm. With stealth, he simultaneously hugged me and got the camera out of my hand.

"Twatwaffle?" Dex asked.

I felt a wad of disgust come up my throat. "His name was Apricot," I sneered into his sleeve.

"Or Jackass," Mitch offered, sounding faintly amused. "What a way to go."

I still didn't dare look, so I kept my head buried in Dex's coat while they talked.

"How does..." Dex began. I felt his muscles tensing. "How does *this* happen?"

"I don't know. I heard him scream, so I ran back out of the woods and saw something bending over him ripping him to shreds."

I shuddered and Dex held me closer, though I knew he was trying to film at the same time.

"You were in the woods?"

"I heard something growling, I thought it was a black bear."

"You keep saying bears, but don't bears hibernate?"

"Not for as long as you'd think. Anyway, I didn't get far before this sorry bastard started hollering. I saw the thing and I shot at it."

"You didn't get a better look at it?"

"I saw the thing and I shot at it," Mitch repeated, his patience being tested. "I didn't have time to figure out what it was."

"Well, shit."

A silence filled the air and I lifted my head up out of Dex's arm to get fresh air. I kept my eyes facing toward the cabin. Besides, someone had to watch our backs.

"Where is the rest of the llama?" I asked. "What kind of animal decapitates another animal?"

"Beats me," said Mitch. "Heads are usually eaten. There's a trail though, all blood, leading right down the slope. I know where Rigby says it would go."

"Into the hollow?" Dex asked.

"That's right."

"Is that what you believe?"

I heard Mitch grunt. "I believe something big and bad lives out there. I don't believe it's Rigby's beast or Sasquatch but it's something I want stuffed and mounted in my house."

"Are we going to be safe tonight?" I questioned into the night air, my nerves still on fire.

"I scared the thing off, didn't I?" Mitch challenged behind me.

"Technically you meant to shoot it, not scare it," Dex pointed out. "And you missed by the likes of it."

Oh God Dex, don't piss off the man with the shotgun, I thought.

"You try shooting in the dark, you punk," was Mitch's response. I felt him push past us and watched as he stormed his way back to the cabin.

I pulled away and looked up at Dex, who was now lapsed back into darkness. "Way to go, dumbass."

He shrugged. "What? He was acting like he was doing us a favor."

"Well he kinda fucking did. Dex, your llama's head is on the ground."

"I feel kind of bad for calling him Twatwaffle now."

"You should feel bad," I yelled. "For all we know, Twatwaffle saved our lives and maybe Mitch did too. There's obviously something out here. Who the fuck decapitates a llama?"

"I'm sure this particular llama was on many a hit list."

I jabbed him sharply with my elbow, so much so that he almost stumbled back onto the bloody area near the head.

"Whoa easy, kiddo," he said. "I'm just joking."

"You're not taking this seriously enough!"

He came up to me, lowering his head until his face was inches from mine. I could barely make out the gleam of the cabin light in his eyes. "I told you we'd look at this rationally first, before we start freaking out."

"Your idea of rational is thinking Christina and Rigby are behind this," I whispered harshly. "And if you think it's not even remotely frightening that they'd go so far as to rip the head of their own precious llama, then you've got a screw loose."

"I have no screws loose," he shot back in anger. I could feel him tense up, on the defensive.

"Oh we both have screws loose. Just fucking look at us, Dex! We're in the mountains trying to find Sasquatch and we're arguing over the llama formally known as Twatwaffle."

He sucked in his breath and looked down at the grainy shape that was the llama's head in the darkness. "All right, all right. So I don't have a fucking clue what's going on."

I coiled my gloved fingers around his coat sleeve and pulled him toward me. "Neither do I. So then what do we do?"

He looked back at me and in the thin light I saw the look of defeat on his brow. "Wait until morning I guess."

I sighed and turned around, heading back to the cabin. He was right as he often was. There wasn't much we could do until morning. There was no way we were going to make our way back to Rigby's at night, which meant we were shit out of luck.

Once we were back inside, Mitch went to make sure the remaining llamas were OK. Luckily they were fine, though thoroughly spooked and uneasy about the whole event. We still didn't know what happened, whether Twat– I mean, Apricot got loose and then was attacked or whether he was taken from the pen. I wanted to think it was the former, because if it was the later, then it meant that we could be taken from the cabin. That's if there was a beast, and you know what, I was starting to think there was. Why on earth would Rigby and Christina decapitate their own llama – something that would have cost a pretty penny – in order to prove a point? There were better ways to do it, however from the furrow on Dex's brow as he sat near the fire, I could tell he was still thinking it over. I knew he had a darker view of humanity than I had and would be quicker to place the blame on a fame-hungry business.

Even with all the doors locked and Mitch taking watch for most of the night, his eyes bug-eyed and creepy as hell, shotgun in his lap, I barely slept. In fact, because I couldn't sleep by our feeble bedroom window, Dex and I ended up bringing all of bedding out into the living area and sleeping in front of the fire. I felt a hell of a lot safer this way, even though trigger-happy Mitch was in the room with me. And unlike my fantasies, this was no time for sex with Dex on the rug.

When I finally did drift off though, I found no respite. I dreamed of teeth, blood and claws.

15

The next morning I felt like my mouth and head were shoved full of cotton balls. The lack of sleep wasn't taking it easy on me and I slogged around the cabin in a half-asleep state. I wish I could say this meant I was more relaxed and chill but though it felt like the world was passing by me like mud, I was still nervy from the night before.

And I was also getting a little cabin crazy, which is probably why, when Mitch suggested we go camping, I didn't protest as much as I thought I would.

I still protested, though.

We were outside surveying the remains of Apricot in the sunshine. It was a piercing blue sky that soared high above the trees and the world around me glistened like a Christmas card. It was warmer, too, and I found myself sweating underneath my gloves and hat, which still didn't counteract the chills I got whenever I caught a glimpse of blood out of the corner of my eye, the slaughter even redder now in the broad daylight.

I was keeping the camera focused on Mitch and Dex as they argued over what to do.

"We really need to get back to Rigby," I told them, Mitch especially.

"Rigby is too far away," he answered, not looking at me. He shoved the sleeves of his army-issued jacket up his arms in a huff. "And the walkie talkies are useless."

That they were. We had been trying all morning, but neither of them could pick up any signal. It was like broadcasting into thin air.

"He's not too far away," I countered. "That was an easy walk, just over an hour. We could be there and back before lunch time."

"Then you guys go ahead," Mitch said with hard eyes. "I'm finding out what happened to the llama before it gets picked up by the raptors."

Oh shit. "Raptors?" I questioned with shaking lips.

"Birds of prey," Mitch said, like I was an idiot. "They'll come and pick off whatever is left behind. I thought you celebrities were all about finding the proof. Well here is your proof, if you want it. If you don't, tough tits, but I'm going and I'm taking a llama with me."

"You're camping?" Dex asked.

"Couldn't pick a better day to do it, could I?" Mitch growled back, raising his arms to the saturated sky. "You're both welcome to join me still. I can take you to the places on the map, just like Rigby wanted."

I remembered the map that Christina had given me, then decided it was best to keep it a secret for now. I looked to Dex. He had his newsboy cap pulled low on his head, his eyebrow ring glinting in the sunlight. He was thinking and thinking hard and I knew that the decision would come to me. It usually did.

As I thought, when his brows couldn't knit together enough, he raised his head and looked at me with wondering eyes. "Well, kiddo, what do you think?"

What did I think? If Dex and I left for Rigby's, we'd be on our own without a guide. It didn't seem like a tough trail to follow but it was one we were unfamiliar with. With luck it would take us a short while to get there. Without luck, we could veer way off course with minimal food, no protection and walkie talkies that didn't work. It didn't seem like a very good plan.

"Will my llama lead us back?" I asked hopefully.

"Your llama will lead you to my llama," Mitch answered confidently. "And I'm the one with the food."

I wiggled my lips back and forth. "What about if we stay behind in the cabin and wait for you to return?"

Mitch shrugged. "If you want to do that, be my guest. Just know that I'm taking the gun and according to Rigby, that thing can open doors."

"Perry," Dex said gently, coming over to me and guiding me away from Mitch with his arm. He lowered his voice and spoke into my ear. "This is totally up to you. Whatever you decide, that's what we'll do."

"That's putting an awful lot of pressure on me," I whispered back. "What do you want to do?"

"It doesn't matter."

I studied his eyes. They were conflicted as anything but I caught a hint of resolve somewhere inside. He knew. He usually did.

"You want to go with Mitch," I supplied.

"I want what you want."

"Are you going to resent me if I make us stay behind?"

I expected a roll of his eyes or some kind of rebuttal.

Instead he took both his hands and cupped my face in them. My skin tingled under the warmth of his touch.

"Baby," he said, his tone gruff yet solemn, "there's nothing you could ever do to make me resent you. You're my light, remember that."

My lungs constricted and a flush of warmth filled my lips and I waited, anxiously, for him to do something like kiss me. Something to distract me from the sincerity of his words. But he didn't do anything except hold my face close to his and stare at me like he was trying to read my soul.

When I realized I wasn't going to get a straight answer out of him other than the one he was giving me, I knew I had to make the decision all on my own. He did not want to be held accountable for anything that happened and I couldn't blame him for that.

Still, I had to remind him, "You don't want to put me in danger..."

He shook his head gently. "No. I don't. And if I thought one choice was less dangerous than the other, then that's the choice I'd be making. And there would be nothing you could say about it."

My swallow felt thick in my throat and I wanted him to keep holding onto me a few minutes longer. But eventually his hands dropped away and my skin was met with sparks of cold from the mountain breeze.

The fact was, Mitch was going. I needed to know where exactly and for how long. I wanted to get some footage – that is the reason we came – but I didn't want to go on a wild goose chase down a mountain. I trusted Dex with my life and I knew he'd do anything to protect me, whether that meant getting me back to Rigby's or guarding me at the cabin. But when it came down to the place we were, the wilderness around us, I had to rely on Mitch. He was a creep who made my skin crawl and I wasn't sure if I could totally trust him, but I felt he was the safest person to be around. He had nothing to gain from the expedition except a hunting trophy of some sort. He wasn't afraid. Maybe we shouldn't have been either.

I cleared my throat and looked around Dex's shoulder to him. He was chewing tobacco and watching us with feigned interest.

"Aren't you scared?" I asked him.

"Of what?" was Mitch's response.

"Of what's out there?"

He chuckled to himself, totally humorless. "No, girly. I ain't scared. Cuz I don't know what's out there. I want to find out though."

"You don't think it can kill us?"

"Hell, maybe it can. Lots of things out there can kill you. You just have to be prepared. If you think I'm some redneck moron who's just going to take off into the bush after something without arming himself to the teeth, you've got another thing coming. I'm a hunter. I hunt things. It's not the other way around."

I exchanged a look with Dex.

"Whatever you want to do," Dex whispered. "I won't let anything happen to you either way."

And you know, I believed him.

I threw my shoulders back in an attempt to appear brave and looked at both of them.

"Well considering I'll go crazy if I have to spend one more day in that cabin and I'm not about trust our abilities to find our way back, I guess we'll be joining you on your camping trip, Mitch."

Mitch's face remained passive at my response, but just as

I was about to head back inside to pack, I caught a gleam in his eye. It was something worse than sinister. It was excited.

BECAUSE THERE WERE ONLY SO many hours in the day, we had to pack fast. Rigby had left us with a lot of essentials but with only two llamas left, we couldn't take everything. We decided protection against the cold was the most important. I was already feeling pretty ripe thanks to the freezing cold towel-showers I had taken from the wash basin, so I figured it wouldn't matter if I lived in the same clothes for the next day or two. It would save on space and instead we packed a copious amount of space blankets. A lot of high energy foods like chocolate bars, nuts and jerky were in all of our small backpacks, as well as the dehydrated camping food. Even though the walkie talkies still weren't getting a signal, we brought them along anyway. I wished we had some other way of getting help in an emergency – our cell phones were useless and I ended up leaving mine behind - but I prayed that they'd end up working somewhere along the way.

Just as we got the llamas outfitted, our packing job not as neat and tidy as the one Christina did, Mitch walked up to Dex and handed him a rifle.

"You know how to shoot, bud?"

Dex raised his brows and then looked to me. "If you remember correctly, Perry's the one who can shoot a gun."

Mitch didn't even give me a glance. "Never trust a woman with a gun, son."

"She'd do a lot better than Charlton Heston."

"Charlton Heston's dead."

"Exactly."

"Um," I spoke up, giving Tonto a nervous pat. "Do we really need two guns?"

"What if there are two of your beasts?" Mitch responded, still looking at Dex. No, he was staring him down until Dex reluctantly took the rifle into his hands. Oh this was just brilliant.

"They aren't *my* beasts," I countered.

Mitch just shrugged. "Ready to go?"

Dex and I exchanged a wordless glance. When were we ever ready?

We started out following the few spots of blood that had been left from the scene of the crime. Considering a llama body had been hauled off somewhere, I was surprised at how little there was to show for it. If it wasn't for the occasional patter of red, we wouldn't have a trail to follow.

The trail also happened to correspond with Rigby's map, which Dex kept looking at every five minutes. I kept Christina's map close to my chest. I mean, it was literally folded up in my inner coat pocket.

The hardest part of our journey came first, the steep, sliding trek down the slope toward the hollow of trees. Thankfully the snow provided better grip this time around and Tonto was extremely surefooted. The llama-less Dex was right behind me too, ready to catch me if I fell.

With the hard part out of the way, the most unnerving part was next – the hollow. Even the llamas stopped their constant chewing, looking nervous and on edge as we entered the thicket of trees. As before, a cold, neverending wind whistled through like we were walking through an underground tunnel. The light from above was blocked off, bathing us all in a dim, grey light and it was completely silent except for our boots and the occasional llama snort.

We had just passed the area where Rigby had found the

footprint when I felt Dex at my side, squeezing up next to me in the narrow path. Branches scraped at his coat as we passed.

"How are you doing, kiddo?" he whispered, keeping his eyes on Mitch in front of us.

"Nervous," I admitted in a low voice. "You?"

"I feel great," he said. Then he grinned at me and patted his rifle.

I shook my head quickly, taking an involuntary step ahead of him. "That has to be the worst idea on earth."

"What? You don't trust me?"

"I don't trust you with a *shovel*, Dex."

"Touche."

We walked in silence for a few minutes, the path growing so narrow that he had to go back behind Tonto, who was raising his head higher than normal, nostrils flared wide. He didn't like this any more than we did and who could blame him. We had to have been walking for at least an hour and there was still no sign that the path would ever end. It was just dark grey undergrowth and ominous treetops everywhere you looked.

I was about to panic, my claustrophobia finally settling in, when the path suddenly widened and the air around us grew brighter. A few happy minutes later and all of us spilled out into the open.

We stopped at the edge of the forest. I looked around me, blinking hard and taking it all in. I guess we had been walking gradually downhill that whole time because we were a lot lower in elevation. There was no snow around us, just a rolling landscape of mossy rocks and scatterings of trees beneath towering peaks that threatened to block out the low sun. It was very green, the air slightly warmer, and in the distance you could hear the growling rush of a river.

"Well if it ain't Rivendell," Dex commented, stretching his arms above his head. I was perplexed at his comment, considering I had just compared the hollow to the Mines of Moria the other day.

"Rivenwhat?" Mitch asked, turning to face us.

Dex gave him a dismissive wave and pulled out his map. "Nevermind, are we there yet?"

"The blood trail has stopped."

"So now what?" I asked, feeling tired and impatient. I wanted to get to wherever the hell we were going so we could set up camp without being in darkness.

"Give me the map," Mitch demanded. I saw Dex cluck his tongue, like he was catching himself from saying something "Dex-like", but did as he asked.

Mitch brought the map up his face, his brows scrunched up as he looked it over. I had the impression that the dimwit needed glasses. Then I imagined a pair of Harry Potter ones on him and had to choke back a laugh. It was nice to not feel intimidated by the guy for one second.

Mitch put down the map and looked around him. Then he brought a compass out of his jacket pocket and raised it to his eyes.

"We ain't too far from where we should camp. Don't matter where the trail stopped, the animal has to be out here somewhere."

He tugged on his llama and we began the arduous process of walking across rough – albeit beautiful – terrain. It was probably for the best that the blood trail had stopped. I wasn't in the mood to follow it all the way to a feasting scene. Whether it was beast or bear or whatever, if we interrupted a meal, there was no doubt we'd be needing both of those guns.

I shuddered at the thought and continued. We walked

past a flight of brown and grey birds that Mitch almost shot at but thankfully didn't. We came across the river we had heard, a bright blue-green torrent of rushing water that looked too deep to cross. We followed it for a while until it veered off down a slope. We continued going straight, not up or down, just across the valley, picking our way through loose rocks and deep earth that had been thawed by the sun.

Mitch told us we were close to the campsite when we entered yet another thick patch of forest. The path here was a little bit wider than it had been in the hollow and it was nowhere near as dark, even though the sun had already disappeared behind one of the white mountain spires.

At this point I was dragging my feet and contemplating riding Tonto for the rest of the journey. Too bad Rigby had warned us that the llamas hadn't been trained that way. Besides, as short as I was, I was no lightweight and would have broken the poor thing's back.

Dex noticed and had just taken over llama leading duties as well as my backpack, when I heard a faint growling in the darkness behind me.

I stopped dead in my tracks and whipped around.

There was nothing behind us except the ominously gloomy forest. The birdsong that we had been hearing had suddenly stopped, like it was listening too.

"What is it?" Dex asked, bringing Tonto to a standstill.

I waited a few seconds, in case I heard the growl again, before telling him what I had heard.

He looked over to Mitch. "Hey, Mitch, wait up a second will you?"

I heard Mitch mumble something rude but I was in no frame of mind to care. Dex watched me carefully, then let his eyes roam over the forest, as if seeing would help with hearing.

Then I heard it again. A low, low growl, so low that it rolled through the forest like a bass chord, heavy sound in my bones. I sucked in my breath, trying to hear past the beating of my heart in my head.

"That was...something," Dex said quietly. I took my eyes off the forest and regarded him. He was chewing gum, fast.

"I think we should keep going," Mitch said blankly. But he still cocked his shotgun with one flick of his wrist.

As curious as I was to find out what the cause of the noise was, I also wasn't stupid. I nodded quickly and, forgetting all about my sore feet, picked up the pace. Dex and Tonto followed and after a few harrowing minutes we were out of the forest and back into the falling twilight of another small valley.

We were higher up now than earlier and though there was still no trace of snow, the wind that seemed to sweep down the mountain sides and funnel toward us was as cold as ice. We paused to pile on a layer of scarves and it took another thirty minutes of walking at a quick clip before Mitch finally stopped and announced we were at our camping spot for the night.

I was relieved to see that it had been used several times before, the faint sign of civilization bringing a feeble sense of security. There was a wide, flattened grassy area where the tents were supposed to go, a bunch of logs gathered around an ash and charcoal-strewn fire pit and there were even roasting sticks propped up for marshmallows and hotdogs.

None of us wasted any time in getting ready. Mitch knew exactly how to get the tents out and ready and with Dex's help it took no time at all. I took care of the llamas, which was basically getting the packs off them, brushing them down, feeding them and tying them up to a nearby tree, keeping the lead long and loose so they could graze around them. Mitch had insisted that if we let them loose they would still stick around, but I didn't want to test that theory way out in the middle of nowhere.

And that we were. I had been to many remote places in my life. D'Arcy Island, Red Fox, but none of them felt as far away and isolated as this place did. It didn't even have a freaking name that I knew of, we were just in some valley in the Canadian Rockies. The nearest town was miles and miles of mountainous cliffs and steep valleys away. Our walkie talkies still didn't work, either, giving me that very terrifying feeling of being inconsequential. If I let myself dwell on it for too long, I'd start thinking about those stories where people go camping in the woods and are never heard from again until a hiker finds their frozen bodies twenty years later.

As if he picked up on that, Dex had me working extra hard and staying busy. At first I thought he was just bossing me around but he just wanted to keep my mind off things. And that's why I didn't mind preparing everyone's dinner for them, even though Mitch could have been a little bit nicer about it.

At least the fire we had going was strong and hot and I made everyone tea to match. Mitch brought out the bourbon again and we all partook, making hot toddies to wash down the cardboard-tasting pasta.

"Is this the first time you been camping?" Mitch asked Dex.

Dex took a sip of his tea and looked at me briefly. "Perry and I were just camping on D'Arcy Island in November. Why? Am I lacking in the survival skills department?"

"What was on D'Arcy Island?" he asked. He sounded

interested but his face looked stony and bored in the campfire glow.

"Ghosts," I spoke up, watching for his reaction.

As expected he didn't look too impressed.

In fact, he decided to take out a switchblade from his pocket and start stroking the blade. Yeah, because that didn't scream psychopath or anything.

"Ghosts," he repeated, sounding almost insulted. "You guys are fucked up, you know that?"

Dex's gaze was a few squints shy of a full-on glare. "Is this going to turn into a pissing contest cuz I'm pretty sure I could outpiss you."

I pulled my coat around me tighter and leaned in closer to the fire. The night was growing colder and possible confrontation between Mitch and Dex was drawing shivers down my shoulders.

"No one's peeing anywhere," I said. I gave Mitch a quick glance. "And yeah we're fucked up. You would be too if *you* saw ghosts."

He chuckled coldly. His cloud of breath bounced in the black air.

"So I'm guessing you believe what Rigby's been spewing."

Dex scratched at his chin thoughtfully as the flames danced on his face, making the hollows of his cheeks look sharp. His face was getting quite beardy again.

"Honestly, we don't know what to believe," he admitted. "Ghosts are one thing and Sasquatch is another. If it wasn't for the decapitation of Twatwaffle – God rest his soul – I'd be ready to call this whole thing a hoax."

"You don't believe Rigby either?"

Dex's eyes flitted to mine and back to Mitch's. "I believed

he might be doing this to raise attention to his business. Wouldn't you think that's more believable?"

For once, Mitch seemed stumped. He shrugged. "I've known Rigby a long time. He's not that type. Yeah, business is down but it's not like he's in real trouble or nothing. He lives simple, like I do, like everyone here does. We aren't hurting for money. Besides, there are always dumb Americans coming here, wanting to shoot some good ol' Canadian moose."

Dex raised his brow but declined to comment on the American comment. "So you don't think this is all a set-up."

"Nah. I don't believe it's real either. Rigby's got an imagination."

"And his daughter."

"She's a dumb young bitch," he said simply.

Dex and I were stunned into silence. The crackle of the fire filled our ears and the only thing missing were the chirps of a few crickets.

Dex cleared his throat in a rough manner and leaned forward, his elbows on his knees, his cutting gaze on Mitch. "Kind of an unfair assessment of a girl who's only, what, sixteen?"

"Women start as bitches early."

Then Mitch looked at me, as if I was some sort of example. I cocked my head, running through the many, many things I wanted to say to him.

Yet couldn't. Because as we sat there, staring at each other across the angry flames, the dark and unforgiving wilderness at our backs, filled with who knows what, he was our only hope of survival. And he had two fucking guns on the other side of his log.

I bit my lip. Hard. Until I tasted copper. I stole a glance at

Dex and from the way his jaw was clenched, I could tell he was doing the exact same thing.

"I think it's time for bed," I announced, gulping back the tea which was cooled from the mountain air, and got to my feet. I needed to remove myself from the situation before I said something I regretted and I could only hope that Dex would do the same thing.

I gathered up my toothbrush, wet-wipes and a roll of toilet paper out of the tent. I fished my flashlight out of my pocket and made my way past the men, who were staring at each other like that pissing contest was about to erupt at any moment. The fact that no one was speaking only added to the awkwardness.

I didn't go too far to do my business, keeping their shadowy figures and glowing fire in my line of sight at all times. They could probably see me if they tried to and I was glad Mitch's back was to me. He was creeping me out more and more and I wouldn't have put it past him to be a peeping Tom of some sort.

By the time I was done, somehow not feeling refreshed or clean or anything, Dex was spitting out toothpaste into the fire. Mitch was staring at the flames with some super nutso look on his face, the bottle of bourbon in his hand. He was beyond drinking out of cups now and was just swilling from the bottle like it was water.

I couldn't have been happier when Dex finally crawled into the tent, his flashlight bobbing as he held it between his teeth.

It wasn't as cold as I thought it would be. The tent was a lot thicker than your standard model, the sleeping bags were heavy and insulated and the mat beneath the tent did an excellent job of retaining heat. And yes, I was a tiny bit disappointed that we weren't sharing a sleeping bag like the last time we went camping together, but I wasn't about to request that I crawl into his. I had my limits and I think I blew past them the other night when I tried to put his dick in my mouth.

I wiped that mental image out of my head and settled back into the sleeping bag as he zipped the tent shut. Like I had done, he kept every item of clothing on for warmth and just crawled right into the bag.

"I was thinking about sabotaging your sleeping bag so you'd have to get in here with me," he said with a grin, quickly zipping himself in.

My face grew hotter than the rest of me. "Thinking isn't doing."

He rolled over, his face now inches from mine.

I moved my head away. "Get away from me, I stink."

"You don't stink. You smell like Perry."

"That's gross."

"Baby, I could drown in your scent."

I looked at him askance and saw the gravity in his hooded eyes. He was totally serious.

"But," he went on, voice low and rough, "if you need to get clean from head to toe, I'm offering my tongue."

I wished that image hadn't caused more heat to flash over my body, this time between my thighs.

I eyed him steadily. "You really are something, you know that?"

The corner of his mouth tugged upward. "I do."

"Is this you trying?"

"This is me playing."

Figured. I rolled away from him and put my back to his face. "Of course. What else is new?"

His arm came around my body and he brought me back toward him, spooning me through his sleeping bag. He gently brushed my hair away from my neck, the skin shocked from the cold air, and rested his chin there, speaking low into my ear.

"I'm not about to try anything with Heston's understudy out there. You know he's drunk, armed and listening."

A shiver rolled through me, lighting my nerves. If Mitch hadn't been sitting just outside the tent, would Dex be trying something? And would I have had the guts to turn him down?

Somehow, I really doubted it.

I didn't know what to say to Dex about that, so I swallowed my fears and anticipation and tried to sleep. With his arm around me and body pressed up against mine, I didn't once think about being in the middle of the mountains with Mitch and some beast. I just thought about his hot breath on my neck, wishing I could fall asleep like this every night.

16

Dawn was just breaking when I woke up. Our tent was shaking and I was frozen in a half-asleep fear before I realized that it was Mitch who was doing it.

"Wake up you bastards," he said, his voice slurring terribly. "Get the fuck out here."

I sat up beside Dex who was unzipping his sleeping bag in the dim light. The air was freezing cold, colder than it had been all night, and I wanted nothing more than to stay bundled up. But when Mitch was telling you to get up, you got up.

Dex opened the tent flap and stepped out into the grey morning. I hurried to shove on my boots and trundled after them, careful not to trip on my loose laces. Mitch was standing by the fire, like he'd never moved all night. The bottle of bourbon was empty at his feet and he was swaying back and forth, his eyes fixed on a spot behind us.

I followed his eyes straight to the front of Mitch's tent. In the grey mist of early morning, a bloody llama carcass laid there, a gruesome mixture of white and red.

"Holy shit," I swore, turning my head and immediately heading back into the tent. My first instinct was to grab the camera and if Dex hadn't looked so disgusted, I could have sworn I saw a hint of pride in his eyes.

"What the fuck?" Dex asked as I came back out and hurried to turn the camera on. He took a few steps toward the carcass, getting into the shot but not going any farther. I couldn't blame him. My pulse was raging and it was only by looking through the viewfinder that I could look at the corpse without wanting to hurl everywhere.

"What...oh my God, he has no head," Dex said, putting his hand to his mouth. He looked back at Mitch for explanation and I swung the camera over on him.

He didn't look too good. He was drunk off his tree, his eyes still fastened on the dead creature.

"I fell asleep here," he said, waving at the logs. So I wasn't too far off with my assumptions. "I woke up just now. Saw that."

"Is it...Twatwaffle?" Dex asked, peering back at it.

"Yup. The other llamas are still here. Surprised they didn't warn us. You guys hear anything last night or are you both too useless?"

I took my eyes off the screen momentarily and glared at him. "We were sleeping. And no, we didn't hear anything. At least I didn't."

"Me neither," said Dex. "Jesus."

"Can't save you now," was Mitch's dry response. He then spat in the smoldering ashes in the fire.

"But he's been gutted..."

"What?" I asked in alarm, craning my neck to get a better look.

"Yeah, come look," Dex said, walking forward, covering his mouth and nose with his sleeve. "He's been sliced up from top to bottom. Fuck man, he's just been emptied out."

"Guess all the good stuff is inside," Mitch commented. I heard a bottle clink and turned to see him stumbling toward us. I quickly moved out of the way and he went up beside Dex to gawk.

"Who would do that?" I wondered, chewing my lip.

"What would do that," Dex corrected. "This is definitely a what now. No way would Rigby go through all of this."

"It's almost like it's teasing us," I mused quietly. "Like it's showing us what it can do."

Mitch snorted up through his nose and then spat again on the llama. The sight made my blood boil.

"Can you be any ruder?" I sniped. My tone made me cringe internally but Mitch only shot me a deadly look.

"You're believing Rigby now?"

"Well I really doubt a bear did this," Dex countered, stepping back from the llama carcass and coming over to me. He laid a supportive hand on my shoulder. "So yeah, I guess maybe we should start taking at least part of his word as truth."

"You two are suckers."

Dex opened his mouth to say something but I quickly stepped on his foot to get him to shut up. Just because I got away with talking back didn't mean he would. He looked down at me, brows dark and angry, and I tried to quiet him with my eyes. It took all the grinding of his jaw to comply.

I took in a deep breath and looked around me, trying to figure out what was happening. It was growing brighter by the second as the sun was climbing above the mountains, still hidden by the low clouds. But it was growing darker in my heart. Whatever left the llama there had been outside our tent during the night. It hadn't come after us, for whatever reason, but that didn't mean it wasn't out there, hiding in the gloomy trees, waiting for our next move.

"So now what?" I asked Dex feebly. "Now that you and I think the beast is real, what does that mean? Shouldn't we, I don't know, go back?"

"Oh we aren't going back," Mitch piped up, a dangerous edge in his tone. "We aren't going back until I kill this motherfucking creature. I told you I'm a hunter. I hunt and I kill and I'm going to be doing both those things."

Fuck, I thought in frustration. *We should have taken our chances the other day and made a go for Rigby's while we were able to.*

Dex gave me a short, understanding nod then looked back at Mitch. His wiped at his beard and then smiled and I could feel the change coming over him, like he was trying a new persona.

"All right Mitch," Dex said in a reasoning voice. "We won't go anywhere. But what do you suppose we do now that we are out here. Wait for it to show up again?"

"That's exactly what we're going to do. We've got guns and nothing but time."

Actually, we didn't have a lot of time. Our supplies would only last us so long. It's not like we were lounging on a beach in Cabo.

"I hear you." Dex smiled. "Now what do we do with the llama leftovers?"

Mitch eyed the carcass eagerly. "I'm going to take it out into the woods, leave it as a trap. Maybe it'll bag us a bear or a cougar in the meantime."

"Cougar, huh," Dex commented. "You like the older women then?"

Would have thought he was a cradle robber.

Mitch wasn't even listening. He had grabbed both of the

llama's hind legs and was dragging the poor dead thing away from the tents and toward the forest, a thick trail of blood left behind.

Dex sighed. "I suppose I should go help him."

I grabbed his coat and held him in place. "Why are you being so nice?" I whispered.

He gave his eyebrow ring a brief tug. "I don't really think we have a choice."

Then he left me and hurried after him, picking up the llama's front legs. Together they disappeared into the woods.

I turned the camera off and brought a bottle of water from our packs and a thing of hand sanitizer. Dex was going to need it after that. Then I wrapped my coat tightly around me and went over to the fire, adding more kindling and wood and prodding it until it was going again. I felt I was safe if I was by the fire, plus the two guns were still right there. I didn't know if I could handle the recoil of the shotgun but I knew I'd be handy with a rifle if it came down to it.

I could hear Dex and Mitch in the woods, even laughing over something, which seemed wrong and out of place. But at least I knew Dex was still alive and they weren't being attacked by some beast. So far it seemed that the attacks only came at night and I was hoping the creature was nocturnal. Not that night attacks were great, but I was going to have a heart attack if I had to be in panic mode 24 hours a day.

I just didn't know what to think. There was something out there, something with the power and the desire to rip the head off and gut a harmless llama. Part of my brain kept arguing with the other, saying that there was no way some unclassified, unknown beast could exist in this world of satellite feeds and YouTube videos. How was it even possible that the fabled Sasquatch might even be true? It just didn't make any sense in my rational mind. Urban legends were just that - legends.

Yet, we now had proof of something dangerous and terrifying and the fact that it still didn't seem possible only made it scarier. I'd dealt with ghosts and demons and I thought things couldn't really get much worse for me. I mean, the only reason I agreed to the whole stupid episode was because I thought none of this was real. I thought none of this could hurt me. I thought I'd be given a break because I'd been through so much already.

I was very, very wrong. And whatever lurked in those dark trees was very, very real.

I rubbed my hands together, trying to get them warm. Even through the gloves, the morning air seeped through, turning them into frozen blocks of pins and needles. I heard one of the llamas snort, so I got off the log and walked around the pile of boulders to my left and over at the patch of grass that the llamas were being kept on. To my relief, they looked fine. Spooked but alive and unharmed. I felt sorry for the animals, wondering if they had to witness what had happened to their buddy.

I carefully walked toward them, wishing I had spare food or treats I could give them. Their heads were raised, snouts to the air, and the whites of their eyes showed as they rolled around, trying to figure me out.

"It's just me," I said, approaching Tonto first. He seemed to calm a bit at the sound of my voice, so I came forward, one step at a time. I didn't want to freak them out and start a stampede - they wouldn't get very far on their lead lines.

I paused and gauged the way the lines were wrapped around the tree. Mitch had said that if we turned them loose, they wouldn't leave. I needed to believe in that because there was no way we were going to keep them tied up and unable to run if some beast was going around killing them.

I had just reached the pine tree and was untying Tonto's lead with fumbling fingers when I heard a low moan from behind me.

I froze on the spot, the terror seizing me from limb to limb. I had seconds to try and process what the hell I had heard when the moan got lower, nastier. And human.

"You trying to make a run for it, girly?" Mitch's depraved, sloppy voice roared from behind.

Before I could whip around to face him, he had grabbed my shoulders and spun me around then he shoved me backward onto the hard ground.

I screamed as I fell and the llamas bolted. I fought to get back up but before I could he placed his boot on my stomach and put the weight down, crushing me.

"Dex!" I tried to scream but he pushed even harder, taking my breath away and replacing my world with pain. My arms flailed, trying to grab onto his leg, to fight back, to do something but I could only lie there, writhing, as Mitch towered over me. His face was drunk, and demented with lust.

"You think I wouldn't notice if you took off with the llamas and left me here?" he sneered. I didn't think the man could look uglier but here he was, looking like a disgusting, red-faced animal. "You think I'm too stupid to catch on to your plan?"

"Dex," I cried again, turning my head to the side and trying to see beyond the spots that were forming in my eyes. Where was he? What had he done to him?

With the last reserves of strength I had, I whipped my hand up and dug my nails as deep as they would go into his pant leg. They broke through the fabric and then into his skin.

He yelped and took his foot off in surprise. I used that time to roll onto my side and try and scramble to my feet. I didn't get far before he yelled, "you bitch!" and reached out. He grabbed me by my hair and yanked me backward until his mouth was at my ear.

"I'm not done with you, girly," he murmured, warm drool leaching out of his mouth and down my neck. He took his free hand and yanked down at the front of my coat, trying to get at my breasts. I refused to panic and going on sheer adrenaline, I took my leg and kicked the heel of my boot back into his shin as hard as I could, then crunched down on his toe.

His grip on my hair loosened but instead of letting go he threw me forward until I slammed against the tree, my cheekbone catching most of the impact. I held on for a few seconds, trying to figure out where I was, what was happening, trying to figure out how to fight the dizziness that was threatening to take over, the grey that was creeping up on the sides of my vision. My cheek throbbed with starbursts of acute pain.

He grabbed my hair again and flipped me around. I cried out and his other hand went to my mouth, covering it and my nose at the same time. I fought for breath, feeling weaker by the second, while this mammoth beast of a man pinned me against the rough bark, that predatory leer on his twisted mouth.

"Pretty girly all bruised up," he jeered. "Don't worry, I'll just have you from behind. Won't have to look at your ugly face."

My heart lurched at the finality of his words, at the separation between my lungs and the air. I was either going to die or I was going to get raped, or both. The whole time I was fearing a beast but I hadn't been fearing the right one.

"Perry!" Dex's voice broke through the haze and Mitch's hand slipped off my nose enough to get a good inhale. I drank it up like water and tried to regain my courage and strength.

Behind Mitch I could see Dex running toward us. His hands were empty and all I could think was *get the gun, Dex, baby get the gun*. I didn't want Mitch dead but nothing short of a gunshot wound to the kneecap was going to stop this man.

Dex slowed a few feet away, his eyes wild but in a rare form of control. He looked at me intensely and I felt only relief and anxiety. He was here. And he was going to get hurt.

"Get your fucking hands off her," Dex threatened quietly. He sounded far too confident for what was about to transpire.

Mitch agreed. He snorted contemptuously. "Oh, is that what you think? You don't even have a gun, you idiot."

"I could run back and get it," he replied calmly, his eyes like blackened lasers boring into Mitch's bald head.

"I'd finish her off before you got back," Mitch told him, practically salivating as he said it.

"*Or* I could stay here and teach you some manners," Dex went on to say. He raised his brows and grinned coldly at him. "Which is it?"

Mitch looked back at me, shaking his head slightly. I watched him with widened, fearful eyes as his grip on my mouth tightened. "Oh this oughta be good, girly."

"So be it," was the last thing Dex said before he lunged forward and grabbed Mitch by the shoulders. I had one thought, *please don't let Dex die*, before he spun Mitch around on the spot. The speed and ferocity in which he turned the oversized man surprised all of us.

All of us except for Dex, who just grinned again, cocking his head to the side like he was examining the psychopath. He took advantage of Mitch's surprise and in an angry flash of fists, he punched Mitch straight in the face.

Mitch actually flew backward with blood spurting freely from his nose. I don't know how, or if it was a trick of my mind thanks to the lack of oxygen but Mitch's feet actually left the ground and he was thrown a few feet, his heavy, hulking body smacking down like a sack of potatoes.

I was free from him now but I grabbed onto the tree anyway, unsure of what to do and if I could and should help.

Mitch staggered to his feet and tried to go for Dex, but Dex beat him to the punch. He leaped forward and tackled him around the waist, shoving him toward me. I yelped and left the tree just Mitch was thrown against it, the back of his head swinging back against the trunk with a sickening whack, pine needles raining on the ground.

Dex tightened his white-knuckled hands around Mitch's throat, face inches away, gazing down at him with intense hatred. I could almost feel the waves of anger streaming off of him, Dex's single-minded mission to hurt the man who had hurt me.

"If I see you within a hundred feet of us," Dex whispered harshly, his words dripping with venom, "I will come back and finish the job. And no, I won't be using a gun, though you can sure as hell bet I won't be leaving the guns with you, you fucking monkey. I'll be using my hands cuz I can just tell an animal like you can't stand to lose a fight to a guy like me."

Dex gave his throat one last squeeze, Mitch's eyes almost

rolling back in his head, his mouth sputtering, before he released him angrily.

He stepped away and had turned toward me, when Mitch sprang off the tree.

I screamed in response and Dex flipped around, instinctively ducking as he went and avoiding the punch that Mitch threw. Dex spun around so he was behind Mitch and delivered a solid punch to the back of his head.

Mitch toppled forward like a fallen giant, the ground shaking beneath him from the impact. It felt like the ground continued to shake but I realized it was just me, shaking where I stood, fear and relief flooding through me like a river unleashed. I couldn't take my eyes off of Mitch's body as he lay there, watching him breath slowly, waiting for him to rise again. But Dex was suddenly at me, scooping me into his arms and pressing me into chest. He held me tight and kissed the top of my head.

"Baby, it's OK," he soothed. "You're all right. I've got you. I've got you."

I fought back tears of confusion. He saved me. But how? Dex was leaner and meaner than ever before. I had felt and seen those muscles on him. They were firm and hard but compared to the fallen meathead, he was in a different class. There was no way someone of Dex's stature, no matter how newly buff, should be able to take on a man of Mitch's size.

I swallowed hard and tried to calm my heart. My shaking was slowing down, as Dex held me in place, stroking the back of my head with gentle pressure.

"Baby," he murmured. "I'm so sorry, baby."

I pulled my head back and looked up at him, blinking my tears away.

"For what?"

"I shouldn't have left you alone," he said, rubbing his

thumb under my eyes. He took his fingers and lightly traced my cheek where I had hit the tree. "This is swelling up."

"You couldn't have known," I said, ignoring my cheek. "I didn't think he was just going to…flip out like that."

He frowned and closed his eyes, shaking his head. "I should have known…I was watching him. I kept seeing the way he was looking at you. As soon as we brought the llama to the woods, I just had this feeling and before I could do anything he whacked me on the back of my fucking head. Thank fuck I woke up in time, I wouldn't have been able to forgive myself if…"

"I should have said something," I admitted. "He was coming onto me a few times before."

Dex's eyes sharpened. "What?"

I looked away at Mitch's body. He was still breathing and still out cold.

"Why didn't you tell me?" he asked.

I chewed my lip, feeling the pain in my cheek creep up to my head. "I didn't want you to get upset. You would have called off the whole thing."

"You're damn right I would have!" he yelled. I flinched in surprise. "Perry, you should have told me."

"Then the show would be over."

"Fuck the show!" he said, throwing his arms out. "I don't care about the damn show. I care about you and only you. You're everything to me. Nothing else even comes close."

He came back and placed his hands on my shoulders, holding me firmly. He eyes roamed my face, and he winced every time they passed over my cheek. "We've got to leave and leave now. We're going back to Rigby's and then we're going home. To our home. Got it?"

I nodded dumbly. He grabbed my hand and squeezed it. "Come on, we can't chance him waking up again."

We scampered back to the campsite and grabbed as many things as we could, shoving them into our backpacks. The space blankets, flashlights, dried foods, walkie talkies, waterproof matches and extra layers of clothing were all we could fit. We decided we had to leave the llamas behind or they'd only slow us down, but just as we were running out of the campsite, we swung up by the llamas and let them loose of their leads. They trotted away from us, then stopped at the edge of the forest and began to graze. I was sure one day they'd find their way back home. They had time that we didn't.

Dex took the opportunity to get the map off of Mitch. He approached the slumbering giant like Indiana Jones snatching a relic. I held my breath, my grip on the rifle tight, until Dex's fingers ripped the map out of Mitch's back pocket. The man began to stir and we both took off running into the woods, trying to find the path we had come on.

We didn't have much luck and Dex didn't want us running around in the open while we looked for the path in. So we headed straight into the middle of it, stepping over rotting logs, uneven ground and brushing past a million branches that pulled at our clothes and hair. We were lucky it was morning and there was enough light in the undergrowth to see but it was hard to look straight ahead when you had branches threatening to poke your eye out.

"I think we've lost him," I said after a while, gasping for breath. Dex didn't slow.

"Dex, please, I don't think he's following us."

"You can't be too sure," he said without looking behind at me.

"But we have both guns," I pointed out. I was gripping the rifle still and he had the shotgun. We made sure the safety was on both of them, knowing how easy it was to trip and have a *major* accident.

"We have guns but he knows this place like the back of his hand. And we're definitely lost."

My stomach flipped. "Don't say that."

He shook his head, still marching forward, brushing past branches and being careful not to fling them at me. "We're lost, kiddo. Once we get out of the woods though, we might be able to find the way back."

"We should have taken his compass," I mumbled.

"It was in his front pocket."

"Do you think he sabotaged the walkie talkies?" I asked, something that had been on my mind for a while.

"I don't know. I don't think any of this was planned, at least not by him."

I mulled that over. We walked some more, my knees tired from stepping, my shoulders aching from the backpack.

"Dex?"

"Uh huh?"

"What happened to you?"

Finally his pace slowed and I was able to catch up. He still didn't look behind at me, though his head was cocked, thinking things over.

"What do you mean?"

"You're not the same anymore..." I said quietly. "Who are you?"

A beat.

"I'm Dex," he replied thickly.

"You're Dex 2.0. You're different now."

"So are you."

I reached out and grabbed his hand, getting him to stop.

Somewhere off in the trees, a bird flew, flapping its wings noisily.

"I mean it," I told him, examining his face. "The other day you picked up Maximus with your bare hands. Now you threw Mitch back with a single punch. You're turning into Chuck Norris."

"Will you make Chuck Norris jokes about me?"

"No," I said sternly. I stepped up to him and squinted at his face. He was hiding something, and despite the grey, dim light, I could see it in his eyes. "Tell me the truth. What happened to you?"

He exhaled through his nose and let his eyes search the woods as he planned his answer. I waited. We didn't have the time but I made the time.

Finally he said, "I don't know what happened to me. I'm just...I'm still me, Perry. I feel like me. Except sometimes I feel this extra energy kind of swirling around. In here." He pointed to his chest. "It feels like adrenaline. Or, like, I'm on a fuckload of meth. And suddenly I know I can do anything. I'm...I just get really strong and I have no fucking clue why. Or how. I just don't know."

He brought his eyes to mine, the corners crinkling gently. "I know how fucked that sounds and I'm right there with you. It doesn't make sense but it keeps happening. I don't know how to stop it and to be honest, I don't know if I want to stop it. Perry, I ripped a fucking sink out of the ground when I was in jail. I don't know how to explain that. I can't."

He tugged down his newsboy cap and looked at the ground. "I don't blame you if you think I'm a freak now."

"Dex," I said carefully. "I've always thought you were a freak."

He chuckled, still avoiding my eyes.

I decided to bite the bullet and be honest with him. Even though the mountainous woods wasn't the most practical place for confessions, it was only fair.

"And I guess I'm a freak too. Because something happened to me. I'm different now too."

He looked at me sharply. "What?"

I gave him a quick smile and shrugged. "It's hard to explain. Ever since I went into the Thin Veil, I've…I've been able to project my thoughts. At least to Ada, and maybe Maximus."

His body stiffened at the mention of his name but I continued, "and I don't think they can hear it all the time. And I don't think anyone else can hear it. But, so far, this just seems to be the way it is. People can hear my thoughts."

A slow smile spread on his lips, causing the dimples in his cheeks to deepen. "I know."

I jerked my head back. "You know?"

He kept smiling and pulled down at his cap again so I couldn't see his eyes.

"Jerkface," I said, punching him on the arm. "You know? You *know*? How could you…oh God. Oh my God. Dex, can you hear what I've been thinking?"

He licked his lips lazily before answering. "Yes."

I gasped. Then I hit him again, harder this time. "Fuck you!"

"What?" he exclaimed, grabbing his arm. "It's not all the time. Only sometimes!"

"What sometimes?" I asked through gritted teeth. "Tell me!?"

Oh dear lord, what did Dex hear?

"Nothing too personal, don't worry!"

I raised my fist at him and he shied away. "I'm being serious. I've only heard you a few times. Like, the other day, you were comparing the woods to *Lord of the Rings*. Stuff like that."

I thought back at all the times when I was certain he could hear what I was thinking. I felt raw, exposed and mortified. I wrung my hands together. "This is terrible."

"It's not. Really, it isn't."

I speared him with my gaze. "Why didn't you tell me before?"

He rubbed at his chin. "I wanted to know the truth."

"The truth about what?"

He pursed his lips and looked down at my boots. His eyes were flashing from some internal monologue. It was a pity I couldn't hear *his* thoughts. How fucking unfair was this?

"I wanted to know how you really felt about me," he answered, his words barely audible.

My breath hitched and I was surprised at the butterflies rolling around my insides.

"And...what did you find out?"

He slowly met my eyes. He looked crestfallen with brows pressed together. "That you don't know."

My tongue felt thick in my mouth and words failed me. I just looked at his face, the way his eyes sparkled sadly, and wished above everything he had figured me out. I wanted him to tell me how to feel because I sure as hell didn't know.

He touched me on the arm. "Come on, we have to keep moving."

We had to leave that conversation under those towering trees. We pushed on through the grey.

17

When we finally made it out of the forest, we weren't at all surprised to end up in completely unfamiliar territory. Not that we knew the area or anything, but we were even higher than where we had camped. Traces of snow coated the trees just north of us and the landscape was full of moss and loose shale. A steep mountainside bled onto our new path and we had to navigate over boulders and rocky outcrops as we made our way across.

Dex thought he had the map figured out, so we followed that best we could. We could always hear the roar of the river we had seen yesterday, but so far it never made an appearance. We just pressed on, him ahead of me, our backpacks straining, feet aching, only stopping to rest and eat something. We were running low on water too, another reason why we hoped to come across the river again.

Even though Dex told me to forget about the show, every time we had a break, I took out the camera and filmed our surroundings. It might have been fatalistic on my part, but in case something ever did happen to us, I wanted people to know what happened and where it happened. Plus, as I told Dex, it wouldn't hurt to have footage of the places we had been, in case we did a complete circle by accident.

"So what do you think, kiddo?" he asked as he passed me a packet of trail mix. We were sitting on a boulder near where a patch of trees flanked the rocky slope. The sun never came out from behind the clouds but I could tell by the weak light that it was around noon.

"You tell me," I said wryly.

"I can't. I told you it doesn't work like that."

"Too bad."

"How do you think we'll get out of this one?"

I took the map out of his jacket pocket and peered at it. Landmarks were drawn, directions were given, but none of them made any sense to someone who didn't know the area.

"We'll get out of it." I wasn't lying. We had to get out of it. Aside from my cheekbone, which was luckily only lightly bruised, and my abs which burned from where Mitch's foot was, we were in good shape. We had food and sooner or later we'd find water. We had space blankets and extra clothes. The cabin was less than a day's walk away, if only we could figure out what direction to go.

To be honest, I just didn't want to think about the severity of the situation. I needed to stay focused and be positive, otherwise I'd start dwelling on the fact that with each passing second we didn't come across the path we took, it looked more and more likely that we would end up spending the night outdoors and without any shelter.

Dex chewed and nodded at the forest. "I'm thinking we might not be making it back before dark. Maybe we oughta prepare for that. Do you remember your survival skills from grade school?"

"Could you hear me thinking that?"

"No," he said, dusting the crumbs off his hands. "We're just on the same level more than you think."

I sighed. I really, really, really did not want to think about preparing for this. To prepare was to give up and I wasn't done yet. We could still do it. It was still early.

"What about Christina's map?" Dex asked.

Oh yeah. Fucking forgot about that.

I fished it out of my inner pocket. It looked almost like her dad's but instead of just being drawn freehand, it looked like Christina had actually taken the time to trace an authentic map. It was a lot more legible and legitimate.

The two of us spent the next five minutes comparing the maps to each other and then to our landscape. Our faces were side by side and I fought the ridiculous notion I had of kissing his cheek, just to taste him, to feel his stubble on my lips. Ever since he'd saved me from Mitch, I was having these weird flashes of tenderness for him. Then I'd remember the whole "I can hear your thoughts" thing and I'd retreat, feeling flustered and hot.

There was also the "you're lost in the mountains so none of your feelings are important or appropriate" thing too.

"Hold on a minute," Dex said suddenly. He snatched up the map and got to his feet, his eyes darting from the page to the mountain that loomed yards ahead of us. He then looked at the fringe of forest and tilted the map accordingly.

"I think we have something here," he announced, sounding cautiously optimistic.

I joined him at his side, peering over his arm excitedly. "What, what?"

He pointed at the map where a squiggly line marked "river" snaked around to the right. To the left of it was an X marked in the trees and even further left was an area dotted with circles, marked "boulder field."

"This," he said, waving his arm in front of us, "is the boulder field. Erratic leftovers in the moraine. You know, the glacier, when it retreated back."

I followed his eyes. It was true. We had been resting on one boulder but when you really looked around, we were surrounded by them.

"And those hollows in the bedrock, the way they disappear into the trees over there, those are the corrie glaciers she's marked."

"Wow, you paid attention in geography."

"I had to in order to sleep with the teacher."

I snorted with disgust. "You were a pig back in high school too?"

"Hey, geography may have just saved our lives!"

I rolled my eyes. "So now what?"

"Now we walk up there," he pointed at the map past the X, "and we find that damn river. Get some water. Then we follow it down to here and that's where this, the path, meets it. Then it's smooth sailing, kiddo."

I couldn't help but grin. His face returned it. And we stared at each other in one of those slow-motion movie moments where the two actors keep smiling until things get awkward.

Without wanting to waste a single second, we quickly dropped our gaze and proceeded to shove the trail mix in the backpack. I wanted to keep filming now that I knew we were going to be OK, so Dex picked up both the guns and led the way toward the fringing forest, like some bad-ass Rambo. And speaking of ass, it was looking good.

We figured we couldn't get lost if we stuck to the edge of the mountain, where the boulders and loose rock ran into the forest. All we had to do was follow that edge for a bit –

distance was a bit hard to figure out – and we'd eventually meet the river.

Because the slope was hard to get footing on, we walked in the forest at the edge, so there was enough light. The glacial thingies that Dex had pointed out meant there were a lot of caves and hollows in the rock face and some of them jutted out into the forest. We navigated around them carefully, taking our time but wasting it all the same. The caves were dank and smelly and water dripped off the moss that hung to the outer rims. I wasn't sure if they were caves that actually led into the rock face or they were just shallow engravings made by an old glacier but they were creepy enough to make me want to move further into the forest so we didn't have to walk around them so closely. But Dex pointed out that the further we strayed from the mountainside, the more likely we would get lost again.

I swallowed my fears and kept on, cringing every time I had to lean my hand on a slimy rock or I caught a glance of a fathomless entrance into the mountains, spiderwebs floating in the archway. I thanked my lucky stars we looked at Christina's map because knowing our lackluster survival skills, one of those gross caves would have ended up being our shelter for the night.

That said, her map was still a bit confusing. For example, the area we were walking in was labeled with an X while every other point of interest on the map had a few words about it. There was the area where Rigby found the footprint, a place she'd seen the sliced up deer, the section near the cabin where she was attacked. But the X was just an X. It usually marked the spot, but what spot?

"Hey Dex?" I began to say when I ran right up into his back. He'd stopped in front of me.

I looked up and saw the reason why. We had wandered

into a cliff-face that cut us off our chosen path completely. It shot out into the forest in a ragged line of rock that disappeared into the trees.

"That's convenient," I said, adjusting the straps on my backpack with my free hand. It was feeling heavier by the minute and a pool of itchy sweat had gathered under the edge of my hat.

"Guess we have to go around it," he said and started picking his way through the brush, following the long, stony trail of the outcrop. We got to where it tapered off into the woods, then rounded the corner. The rocks trailed back again so it looked like we were back on track until a few minutes of pushing through the underbrush.

That's when we came across another jut of rock. It cut through the middle of our path just like the one before, only it stretched out longer, its ridge soaring high above our heads with no signs of stopping. You couldn't even see where it stopped into the trees.

"Fuck," he muttered under his breath.

"Yeah," I said slowly. "It's probably the wrong time to bring this up, but I was just noticing on the map the giant X that's drawn where we are. And, uh, I have no idea what it means."

"Uh huh," he said absently, scanning the rock face before us and the way it stretched into the mountain side, disappearing into another fathomless cavern.

"So what do you think it means?"

"I don't know, isn't there a legend or something?"

I looked down at the map. It was harder to read now that we were covered by the tall trees and the mountainside had blocked out the hazy sunlight, but from what I could see she hadn't provided any kind of legend.

"I don't think so."

I flipped it over in my hands. Lo and behold, on the back, at the bottom corner of the page in light pencil were a few sentences. The first one said *Sorry if it's not clear, I didn't have much time. You'll want to explore all the spots I've noted if you want to get a glimpse of the creature for your show. I've marked the caves where I think the creature lives with a big X.*

Oh. Fuck.

"Uh..." I started, my mouth flapping uselessly.

Dex sighed. "I suppose we'll just have to go around this motherfucking thing now."

"Uhhhhh," I tried again. "Oh shit. Dex. Shit."

He finally brought his attention to me, folding his arms across his chest. "What is it?"

I wiggled the paper in the air. "Shit, fuck, shit."

"Oh really?"

I thrust the map into his hands and jabbed my finger at the writing at the back.

He looked it over and sucked in his breath.

"Ah, just your regular old Sasquatch breeding caves. Maybe we should try and get out of here?"

"You think?" I whispered harshly.

The smug look on his face vanished. He gave me a quick nod.

"You all right with running for a while?"

"Oh I can run," I told him, getting a better grip on the camera. There was no room in the pack for it so I had to make sure to hold on tight. Then I remembered my plan and quickly pushed the SD card out. Dex watched, perplexed, as I brought the tiny baggie and card holder out of my jean pocket and stuck the card in them. Then I shoved the bag and card into my inner pocket.

"What the?" he asked, a brow cocked to the heavens.

"You think I'm going to lose all my footage if things go wrong?" I asked.

"Clever girl," he remarked with a wry smile. Then he nodded toward the dark forest and we took off running along the edge of the intruding cliff face.

We ran along it for a few minutes, him just ahead of me, both of us traversing mossy outcrops and sliding boulders. The occasional tree would scoop down toward us with open branches and we had to duck under those as well, my hair and clothing getting caught and torn as we went.

I was starting to wonder just how long this rocky arm would go for when Dex suddenly drew to a stop. He held his arm out, blocking me from running past him, and took the safety off the shotgun.

I swallowed hard, my lungs wheezing, my heart racing up to speed.

"What is it?" I croaked. I looked around us but only saw the same old trees and dim light.

He didn't say anything but motioned for me to be quiet.

I clamped my mouth shut, trying to control my breathing. I couldn't hear anything except my heartbeat and that in itself was overpowering.

Then it came through. That low, bass-like growl. Inhuman and otherworldly.

Supernatural.

As soon as I realized it was coming straight ahead of us, I heard another sound. A high-pitched snort like something sniffing the air excitedly. It was followed by something even worse: the sound of branches breaking. Whatever it was, it was running and running toward us.

Dex took the safety off the rifle and thrust it into my hand, then we both ran back the way we had come. We were heading toward the cave again but we didn't have much of an option. We crashed through the underbrush, stumbling over logs, sliding over rocks until we came across a very thick row of bushes that hugged the side of the bedrock.

He slid to a stop and reached out for me to stop, careful not to set off the guns. There was the rockface beside us, the caves in front of us, the beast somewhere behind us and another arm of rock across from us. We were as good as cornered.

Dex climbed deep into the brush and I followed. It was like crawling into a thicket, nothing but harsh branches and leaves blocking your way. When I was little I remember trying to make a fort out of a bramble bush in our yard. Even armed with clippers, I still wasn't able to do it. Now I was forcing my way, ignoring the pain as my body bent the branches, and made it work for me.

Once we were both fully merged in the bush, protrusions poking every inch of us, I followed Dex's lead and lowered myself until I was lying flat on the ground. The guns were to the sides of us, and I kept one hand on my rifle just in case. I was pretty confident that if something walked past the bush, they wouldn't see any sign of us. We couldn't see much ourselves except for the ground right in front of us and only about half a foot off of that. Branches and leaves blocked the rest.

Dex's hand moved over until it was on top of mine, the camera safely tucked between us. He squeezed my hand and I could only see the shine of his eyes glinting in the darkness. He was trying to tell me not to worry, not to panic. But my heart and lungs weren't having any of that. I was trying not to make a sound while breathing, yet my chest gasped for oxygen and my heart was racing a mile a minute, my pulse threatening to leap out of my veins. I prayed that no matter what these creatures were, that they weren't vampires. I'd be totally fucked.

We waited like that, our breaths quiet and controlled as possible, feeling hidden yet immeasurably vulnerable at the same time. We waited, wondering, until we heard a branch break a few feet away from us.

Dex's grip on my hand tightened and I squeezed back just as hard. Both our eyes stayed focused straight ahead, the anticipation feeling as loud as our heart rates.

Another snap. Then a scraping sound.

Right before my eyes, right in front of the bush, I saw a foot step into view.

It was unlike any foot I'd ever seen and I struggled even trying to explain it. It looked like the leg of a small kangaroo, if anything. The foot was covered with dense brown fur, matted and rough. There were three or four toes with sharp black claws at the front of the foot and it was the ball of this that touched down first. The second part touched down seconds later, not really part of the foot at all but looking like it if you were to only examine the print. That deep narrow mark we thought was a heel was in fact the hock of the animal, briefly touching the ground.

My mouth was filling with saliva I couldn't swallow in case it made a sound. I had never been so still, so silent, so fucking frightened, in my entire life. Dex and I were lying in a bush, just inches away from some unknown creature that was slowly walking past us. Even with guns by our sides, I had never felt so damn unsafe and ripe for the picking.

I waited for that creature to stop its trek, to just sit back on those hocks and perhaps sniff the air around it. I couldn't see any other part of it and as curious as I was, I was pretty sure that was a good thing. I could only imagine the human like fingers and black claws on its hands, the way that Rigby had described. No, this was no hoax. This was the real deal and with every second that passed, it was a wonder that we weren't dead.

But, somehow, the creature kept walking. It walked until it was well out of our line of sight.

I finally had the courage to rip my eyes away and look over at Dex. He was watching me carefully, maybe gauging how well I was holding it together.

I stared at him, then closed my eyes and projected the thought, *can you hear me?*

After a few seconds I opened my eyes but he was still looking at me with a concerned expression. I shot him a weak smile to show him I was fine and decided to ignore the experiment. I knew the more pressing question was when we were going to make a run for it.

I never had to ponder that long.

Without warning, the camera in between us flashed red three times and let out an extremely loud beep.

God damn fucking thing had been left on this entire time, despite no memory card. And now, it was running out of battery.

And it decided to let us know about it.

My eyes widened and the most God awful fear stuck its clammy hand into my heart and squeezed it until I couldn't do anything but stare at the camera in a frozen panic. Terror had taken over and left nothing of me except a husk.

Thank God for Dex. What felt like ages to me was probably only a few seconds. At the beep, he looked at me in shock, the whites of his eyes shining. Then he burst forward out of the bush, grabbing me only by the collar of my coat. With his crazy strength he yanked me clear out of the brush, branches breaking with a sickening snap, leaves flying everywhere like confetti. The only thing I could do was hold onto the rifle with all my might as I was dragged a few feet out of the bushes.

Then by Dex's help or some deep-honed instinct I found my feet. I found my footing. I found my strength. And I ran.

I ran like I'd never run before. There was no time for thoughts. No time to wonder if the creature had heard us or how far away it was. It was just one foot in front of the other, one boot leaping above a log, the other boot stretching over a rock. It was Dex and I side by side, leg going in front of leg, knees reaching up and down, arms pumping like cogs in a clock, the rifle never leaving my grasp.

We ran and ran and ran, past branches that scraped at my cheek, a pain I didn't have time to feel. We ran until the rock face disappeared into the brush and the way became dark and crowded with trees, rough trunks that we both bounced off of but kept on going because to quit running meant to die.

And all this time we were both very aware of something on our trail. Something that growled and snapped and broke through the same obstacles that we had. We hadn't slowed down and neither had it. It was coming, maybe just one, maybe many, but it was coming and if you listened hard enough past your own breathing you could hear its breathing, the proof that something alive was still out there, still chasing you.

In my fear-addled, adrenaline-fueled state of delirium, I was certain I could run forever, and if I died, it would be on my feet, legs extended, arms shielding my face against the next tree branch. I would die running and it was a better alternative than being decapitated and gutted by whatever was behind us. The thing I didn't dare once look behind me to see.

I kept these thoughtless thoughts circling my brain, the

shallowness of it all keeping me from totally losing it, from realizing what a hopeless situation we were in. It kept me from realizing something had to give.

I just didn't know what until I noticed another roar fill my eardrums and the forest petered out into an open space of soggy late winter grass. The sun was out, the light was blinding and disconcerting, and after a few uncertain strides I realized that Dex was no longer beside me.

I slowed momentarily and took the chance to look behind me. Dex had fallen on the wet grass and was just getting to his feet, his face filled with panic and his eyes screamed at me to keep running.

I swallowed, my breath nowhere to be found, and convinced my legs to keep going again, faster this time, knowing that Dex would eventually catch up.

I ran and ran and ran through that brownish-green grass, through that open meadow, hearing that rush of water fill my ears like an overflowing symphony.

I ran until an extra step meant another form of death.

My feet skidded to a halt just as the meadow ended abruptly. I was a foot away from going over the edge of a cliff, a forty-foot drop down into the river that ran below it in a deep blue rush that sliced through the trees.

My hands went out to balance me from pitching forward and I quickly turned around to look back at Dex.

He was running toward me at full speed.

And behind him, yards away, was the beast.

It was sprinting with long skinny legs, a creature of thick brown hair, muscular arms and protruding claws that hung from the ends of its human-like hands. Its head was shaped like a small-watermelon, black lidless eyes and a razor-toothed mouth that resembled a cross between man and ape.

I opened my mouth to scream at its proximity to Dex. I opened my mouth to scream at its proximity to me.

And I opened my mouth to scream because I was standing on the edge of a cliff and Dex was not slowing down.

He wasn't slowing down at all.

The next thing I saw was the determined look on Dex's face as he came at me, his body jerking low at the last minute. He lunged at me in a tackle, propelling himself forward and wrapping his arms around me.

Together we flew off the edge of the cliff, the rifle flying out of my hand. For one empty moment it was just he and I in an embrace, weightless, effortless, floating in mid-air, a beast snapping viciously at us from a piece of land it refused to leave.

Then we were falling, Dex on top of me, and I saw the sky get farther and farther away as my back crashed down in to icy cold water.

My torso constricted as I gasped for breath. Then my body submerged and I felt nothing else.

18

I could have fallen asleep underwater in that numbed dreamstate of vibrant blue and effervescent bubbles if my shoulder didn't immediately crack against a boulder as I was pushed violently along.

The pain shook me awake and in seconds I was bursting up through the surface, catching my breath in giant gulps, my unfeeling arms flapping to keep me afloat as the river carried me quickly downstream.

I looked around the raging water. There didn't seem to be any more big rocks in the path before me, but my knees and legs were sure catching the tops of ones submerged beneath, slamming into them as I went.

"Dex!" I cried out, the panic climbing up my throat as I wildly tried to tread the water. The backpack was still on my back and I was tempted to take it off until I realized it was helping me stay a bit buoyant.

"Perry!"

I looked behind me, my heart swelling at the sight of him. He was just a few yards away and once he spotted me, he was at my side in a few powerful strokes of his arms.

"Hang on to me," he said through chattering teeth, wrapping one strong arm around my waist, keeping me up. "We have to get out of the water now or we'll die in here."

I nodded, not having the strength to speak.

He held me tighter to him and as we approached an upcoming bend, he yelled in my ear, "Now kick to the left with all you've got! Go! Kick, Perry, kick!"

I did what I could, bringing up the last reserves of strength and soon I felt pebbles underneath my feet. Dex got out first then pulled me up and along, my legs weak and shaking. Out of the water, my boots and coat were as heavy as sin and soaking me to the bone with a cold that only increased with each second that passed. I made it a few feet onto the grassy riverbank before my knees gave out and I collapsed to the ground.

"Hang in there," Dex said. "We've dealt with this before. We'll be fine."

The first part was true. On D'Arcy Island we had both been in the ocean for an extended period of time. The last part was unknown. I didn't understand how we'd even begin to be fine. The sun at the moment was strong because of the elevation and it was warm but it was still March, still Canada, still the mountains, and we were totally alone, with no shelter or dry clothes, soaked in glacier water. How could we be fine?

Dex took my backpack off, as well as his, and started emptying the contents. Most of the items, including the extra clothing, were soaked. He quickly laid them all out on the grass, then started ripping open the packets of space blankets.

"Take off your clothes," he said without humor.

I tried to make a joke but shivers rocked my body from

the core. In seconds he was at my side and quickly pulling my clothes off.

"Please baby," he said quietly, trying to quell his own chattering teeth. "Try."

I did, finding my boots too intricate to undo with numb fingers, but my sweater came easily.

I stole a quick glance at Dex. He was throwing his jacket out on the grass, spreading it wide for the sun to warm and ripping open the remaining space blankets with shaking hands. There were five of them in total and he spread out two on the bottom and three on the top, like a makeshift sleeping bag.

When he was done, he slipped off his boots in a hurry and came over to me, making sure I could get mine off.

"Get in under the space blankets as soon you're naked," he ordered. "Don't go in there with wet clothes; it'll stop you from retaining heat.

I nodded and pulled off my wet jeans, wincing at the feeling of the legs being rolled down over icy blue thighs.

Soon, both of us were naked and as blue and mottled as a newborn baby. I didn't have time for modesty, didn't have the chance or strength to care. I just crawled onto the reflective silver blanket, noticing that the silver sheets on the ground were thicker than the ones above us.

Dex joined me, wrapping his body around mine and pulling in the sides of the blankets, tucking their crinkled edges beneath our bodies until we were entirely encased in them, like butterflies in metallic cocoons.

We held each other, limb around limb, blocks of ice against blocks of ice. From time to time the shivers would rock us, and then they'd slowly increase until we were both shaking. But with the shaking came the feeling as our skin tingled and nerves became alive again. Our heart beats returned to normal, I could feel the pulse of his neck as it pressed against mine, our heads against each other. Our breathing became less labored and more natural. If the grey morning hadn't burned away to bright sunshine, it might have been a different story. But after a long time of our skin on skin, I knew we were going to be all right. We weren't out of the woods – in fact it was all around us as we lay entwined on the grass together – but we escaped the beast and we would live to see another day. Or at least see the moon rise.

"How are you?" Dex whispered into my ear, his breath reassuringly hot and tickling my ear.

"Warm," I answered, my lips grazing his earlobe. "Dry. Safe."

"Good." He pulled his head back and kept the tip of his nose grazing the tip of mine, peering down at me with vibrant eyes. "Good."

A lock of dark hair fell down on his forehead and I reached up with my hand to push it out of the way. It was still wet but drying quickly. I knew my own hair was spread out the side of me like a spilled can of black paint.

The muscles in his face tightened for a moment while a wash of darkness spread across his eyes. "Did you see it?"

I nodded slowly, enjoying the feeling of the side of his nose against mine. It contrasted with the horrific image I was desperately trying to keep out of my head. I closed my eyes and his fingers trailed down the side of my bruised cheek.

"Don't tell me now," he said. "Later. There's always later."

I swallowed hard, keeping my eyes shut. The monster wasn't the only thing I was afraid of seeing. If I opened my eyes again, I know I'd see the thing I feared the most. Dex's face, above my naked body. The man who saved me twice today. The man I couldn't figure out how to forgive. The one who broke my heart yet seemed to offer up his in exchange.

"Baby, look at me," he coaxed.

And that was the other thing. He had been calling me baby and I hadn't been saying anything to stop it. Because, against everything my head was telling me, deep in my heart, in my loins, it felt right. All of this felt right. How did something so wrong get turned on its head?

"Please," he whispered. I felt his nose slide closer and his lips touch mine. They were soft and light. They didn't assume, they didn't ask anything from me. They lightly kissed my own, a brush so bare it almost didn't exist.

My eyes flew open and I only saw him. It didn't matter where we were, what had happened now or what had happened in the past. It was just Dex and Perry in this moment, in this now, in this rush of hearts that were speeding up their beat, in our breaths that were catching in our throats in anticipation. We both knew what was happening and neither of us was going to lift a finger to stop it. Because it needed to happen. Because we both wanted it like we wanted oxygen to breathe and water to drink. Like we needed it in every cell in our body, some driving mechanism of our evolution. It wasn't until that moment I realized how starved for him I had become.

Our eyes only met for that brief second and in that brief second we said everything we could. That drive, that need, that *want*, took over after that. There was nothing that words could say. Only eyes, lips and hands.

He brought his lips down hard against mine, crushing my head against the silver ground. Our tongues fought for each other, gently at first then harder as the needs became more insistent. He kissed me like I represented another plane of life, another existence to live on. I returned the favor, my feelings deepening with each soft caress of lips and skin and wet.

Then any memory of being cold was banished out of my mind. My body felt ripe and alive, refreshed and clean from the water and burning hot from unrequited desire, a lust I had tried so hard to bury. Unlike the other night, I was sober to the point of being spiritual, every sense awakened and ready.

Dex's hands found their way off my face and down the soft curves of my body, my skin shivering from his touch, even though I was warming beneath his gentle fingers as they trailed along from my ribcage, into the thin of my waist and out along my hips.

Suddenly he leaned back, sitting upright, and I got a full view of his softly rippled abs and taught, wide chest, those infamous words inked on them, before he grabbed me by the arms and hoisted me up like I was made of feathers. He pulled me on him as he leaned back on his legs in a kneeling position and positioned my legs in either side of his torso so I was straddling him. He was in charge and I was prepared to do pretty much anything he asked.

He brought his arms around me and pressed my breasts against his chest. I could feel his erection pressing hard against my slit, the heat vibrating off of him.

"Are you all right?" he whispered with a wicked grin on his face.

"I'm feeling no pain," I said.

His grin faltered as he put his hand past my ears, burying them in to the depths of my hair. "Are you having doubts about this?"

There it was. There was no question about what was happening. About what *this* was.

"What if I said I was?" I challenged softly, keeping my lids heavy, my eyes focused on the heaving of his chest.

"I'd keep going," he said huskily. "Because I know I can change your mind. You think you want to say no – baby, I see those wheels turning in the back of your skull – but you won't want to say no. I'll make sure of that."

"Is this you trying?"

"This is me. I'm just me. And I'm right here."

I licked my lips and found the only words I could say. "I'm right here too."

That grin wiped the graveness from his eyes and in seconds, his lips were back on mine, kissing me so hard I thought we were going to draw blood.

His fingers found their way out of my hair and slinked their way down my collarbone toward my breasts where he caressed them like they were precious gems he'd been searching forever for. A few moans escaped his lips as both hands were there now, cupping them, holding their weight, relishing them. I leaned back slightly, my neck open, my hair trailing down my back. He went at my neck first, licking and sucking down the windpipe, then swirling down the bones of my breastplate until his tongue found my nipples. Now it was my turn to moan, letting out days of pent-up frustration.

"That's my girl," he said between sucking.

Those words, those lips, that tongue. There was no turning back.

I took my hands and ran them up and down the planes of his back, tracing the hard muscles that ran along each side of his spine. I felt his strength between his fingers, felt the urges rippling through him. The silver thermal blankets fell away from him and we were just us, naked and wrapped around each other, beneath a sunny mountain afternoon.

We could have been anywhere. All I felt was his heat on my heat, his needs and my wants, both of us trying to find a compromise of pleasure.

He reached down and began positioning himself. I couldn't help but steal a look at his cock while he wrapped his fingers around it. Nothing turned me on more than that.

I raised my brow at him, my hair sticking to the newfound sweat at my back.

"No time for foreplay?" I teased breathlessly.

His smile was sly. "Oh, we've had nothing but foreplay from the day we first met."

He slipped his hand between my legs and bit his lip before speaking. "Besides, you're more wet now than when I dragged you out of that river."

I felt a flush creep up my neck and onto my cheeks, turning them hot and tight.

"Keep blushing baby, that only turns me on more."

And naturally my skin went to the level of an inferno but Dex was quick to make me forget about it. With one hand he stroked himself and with the other he stroked me, rubbing and pressing my bud until I was starting to lose the inclination to stay upright.

So I lay back, my sweat sticking to the blanket beneath, while he guided himself in. I couldn't have asked for a more magnificent sight; him towering over me in fine form, his black hair in messy strands across his forehead, his eyes deep and searching every part of me, his lips parted and full, ready for anything. Below, his chest, his tattoo, was wide like a beacon and every muscle in his arm grew as he placed his hand at the curve of my waist and with the other hand, made sure he was going in straight and going in slow.

I felt fulfillment, an answer to that other night when I

felt hollow. As dumb as it might have seemed, I felt whole. I felt filled and fulfilled. I was not just a body, I was a heart.

He squeezed into me and our breaths became shorter, the sweat between us increasing. I felt no pain at all, just an expansion, like this was how it was supposed to be. My brain wanted to think about the last time and what happened then, it wanted to compare. But somehow I was able to push those thoughts to the very back and stripped them of their power. They had their power over me for too long and though that battle was far from being over, my body won.

Dex started driving in, his hands tight on the sides of my hips and he pushed forward, each pump harder than the last, a light sheen growing on his forehead, his eyes dark with determination and totally lost in a lust I rarely saw in him.

He came at me over and over again until I was certain he was trying to nail me to the ground, and then his fingers found their way inside me as well, circling around his shaft and tracing my edges.

I leaned back into the ground, raising my hips higher. He groaned in response, his breath getting caught in his throat. He leaned forward and held my arms still above my head, as if I would try and get away, like I was some prey of his. That said, I might as well have been. With his other hand he brought me to an orgasm that rocked me from the inside out. It snuck up on me and caught me blindsided, until I was panting for breath and wondering what the hell just happened, the world spinning deliciously.

I tried to raise my head but he tightened his grip on my arms.

"You're not done yet, not by a longshot," he murmured.

I couldn't protest. He was still driving deep into me, his

eyes searching mine and every now and then I felt like he found what he was looking for. Though I forbade my brain from comparisons, I couldn't help but feel this Dex was all man compared to the last time. We weren't the same people anymore. I know I wasn't.

I definitely hadn't been this woman, the Perry who dug her nails into his ass and begged him to take her home again. Dex did nothing but oblige. He pounded me harder, his fingers swirling until I came again, a multi-colored torrent of sensation that swept me along, tugging at my insides, making feel things I couldn't dare feel. I was probably crying, probably crying out, probably screaming, and none of it mattered.

And then he finally let loose. His breath thickened, his chest heaved and every single muscle in his body clenched. He wasn't shy either. His cries echoed from the forest floor to the tree tops and disappeared somewhere where the sun was threatening to make its decline. I'd never heard one man be so vocal before and it only added to the waves of pleasure that were still rolling through me.

When the last of him was milked dry, he fell forward, careful not to crush me on his descent. There was a small moment when I was sure he'd bolt up and walk away into the forest to "think" but that never happened. Instead, he brought both elbows on either side of my shoulders and leaned forward until his nose was flush against mine, back to the same way we'd started.

He kept himself inside me still as our breathing returned to normal. His eyes closed and he whispered, "I want to feel like this for the rest of my life."

If there was anything left inside of me to melt, it would have. My emotions were drained but still there, simmering under the surface, waiting to surprise me.

19

The longer Dex lied on top of me, his naked body held firm against mine, pressing me into the silver blankets, the more confused I became.

Because I began to think and have thoughts again. And my brain started to analyze. And I realized what the hell we had done and where we had done it. We had almost died, were chased by a creature, then swept by a wild river, almost succumbed to hypothermia, yet we found the time to have sex?

Sensing the change in me, Dex's eyes flew open and he stared at me intently. "What's wrong?"

I turned my head and looked away. Our clothes were scattered around us, drying in the sun. "Nothing's wrong."

A chill began to spread on my body and I tried to move out from underneath him.

His nostrils flared. "Where are you going?"

He pressed down on me hard but I was already rolling out of the way.

"I'm not going anywhere," I told him, getting to my

knees, painfully aware I was naked and in broad daylight. "There's nowhere to go."

I quickly snatched up one of the space blankets from the ground and wrapped myself in it before the chills had the chance to set in. I grabbed another loose one and handed it to Dex who was on his knees.

"Here," I told him, placing it in his hands. I walked past him and examined our clothes. They were all still wet, though drying faster than I had thought. "This might take a while."

"Perry," he said, sounding confused.

I bit my lip and looked behind me. He was still holding the blanket and it was doing nothing to hide the erection that was barely fading.

"Cover up," I told him quickly, looking away. "You'll freeze. And I want to use the blankets underneath you. Maybe if we lay our clothes out on them, they'll dry faster."

"Perry, let's talk about this…"

My mouth twisted. "Talk about what?"

Dex raised his brows and slowly got to his feet. Still naked.

"We just had sex."

I tightened the blanket around my shoulders. "I am aware of that."

His eyes grew soft. "That didn't mean anything to you?"

I jerked my chin into my neck, blinking hard. "Um."

"Because it meant something to me," he said, coming forward. His voice quivered slightly. "It meant *too* much to me."

His words tore me up inside. I couldn't handle that. I didn't even know what it meant to me. I didn't even have time to think about it. I didn't want him to think that just because we had sex, that all was forgiven between us. I didn't want him to think that he "won," or he had me or that it was fine that he left me broken before.

He placed his hand on my cheek and brought his face close. "I'd give anything to know what you're thinking right now."

I looked down, feeling the warmth from his lips. I closed my eyes and took in a breath for strength, then moved away from his hand.

"I think we need to start figuring out what to do next."

"Between us?"

I shot him a look. "No, not between us. There's no time for 'us' right now. We're in the middle of the fucking forest Dex and I'm pretty sure that, that thing, is out there looking for us!"

He cocked his head, eyes turning hard. "There's no time for us?"

"Are you deaf?" I knew it sounded nasty the minute it left my mouth, but it was too late.

Dex was caught off guard, looking stunned. "You're angry. Why are you angry?"

"I'm not," I told him and walked away, back to the clothes. Or maybe I was. I wanted to get out of here, I wanted to run away and I couldn't. We were stuck there, naked except for the space blankets that Dex was finally wrapping himself up in, and there was nowhere for us to go. Nowhere for *me* to go, to just get a handle on things and think. I felt trapped, scared and confused.

His brow lowered, his hands gripping the edges of the blanket. "Are you trying to punish me?"

Now it was my turn to be surprised. "Punish you?"

He smiled with eyes that remained cold. "Yes. For what I did to you. Is this my payback? First you fuck Maximus and now this?"

My eyes nearly bugged out of my head, blood whooshing loudly in my veins. "What?!"

"Don't tell me you actually wanted to do him."

I threw my hands up in the air, nearly losing my blanket in the process. "What does that have to do with anything? This isn't about punishing you, this is about how fucking inappropriate it was, what we just did, with all this shit going on. Dex, this is a life or death situation we are in and I need you to focus on that. Not this 'us' bullshit!"

He swallowed hard, his eyes never leaving my face. They were growing darker and harder by the second. "You think all of this was bullshit?"

I buried my face in my hands, growling in frustration. "I'm not even wearing fucking clothes."

"Do you?" he repeated. His voice was louder, causing my heart to shake. "Do you think we're bullshit? After everything we've been through..."

I still didn't look up. "There isn't time."

"You were fucking possessed when you slept with him!" he yelled. I couldn't believe he was still hung up on the whole Maximus thing. I should have known that he was harboring a grudge about it.

"Don't tell me then there isn't time, because you fucking made time to fuck him and deal with that! Why not me?"

My eyes snapped up and I felt my chest shrink at the wild, pained look that was raging across his face. "You broke my heart!" I spat out. "I don't owe you anything."

He took a step toward me, shoving his finger in my face. "And you need to get the fuck over yourself!"

I gasped and stumbled back from him, feeling blind and stupid in my anger. "How dare you!? After everything you put me through!"

"Oh, I dare," he said, baring his teeth. "I dare and I'll continue to dare until you can just give me a fucking break."

My head felt like it was going to cave in; the frustration was rising up in my throat, tasting sour. "I don't understand this, I don't!" I cried out. "We just had sex, who fucking cares, it was just sex and it's over and now we have more important things to worry about. Why can't you see that? Just drop it. Why do you care so much about this?"

"Because I love you!" he roared. A sledgehammer swung right into my heart. The words took their time to soak in, permeating each bone in my body, sticking to the marrow. I was speechless. Breathless.

Then heartless. The injustice spewed right out of me.

"You," I sneered, unable to control myself, my eyes slicing into his. "You don't get to tell me that. That isn't fair."

"You want to talk about fair? You lied to me! You're going on like I ruined your whole world, like you're some holy, pious creature who's never done a wrong thing in her life, but you lied to me. You switched my pills just to see what would happen, with no regard of what the fuck that would do to me, then when I asked you if you loved me, you looked me straight in the eye and you said *no*. You lied. You. Loved. Me!"

"You're right! I did! Past tense!"

"I know it's past tense. You couldn't be more obvious about it!"

Oh good, because I wasn't done.

"You slept with me, then freaked out and treated me like, like a used condom!" There was no turning back now. It was all out on the table, every feeling either of us had ever felt.

His hands gripped his blanket even harder and he marched up to me, his eyes crazy in the heat of our words, his jaw clenched tight. "How poetic, Perry," he said, struggling to bring his voice down, to stay calm. "Do you know why I freaked out? Because I realized I'd fallen in love with my best friend. The very same person who had just told me she didn't love me. Call me an asshole for overreacting but that's what happened. You're not the only one who is hurting here, Perry. At least I didn't do it deliberately."

My forehead scrunched up but I refused to back away from him.

"I'm not doing anything deliberately. What are you talking about?"

He took in a steadying breath and let his eyes fall shut. "For the last couple of weeks, you've been doing everything you can to spear me, to make me hurt. And if you keep on thinking that nothing can hurt me, well then maybe you don't really know me at all. You're not just hurting me Perry, you're *killing* me."

I gulped, my throat closing up. I felt a pinch deep, deep inside, like my soul was getting cut. It started to ache.

"*This* is me trying, Perry," he said softly, the anger being drained of his face. "This is me taking my heart out of my chest and putting the bloody mess in your hands. I can't give you much more than that."

The ache grew. So did the fear.

Dex was saying he loved me. Beneath our anger, our words, our mistakes, he was telling me he was in love with me.

Me.

I just didn't know what to do with that. It didn't fit anywhere inside of me, didn't fit into the world I had created in his wake. Why couldn't it have happened months before? Why now? Now was too late. It was far too late. He loved me but I didn't love him. I *couldn't* love him. The risk was far too great and there was no way I could go through all that pain again if things were to go wrong. Fool me once, shame on me. I didn't want to get fooled again. The shame was enough. It was more than enough.

I swallowed hard and looked away. "Then stop trying."

"You don't mean that," he said quickly. "I know you don't. Oh baby, you can't mean that."

Now my heart was aching as well, bleeding out with my soul. I fought back the tears that were teasing behind my eyes. It wasn't fair. It wasn't fair that it had to be this way. It wasn't fair that the pain I felt wasn't going away. It wasn't fair that I finally had everything I ever wanted and I was too afraid to reach out and grab it.

"I do."

"Please," he voice cracked, his eyes begging mine. "Don't just dismiss this. Just...please baby. I need another chance. We both deserve it."

I shook my head, the tears now coming loose.

"I can't. I can't get over it," I sobbed. "I can't. I'm sorry. I just can't turn that part of me back on. It's gone."

"Let me bring it back."

"And if it fails? I can't take that chance. I have you back in my life, as my friend. Maybe that's all we were supposed to be. How do you know?"

"I'm not supposed to be anything else than a man that's stupidly in love with you. That's what I know."

And now, it's what I knew too. But he had to step back and look at us. We couldn't make it five minutes after sleeping together without everything blowing up in our faces. I didn't know whose fault that was. Maybe it was just the way we were together. Dex and Perry always leads to trouble. Maybe this was a sign that we really were better off as friends.

"I'm sorry," I whispered, torn between wanting to touch

his face for comfort or to wipe away my own tears. "I don't mean to hurt you."

His eyes fluttered with disappointment. He didn't believe me anymore. And why should he?

Then came the most painful part, the right thing to do that felt oh so wrong. "I'll be moving out when I get home. I don't want to put either of us through this again."

He nodded, seeming to accept it. I hated that he accepted it. I hated that I made him accept it. "Just know, if you do find you can get over it and until you move out, you know where I'll be."

"The room next door?"

His smile was sad. He nodded gently. "The room next door."

He turned away from me, hugging the blanket close to him, and walked back along the green grass. I watched, numb from the inside out, as he began to lay out our clothes on the reflective silver, hoping they'd dry faster. I waited, summoning up a little courage, then joined him at his side.

OUR CLOTHES WERE PRETTY MUCH DRY JUST as the sun was beginning to set behind the mountains, the dying streams of orange light gleaming on the dark water. Though the space blankets did a good job of keeping us warm as we sat there together on the grassy banks, both of us tired, drained, and lost in our own heads, it felt good to be able to put on our clothes. We were wearing everything we had with us, not caring if we resembled Stay-Puft, and set about finding our way back.

The river had the most light to see by, so we walked along that as Dex examined the map, trying to figure out where on it we could be. He seemed to think that if we followed the flow of the river, it would eventually lead us back to the path we had been seeking. The only problem was there was no way of knowing how long it would take to get there and a night in the woods seemed looming. We would have to find shelter before it got completely dark. Twilight fell hard out here.

I was just about to pull the flashlights out of the backpacks when Dex came to a stop.

"What do you think?" he asked me. He hadn't been saying very much to me and his voice came as a bit of a surprise.

I looked around his body. We had gone a few feet into the forest and stopped at the base of a giant, partially hollowed-out log that had fallen on its side. The interior was big enough for us if we squished and looked dry thanks to the overhang. There was some soft moss as well, that looked nice to sit on after the day we had, and would probably help provide some warmth too.

Still...

"Do you think we're stealing an animal's home?" I asked, peering at the log closer. "This looks like prime real estate."

He sighed. "Do you want me to clear it out in case there are bugs?"

I grinned sheepishly, looking up at him with pleading eyes. "You don't have to..."

He rolled his eyes but set down his backpack and started wiping away at the log with his hand, brushing away cobwebs, dirt and leaves.

"She's been possessed yet she's still scared of a few insects," he muttered to himself.

"Oh, well you try taking a bath in a tub full of spiders

and tell me how you feel after that!" I pointed out defensively.

"I'm not even going to ask. There." He stood back and displayed the somewhat cleaner log. "Your home for the night."

"Thank you," I said and started to rummage through the pack. Dex was being nice and acting like everything was fine, but I could tell he was still smarting from our fight. I definitely was. Every time I ran the words "Because I love you" through my head, my heart sank. And when I remembered what I said, how adamant I was that my feelings were in the past, it sank even more. I was cruel, unnecessarily cruel to a man who said he loved me, just because I couldn't let go of the anger I had inside. It wasn't fair. I needed to apologize again but I wasn't sure how. Or if it would even matter at this point.

Before I got swept away in my own self-loathing, we quickly made sure we had everything we needed. The space blankets would keep us warm overnight, providing the temperature didn't drop too much. Clouds had started to move in over the darkening sky, bringing the threat of snow but also better insulation. We spread out the two thicker ones underneath us and the rest on top. I felt myself getting embarrassed as we made our makeshift bed – I was never going to look at a space blanket the same way again. Hell, I wasn't going to look at sex the same way. Dex's performance had ruined every other man for me, I just knew it. My blood throbbed at the memory.

We went through our packets of food, rationing them out with the bottles of water we had filled at the river. Tonight our dinner was more beef jerky plus chocolate covered raisins and an apple. Not gourmet, but not bad considering the circumstances.

"We just better find that cabin tomorrow," Dex said, turning on the flashlight so we could see what we were eating. "We just have the trail mix and the dehydrated soup left."

"We could always light a fire and try to boil some water."

He shook his head. "Can't risk a fire. We don't want to attract attention to ourselves."

"I think we *should* attract attention to ourselves," I said. "Maybe someone will rescue us."

He shot me a sidelong glance, his eyes shadowy in the dark. "We don't need rescuing, kiddo. We're getting out of here tomorrow, I can promise you that. But until then, we have to stay hidden. You know what's out there."

I swallowed hard and gathered the blanket around me. I did know.

"You saw it," he continued in a grave voice. "Tell me."

I sighed, wishing my brain was made of steel. My nerves were shot and the last thing I needed was to see that creature again in my head. But Dex deserved to know and I couldn't keep the sight all to myself.

I picked at some jerky and explained everything I could remember about it.

After I was done he stroked his chin thoughtfully, his light beard scratching against his glove. "Legs like a kangaroo. I remember thinking that too when I saw it walk past."

"But it didn't run like one. Like, it wasn't hopping. It was sprinting. Like a person would. I hate to say it, but Christina wasn't that far off with her impression. It kinda did look like a velociraptor from the way its hands just hung in front of it, the way it was all hunched over and decrepit looking. Those...claws."

I shuddered and for once I wasn't cold.

He exhaled loudly. His eyes were thoughtful. "I just don't believe it. You know? How...how? How is this shit real?"

"I don't know. But it was."

"There's some Twatwaffle-gobbling monster out there."

"I think a monster is a pretty good way to describe it. Or an ape, kangaroo and raptor hybrid."

"Fucking terrifying."

"Fucking right."

"And that's the infamous Sasquatch. Man, Harry and the Hendersons were way, way off."

I managed a smile. "I don't know what the hell it is. It doesn't matter, does it?"

"Guess not," he said, furrowing his brows. "Too bad we lost another camera."

"But," I said, reaching into my coat pocket and pulling out the small baggie. "We have this."

He snatched it out of my hand. "Did it make it?"

"I think so. It stayed dry."

He turned it over in his hands, a smile tugging at his lips. "You know, for once, we might actually have a damn good show."

"I thought you didn't care about the show," I teased, watching his face carefully.

"You'll always come first, as long as you let me put you first," he said softly. Then his eyes perked up. "But I care about a paycheck too. And so do you."

I sucked in my lips and watched the trees around us grow dimmer in the fading light. Soon it would be totally black and we'd be alone, waiting for morning.

"You know," I mused quietly, conscious of the night fall, the need to keep quiet and hidden, "I don't know why I thought being the camera person would keep me out of danger."

"Perry, you couldn't have known this would happen. I sure as fuck didn't."

I shrugged and took some more jerky out of the bag.

"I guess I always felt like you were always so removed from everything," I admitted between chews. "You know, being the host, you have to go first. I mean, you always had me out there ahead of you. I had to face everything alone, at least that's what it felt like. I just assumed you were never as scared as I was, that you weren't at risk. But...now I know you were. You've been with me every step of the way. Every scary ass door you made me open, you were right behind me. I'm sorry if I seemed..."

He raised his brows. "Disagreeable? Wussy? Wrong?"

I tapped his hand lightly. "You know what I mean. Now I know. We've always been in this together."

He looked straight ahead into the forest as he brought his knees up to his chin and rested his arms on them. "I'm glad you finally caught up."

A silence, heavy as paint, sank on top of us. With no roar or crackle of the fire, there was nothing around us but the quiet of the trees and the occasional chirp from an insect of some sort.

"Well, I don't know about you, but I'm thinking about turning in," he said after a yawn.

"It's like six."

He shrugged. "And I've had a long day. I don't know if it's the same with you and your...Jean Grey thing...but having to fight off Mitch really tired me out. I guess that's the drawback for being Hulk. I feel like I could sleep for days."

I was tired too but my mind and heart were too jumbled for sleep.

He eased himself out of the log and disappeared behind

the trees, taking a whiz somewhere. When he came back, I was lying lengthwise in the log, my back to the wood.

"You don't have to turn in too," he said crouching down so he was at my level.

I nodded. "I know. And I don't think I could sleep anyway but it'll at least keep us warm."

"How about you keep the first watch and I'll take over the rest?"

That sounded like a plan.

He lied down in front of me, back against my chest, and I brought the blanket around so we were both tucked in. Despite the odds, it was actually comfortable.

A few moments passed in the dark, each second feeling infinitely longer than the last as I wrestled with my conscience.

Finally I whispered, "Dex?"

He twitched and grunted in response.

I waited some more. Then I said, "I'm sorry."

Silence. I was starting to think he hadn't heard me and was about to repeat myself when he answered.

"I'm sorry too, kiddo."

And that was that. He sounded sincere and he sounded sad. And even though my forehead was almost pressed to the back of his neck, I felt the walls going up around him. A distance settled in where there wasn't distance before.

I didn't want to lose him. I couldn't lose him. But I hadn't given him much choice. It's all I could think about as the minutes turned into hours and the sounds of the forest intensified.

The night was long.

20

Dex kept his word and after he had at least six hours of solid sleep, he stayed awake while I went to sleep. By that point my mind and body were exhausted, not only from the day, and the constant fear that the creature was lurking somewhere in the woods, but from the turmoil my heart kept spitting out at me.

When daybreak finally rolled around, another hazy grey morning in the mountains, Dex had gently shaken me awake. There was no time to sleep in. We had to get moving while we could.

We packed up and left our log home behind, heading back the way we came to find the river again. I couldn't quite keep up with him; every single bone in my body ached, from my shins all the way up to the bruise on my cheekbone. I had taken a hell of a beating yesterday and it was all finally coming down on me. With no adrenaline to keep the pain at bay, it was almost distracting at times.

Dex helped me when he could and soon we reached the roaring blue river. I went as fast as I could, wincing every couple of steps, telling myself that as soon as we got back to the cabin, I'd be stuffing myself full of Advil and any leftover bourbon. The small first aid kit we had packed had everything except bloody painkillers.

We had been walking for about two hours, taking more breaks than we should have, when the clouds overhead thickened and a slight breeze picked up. Seconds later as I finished off a glass of icy river water, a light snow began to fall. It was beautiful, the way the delicate flakes danced on their descent but I knew sooner or later it would start to trip up our journey back.

"We have to keep moving," Dex said and brought out the space blankets to wrap around our shoulders like a cape. We were dressed warmly but at this point there was no such thing as being too careful.

He shot me a glance as I winced my way around a slippery rock bed.

"Do you want me to carry you?" he asked.

I waved him away and put on a brave face. "Don't worry about it."

"I'm serious. I could actually carry you the whole way. Remember? I'm Hulk now."

I rolled my eyes. "Are you going to let this thing go to your head?"

He tried not to grin but he failed. He let out a laugh. "Oh, it's already gone to my head."

"I can tell," I said. I straightened up and tried to ignore the burn in my bones as my boots slipped on the fresh snow.

He studied me for a bit, pursing his lips. Then he said, "All right, but if I see any more painful looks from you, you're going on my back. Got it?"

I knew better than to argue with him. I just nodded,

focusing my attention forward and keeping my facial expressions at bay.

Why are you being so nice to me? I thought to myself even though I knew the answer. The answer hurt too.

The more we walked, the more I was able to take my mind off the pain. Nothing was damaged, really; I just had to suck it up. But after a few hours we came to something we couldn't quite get past.

"Ah, shit," Dex swore. He brought out the map and looked it over.

The river banks had been slowly but surely tapering off until there was nothing left. The river decided to cut right through a mountain, bordering by towering cliffs. There was no way we could follow it directly anymore unless we felt like taking another dip.

"Now what?"

"I'm thinking," was his answer. He put the map down and looked up at the cliffs. The only choice we had without going off course again was to go straight up but that was ludicrous. Even if Dex was stronger and I was on his back, he wasn't Spiderman. Or a spider monkey for that matter.

"Don't worry," he commented without looking at me. "We'll try and find our way where it's less steep."

Once again, could he hear me? I decided it didn't really matter. He was right when he said we were always on the same page. At least, we were most of the time.

It didn't take us too long, maybe ten minutes of picking our way through the forest again, before we were able to hit the mountain slope. It was about as difficult as a steep hike, hard on the knees and the lungs, but not impossible, even though I was occasionally grinding my teeth in pain. I kept imagining lying in a bathtub at home, soaking in a pile of

Epsom salts and relaxing with a glass of wine and I worked toward that thought.

The funny thing was, when I had that mental image, it was of the bathroom back at my parents' house. It hit me like a blow to the gut, the fact that I wouldn't be returning to that place. I couldn't even think about my entire life prior to this without feeling a bit sick at the way things were left.

Then I was reminded of the bathroom I had now. At Dex's. The thing was, when I really thought about it, I didn't want to actually move out. Logically, it made no sense for me to stay if I was so hell bent on returning our relationship to normal – living with him would be too hard if we were just friends, the friends I said I wanted us to be.

But I told him I was moving out. That was the original plan and I had to stick to it now.

I guess I had been mulling all of this drama over in a daze of sorts because before I knew it, the climb had softened its intensity and was leveling out. We were much higher and the snow was really coming down.

Dex paused, catching his breath, and looked around us. My eyes followed. Everything was grey and white, like we had climbed up into a cloud. Scratch that. We *had* climbed up into a cloud. The white mist blew past us, almost tangible, like something you could hold in your hands, dumping snow on our heads and shoulders.

"Is this it?" I asked.

He kept his head raised high in the air, sussing out the situation. "I guess we either plateau for a bit or go down again. I think we've been walking in a straight line, which means we will eventually meet the river again. We're just way ahead of the path, that's all."

"You *think* we've been walking in a straight line?" I scoffed.

"I don't see a river to follow and I don't have a compass, do you?" he answered, still eyeing the hazy landscape around us. "So yeah, I think. I've been keeping track, don't worry. I guess we're caught in some low crest that's not on the map."

"Will we still make it back before it gets dark?" I asked, swallowing the dull panic in my stomach.

"I promised you we'd make it," he said, finally bringing his eyes to meet mine. "I meant it."

You know those times when someone just takes your breath away out of the blue? When you see them day after day, and then one day you just *see* them. Like a layer has been stripped away, leaving the core exposed. This was one of those times. I don't know if it was the stark and moody backdrop behind him but I suddenly saw Dex Foray so clearly. He seemed taller, even though he wasn't, and just rippling with determination. It had settled in his dark brows, causing shadows to be cast on his eyes. Only occasionally could you pick out the rich brown of his irises, otherwise it was just a feeling you got from looking at him, not an image. His jaw was wide and tense, and maybe his cheekbones were sharper because of the stress we'd been under but it was accented by the dark facial hair that hugged all the right places. It all wrapped together under a package of black messy hair and taut, tanned skin, a man of virility and strength, and most surprising of all, of heart. This wasn't the Dex I used to see. No, I finally saw Dex as the man he was.

What a strange, strange place to have an epiphany.

"What is it?" he asked, the wind whipping the map in his hands.

"Nothing," I answered robotically, still caught in his gaze.

His frown deepened. "Are you worried?"

Yes, I thought. *But about the wrong thing.*

'No." My tongue felt too big for my mouth.

"All right. Let's keep going then."

I watched him take the lead, his black on black form fading as he walked. Then I shook the crap out of my head, the loose thoughts that weren't going anywhere. I followed closely behind him, my feet being careful on the snow-slick rocks. Up here there were no trees, just boulders, loose shale, and a powder-fine grey dirt that stuck to my boots. Everywhere I looked, we were surrounded by a white mist of quickly drifting particles.

We'd been walking for a bit on uneven but slowly descending terrain when things suddenly took a turn for the worse.

For one, the land started sloping upward again, presenting us with a trail of ragged rock that seemed to spear out of the earth like teeth. For two, though the air was growing lighter and the clouds seemed to be passing farther above our heads, the ground beneath our feet had snow coming up to the tops of our boots. I could feel the icy chunks trickling down into my socks.

And then, as we were picking our way across the dangers, trying to find our footing on a ground that only grew steeper and slicker, we heard a terrible scream.

I had no idea what direction it came from, except that it was human and it was a human in utmost agony, a torturous pain that struck fear in the deepest recesses of my being.

Dex stopped dead in his tracks, almost falling back onto me. He leaned forward, hands grasping to the nearest rock and we both paused, waiting, listening, wondering.

The scream came again. It almost sounded like it was yelling "help" and it was loud enough that I couldn't tell if it had come up from the valley, bouncing off the mountains, or was coming from somewhere nearby.

"Mitch?" I whispered. I couldn't pick it out but it was certainly male. A male screaming for his dear life, a male who was getting ripped apart. And we now knew by what.

"All signs point to yes," Dex said, his voice low. He adjusted his lean on the rock and we kept still for another minute, waiting to hear something else.

But it never came. To tell you the truth, it was enough for me. His scream nearly made me pee my pants, a fright that caused some sort of chill that began below my lungs and bled outward in a slow paralysis.

"What should we do?" I eked out.

"Keep going," was Dex's bleak answer.

He straightened up as much as he could on the slope without losing his balance and started going forward again. I followed right behind at a 45 degree angle, trying to avoid the rocks and snow that was inevitably pushed toward me. My fingers fumbled as I tried to gain traction on the ground, feeling lame and unfeeling in my gloves. My chest heaved underneath my coat, the cold air jarring my throat, the occasional breeze icing my nose and eyelashes.

"I think this is it," I heard Dex say from above me. I paused and raised my head. He was quite a bit ahead of me but it looked like he was standing straight up on flat ground. "I can see the river!"

He sounded excited and that was enough for me to push through the next steps, hand above foot, rock and snow falling away from me as I climbed.

I was just reaching for the final boulder to get extra traction that would propel me to the top, when Dex walked a few steps away. He stopped.

Looked stunned.

And then disappeared entirely.

I had to blink hard. But he was gone.

And it took hearing his own scream to make it all real.

My heart seized from the sound and the next thing I knew I was screaming too, pushing off with my legs until I was off the cliff face and on flat earth. I looked around me wildly, spotting the surrounding mountains that had emerged from the mist, the river and the valley below but not Dex. In the narrow crest we had found ourselves on, Dex suddenly ceased to exist.

"Dex!" I screamed from the bottom of my lungs, the word ripping out my throat.

I ran to where I had last seen him and found the truth too late.

The edge was too sharp, too near and I was standing right on it. My world began to slide beneath my feet, my balance thrown off.

I fought to run, to scramble back to the earth that wasn't moving. I threw my body forward and to the left, trying to go for the most stable looking part of the cliff face.

I made it for a few seconds as my fingers tried to wrap around the edge of a jagged black rock, my feet scrambling wildly below me as they fought hard for something solid beneath them. There was nothing, the ground kept moving, a slide of rock and snow, a symphony of falling objects that was deafening to my ears as I held on for dear life, the world beneath me disappearing in a blink of an eye.

I managed to haul myself up as much as I could by my arms and pecs, my muscles screaming for me to stop. But I couldn't. I was almost there. I was almost safe. I was almost still.

I swung my legs up and around, my boots catching on a side of snow and earth that hadn't crumbled away. I leaned on my legs, hoping they had the strength to pull me up and I pushed away from the black rock, my gloves sticking to the snowy crevasses and being pulled off.

For one moment I had made it. I was hanging sideways but I wasn't moving. I was staying put. It took that extra push to get myself from a horizontal position to a vertical one and what I should have done was put my trust in the rock that wasn't moving.

But all my power, all my weight, went to my legs. And there was that horrifying instant, that first slip of earth beneath you, when you realized you made the wrong choice.

The ground fell away and there was nothing I could grab to save me from it. I felt my body fall, being swept downward in that brutally loud avalanche. I was bumped and thrown, not freefalling but dragged, like Mother Nature herself had reached out from the ground with stony fingers and pulled me down toward her belly.

I don't remember ever coming to a stop.

21

Whiteout.

That's what I saw when I finally pried my lids open, my lashes stuck together with the glue of tiny snowflakes.

White. White. White.

Where was I?

I rolled over with a groan and felt an explosion of pain in my side. I looked down and as my vision began to right itself, I saw a rock jutting into my stomach, protruding from the cold, snow-blown ground like a weapon.

I eased onto my back, the chill seeping through my jacket. My bare fingers tingled as I ran them over my body. I felt intact, nothing bleeding or broken.

But how did that explain the rich, acidic smell of blood in the air?

I slowly sat up, surveying my surroundings.

I was sitting on the barren, rocky ground up the side of a mountain. Snow swirled in the air from all directions, some of it falling on the icy white patches on the earth, the rest blown away like angel dust.

Because of the infinite white, I could barely make out a forested valley below, and across from me, in the haze of snowfall, a few jagged peaks.

Beneath me the ground sloped off gently, alternating between sudden drop-offs. Vertigo swept through me and I dug my frozen fingers into the hard ground, suddenly afraid I'd roll off the side and fall to my death.

A soft rumbling came from my left. I turned, painfully, my side still smarting, and saw a slight overhang where snow fell off in gentle lumps. My heart sped up a few beats.

I let out the breath I was holding, watching it freeze and catch in the air before drifting away, and noticed a trace of red where the snow had just fallen.

My bones seized with chill.

I peered at the red spot, my eyes widening as it began to spread and bleed across the snow.

Glancing up at the overhang where the snow had come from, I saw another clump of it come sailing down, landing on the red with a poof.

It too had a spot of red in it that slowly spread like a stain on a paper towel. Curiosity getting the better of me, I carefully got to my feet and walked over to the patch of silky wetness. Hunched over, I tried to figure out why the snow was bleeding. I felt a drip on the back of my neck.

I reached back with my hand and when I took it away, it was slick with blood.

Did I even want to turn around?

I did, anyway.

Above me was a limp, lacerated arm, its torn and bloody fingers dangling over the edge of the overhang.

Claws. Teeth. Blood.

Tearing. Gnawing. Eating.

The images and sounds ripped through my head in a flash of smoky darkness.

Dex! I remembered Dex.

My chest collapsed in on itself as I tried to recall the last time I'd seen him.

Where was he?

What happened to him?

I eyed the arm above my head and felt the world drop away beneath my feet.

I propelled my body up, grasping onto a rocky outcrop as a tiny bit more of the earth slid away beneath my feet. I was still on the side of this God damn mountain and it seemed no matter where I ended up, I couldn't trust the ground.

I pulled myself up, amazed that I hadn't been injured in the fall. It all came back to me. Dex. He had fallen away and then I followed suit.

I looked around me in a growing panic. Beneath was the river, cutting its way into the trees. Above me was a bloody limb.

The reality set in. The fear set in. It started in my bones, then made its way to veins, an icy, suffocating liquid that soon saturated every part of me.

This wasn't fear for me. This was the fear for Dex.

Even though I felt I could ignore it all if I kept sitting the way I was, perched on a rock, watching over the world like a weary falcon, I knew I had to look up. I had to look at the arm. I had to make sure it wasn't Dex.

Because if it were him...

I could barely swallow, my heart constricting painfully. I couldn't think about it. I just had to see. I had to know. And then, if I was lucky enough, I could go on my way off the edge of the world.

I took in a deep breath and started climbing up the slope, the blood spattered rocks coming closer to me. My mind buzzed just behind my eyes, so many thoughts, so many fears at once that not one of them got through. I was in a text-book perfect state of shock and if I could survive this by just going through the motions, then that's what I was going to do.

I made it to the top of the overhang, my eyes purposely avoiding the thing I came to look up. Instead I looked straight up into the sky and concentrated on the high clouds that moved swiftly, the winter sun that tried to punch through them. I tried to remember the moment, the last moment I'd have in my life before everything changed completely.

Closing my eyes, I braced myself and turned in the direction of the arm I'd seen.

I steadied my breath as much as I could, ignoring the weakness at my knees, and opened my eyes.

It was an arm all right. But it wasn't Dex. The coat was an army green. Or it had been an army green because it had been ripped off at the sleeve. It lay there on the snow in a pool of its own blood, the redness still creeping along each crystal of snow, the warmth of it melting it on contact.

It was Mitch. I knew that hand, saw the way it had pushed back those very sleeves in anger, when it had pawed at me, when it pulled back at my hair in a vicious yank. I couldn't say I felt bad but I wasn't relieved either. Because even though Mitch was gone, whatever had done this to him, well that wasn't gone at all.

And now I was alone on the side of a mountain with that beast somewhere nearby. Nearby enough to rip the limbs from an elephant-sized man.

Above all of that, Dex was still nowhere to be found.

I stepped away from the arm and looked up. I could see where I had fallen from, a narrow ledge of rock that sloped off as it went down. The path my body took was scattered with rock debris, marring the snow that barely clung to the ledges, but at least it was a somewhat gentle descent without too many obstacles in the way. It explained why I wasn't in as much pain as I should have been, although I must have hit something that made me lose consciousness, albeit momentarily.

The world slowed down as I stood there, coaxing my brain to come alive, to push through the imposing panic and come up with some way out of here. I was on a mountain side. I had to get to the river. I had to get there alive. I had to find Dex. So what did I do first?

Well, I couldn't find Dex if I was dead, so leaving the scene of the bloody crime would be the first step. I searched the terrain around me for some way down, then when I spotted an area where the descent wasn't as steep, I went for it.

I was trying to be careful more than anything, but when I heard some rocks scattering from somewhere above my head, I threw caution to the wind and just started scrambling down. It was easier now that I didn't have a backpack – I guess it had fallen off during the tumble – and that burst of adrenaline was keeping the pain at bay. The rocks may have scattered on their own, or it was the mark of the beast, searching for me, but I wasn't going to stand around and wait to find out.

When the ground finally became flat again and it looked like I was on another plateau, that's when I started giving it all I had. I ran as fast as my legs could take me, and now that I was away from the cliff face and couldn't see the river, I could only head in the direction I thought the river would be.

I was running so fast, so blindly, that I almost missed it.

The shotgun. It was lying on the ground, looking like it was discarded in a hurry. I came to a skidding halt and then quickly scooped it up in my hands. This wasn't the shotgun that Dex and I had taken from Mitch. This was another gun all together. I closed my eyes and quickly racked my brains for an explanation. Could Mitch have had another gun that we didn't know about? Judging from the size of the pack he had on his llama and the fact that he was a psycho, potential-rapist and NRA-worshipping bastard, I decided that it was very likely. And now, the gun was with me and he was dead. For all his spewing about being a hunter, he was the one who got hunted in the end.

And I was next.

Knowing time was of the essence, I flipped open the action and checked to see if it was still loaded. I could only see the shine of one shell in there. Good, but I hoped there were more because when it came down to it, I would need as many chances with this thing as I could get. Hand guns I could do. I had no fucking clue how to wield this weapon.

I shut it and flicked on the safety catch. I got a good grip of the gun in my hand, ignoring the weight of it, and started running again.

After a few yards of rock and a few boulders to leap over, the slope was starting to run into the forest again and the roar of the river filled my ears. I tried to look around me for Dex, to see where he could have gone, but I didn't see anything. I kept going until I met the first tree trunk, then I pulled myself around it, concealing my body, and took in my first gulp of proper air. My heart was racing loudly, filling my temples with pressure and sound.

Slowly, very slowly, I poked my head out around the tree. The mountain rose up in front of me and from down where I was, I was amazed that I had run – and fallen – my way down it. It was imposing and massive and I scanned it from top to bottom, side to side, looking for anything that moved. I didn't see anything except putty-colored rock and ivory snow. No creature. No Dex.

I tucked my head back and leaned it against the trunk, closing my eyes, mind racing. What was I going to do? I had to get to the river, I had to get somewhere safe, but I needed to find Dex. If I couldn't find him, there was no point to any of this. There was no drive to stay alive. There was nothing.

DEX! I yelled inside my head, hoping he could hear me. *Dex, please hear me! Dex I need to know you're all right. I need you to find me!*

My head ached from the throbbing of yelling internally but I kept going. *I'm at the base of the mountain where the forest begins. I have a shotgun. Mitch is dead. Please, please come find me. Please be OK!*

Hot tears began to flow down my cheeks and I started shaking from the uncertainty. I tightened my grip on the shotgun and tried again. *Dex! Please find me! I can't find you. You need to get to me, I need to know you're OK! I'm going to stick around the trees, look for me in the trees! Look for me!*

I sniffed back my runny nose and cursed the gift the Thin Veil had given me. It had to be such a one-way street. I wanted to hear him, more than anything I wanted to hear *him*.

My breath slowly came under control and I poked my head around the tree again. Still there was nothing unusual marring the side of the mountains. It only made me edgier. How long was I going to have to wait in the forest, wait for Dex who might never show up? I was going to go stir crazy, unable to do anything but yell inside my head until I felt my eyeballs pop.

An idea suddenly slammed into me. It was probably a stupid idea, but it was better than nothing.

I had a shotgun. My voice could only carry so far, whether I was screaming in my head or outside of it. A shotgun blast could be heard for miles. Yes, there was a chance that the creature would come after me if it realized I was out here but at the same time, maybe the sound of the gun would scare it off or at least keep it away from me. Dex, though, if he was alive, and I had no choice but to assume he was, he would hear it. He would know I was alive and hopefully he'd be able to pinpoint where I was.

The only problem with this idea was that I'd be losing a shell and if it happened to be the last shell, I was totally screwing myself over.

Unfortunately, I didn't really have a choice here. I could save the shells for when I might need them, or I could use it now and hope there was another one in there. This was a need for now. There was no telling what would happen later.

I stepped out from behind the tree and walked a few feet into the open. I leaned back on my leg, keeping my center of gravity low, my arms steady and strong and I put the gun on my shoulder, adjusting its position until I felt secure. I aimed it up high so there was no chance of me accidently shooting someone.

Taking in a deep breath, I thought about what I knew about shotgun recoil, the "kick" it left. Somewhere along the lines of my training, when I was just practicing at the range, I remembered hearing some 10% formula about shotguns. It was either the 10% lighter the gun was, the 10% more of a kick it had. Or it was the other way around. I couldn't remember, I just had to be very ready for that burst when it came, even though it made me extremely nervous. The gun was powerful and I was a tiny woman.

I took a breath and flicked the safety off.

Here goes nothing, I thought.

I pulled the trigger.

The explosion drove me back into the ground with one sharp, quick motion, like I was a tent peg getting hammered. My ears rang with the reverberations of the shot and when I opened my eyes, tiny white and black dots were dancing around my vision. My heart felt like it was on fire, squeezing in my chest from the shock.

But though I was knocked back on my ass, the gun was still in my hands and the shell had gone somewhere. The noise was made and from the way it echoed over and over again, bouncing back from the mountains, I knew that if someone was around to hear it, they'd definitely hear it.

"Fuck me," I muttered out loud, getting to my feet. I had no idea why people even used shotguns if you had to contend with that pummeling every time you shot one.

It also made me wonder if I could even get a straight shot at something if I had to protect myself. Probably not.

I flipped open the action and with a wary breath, peeked inside. I could see a golden gleam in one of the barrels. I exhaled in relief, knowing I had at least one more shot. I wished I could make it count.

"OK, Dex," I whispered. "Come find me."

I gripped the gun and walked back to the trees. I felt like I was in a limbo of some sort, not wanting to stray too far away from where I shot the gun, but feeling exposed and vulnerable out in the open.

I paced back and forth under the shelter of the forest, my eyes darted around me. I walked and waited, like a soldier on patrol. My ears were open and listening, my attention was focused and I kept at it until my feet began to ache, my bones began to hurt, and the sun left the highest part of the sky, beginning its gradual descent into twilight.

We had maybe two hours until it got dark, at the very least.

We. It sounded funny now that I was alone. I was trying very hard not to think about the alternative, if Dex never came. He had to be out there, he had to be. As silly as it sounds, I could almost feel his energy. If something had happened to him….if he had been killed…I just knew that I would *know* it. I'd feel some horrible separation from this world, like I one day found myself without a leg or lung. I'd feel like something was missing, something I needed desperately to survive.

I stopped pacing and sat down on the ground. There was no snow under the trees but the earth was cold, hard and littered with dying pine needles and dried-out cones. I placed the shotgun beside me and hugged my knees tightly. If I ever made it out of here, I was never going into the mountains again. I could add that to the list, which included secluded leper islands and isolated towns in New Mexico. Experiment in Terror sure ruined a lot of vacation spots for me.

My eyes were drooping shut, my chin dipping to my knees. Maybe I could just rest here. Just for a few minutes. Maybe when I woke up, everything would be OK. Maybe I wouldn't be in this God awful forest.

I must have fallen asleep for a few minutes, because I suddenly jerked my head up, aware of something my conscious mind was quickly trying to process. I was still in the God awful forest, but something had woken me up.

But what was it?

22

I warily got to my feet, quietly, afraid to make a sound. I listened hard, frowning at the mountain. In the distance the river roared, always making its presence known, but I thought I heard something else. A low rumble.

I searched the crags and undulating ridges of the bedrock, the plateaus and cliffs. I couldn't see anything. What was it?

The rumble got louder. It wasn't constant and it dipped in and out in its level and frequency, scattered and all over the place.

I picked up the shot gun and slowly stepped forward out of the cover of trees. There was something coming for me, I felt it. I heard it.

I saw it.

Up ahead, not too far up, a black figure darted out of a mound of boulders, legs pumping fast.

"Dex!" I screamed. It was a happy scream. It was Dex, I could see it as he got closer, seemingly uninjured. My heart felt like it was going to explode.

I started running toward him, waving my hand in the air.

"Perry!" he yelled back once he spotted me. He didn't stop coming. "Perry, run!"

"What?" I said absently, watching him come closer and closer, his speed picking up as the slope grew flatter.

"Run!" he yelled again. He looked over his shoulder and my eyes followed.

Another dark figure came to the top of the boulders he had emerged from. It sat on the top of the rocks like an ape, surveying the scene below with a few quick twists of its ugly head, then leaped off into the air with surprising grace, hitting the ground with a thud, rocks and dirt flying everywhere. It gathered itself with ease, then started bounding down the mountain on all fours, coming right for Dex.

Coming right for me

Oh fuck.

"Run, God damn it!" Dex yelled again, the panic and exhaustion tearing out of his mouth. He was less than a hundred meters away and I could clearly see the anguish in his face, his eyes imploring me to start moving.

But I couldn't. Because unlike before, that beast was now running on all fours, its back legs propelling it forward with quick, wide strides that covered a lot of ground. We didn't have a chance in hell of outrunning it.

So we weren't going to.

Dex was closer now and the beast right behind him, a flurry of dirt and snow torn up in its wake.

I gripped the gun hard and raised it up on my shoulder. I lowered myself into a small lunge, all the weight distributed between my back heel and my thighs. I knew what to expect now from the kick. I knew it would try and drive me backward. I had to make sure that this was going to be a sure shot. I had to hit this target.

And it was a moving target.

Dex was almost at me now.

"Get out of the way!" I yelled at him without taking my eyes away from the sight on the end of the barrel.

He veered to the left so the only thing in front of me was the beast, matted brown head to the ground, black liquid eyes flashing, jaw open and baring a row of nasty teeth. The claws dug into the ground as it ran, leaving destruction behind.

Dex ran to my side, keeping back and I thought he said my name or something like that but I didn't hear him. I didn't hear anything except the rumble of the beast as it ran. Almost at us now. We had seconds left.

I closed one eye, my arm muscles straining to keep the gun still, and just when I had the sight lined up with the beast's head, I pulled the trigger.

The shell blasted out of the gun, the sound of the explosion mixing with the cry of the beast as the shell slammed into it. I was thrown back but managed to stay upright with the help of Dex, whose arm shot out behind me. My ears were ringing, the dots were back in my eyes and the creature was down on the ground.

Well, kinda. It was getting back up, or trying to. I hadn't hit the head at all, but from the looks of it I took off part of its shoulder, leaving a wide, bloody wound that left bone and muscle exposed. I would have been grossed out. Maybe even proud of myself for actually hitting it. But there wasn't any time. Because it wasn't dead. And when I tried to pull the trigger again, nothing happened but a dull click.

I threw the spent shotgun on the ground and turned to Dex with wild eyes.

"Now we run!"

His eyes grew narrow with grim agreement and soon we were running again, as fast as we could. I only looked behind me once to see what our chances were. The beast wasn't on its feet yet and kept collapsing to the ground. With luck on our side it wouldn't follow us. But our luck had a strange sense of humor.

We ran through the forest until we saw open space and found ourselves at the river's edge again. I did a little whoop of joy inside my head, too breathless to make an actual sound. We ran along the river side, not going crazy with speed, but at a fairly comfortable and steady pace so we didn't tire ourselves out. Not that I wasn't absolutely dying inside, my lungs burning with each shallow breath I took. But we just needed to make sure we kept going.

It was starting to get a bit dark – Dex didn't have his backpack either so flashlights were out of the question – when we found the entrance to the trail.

This time I did allow myself a squeal of delight, even though it came out ragged and hoarse.

"Fuck yeah, we're making it. I told you so," Dex said between breaths. He slowed down as we entered the hollow and shot me a tired look. "Are you OK to keep running?"

"No," I said, sweat streaming down my forehead, my skin uncomfortably hot and tight. "But I'll do it anyway."

I waved him forward with my hand to encourage him to pick up the pace. If I slowed down too much, I wouldn't be able to continue. "Please, seriously, go."

He nodded and we ran together into the hollow. Unlike the last time we had come through here, we weren't afraid. We had seen the worse and we knew it was behind us. At least, we hoped it was.

We ran through the darkness, our feet never straying from the path. It sucked that the whole path went gradually uphill, adding more strain to our staggering bodies and testing our endurance to the max. I ceased to have thoughts of any kind, just the constant push of my brain to body, coaxing myself over and over again to move my legs, ignore the burn and keep going.

There was only one more obstacle between us and the cabin – the steep, sliding slope. As we burst out of the trees, it loomed in front of us like the final challenge.

I didn't even stop to think about it. The both of us ran forward and scrambled up the slope, grasping for rocks, kicking away the loose ones. We fell on our faces many times but we always picked ourselves up and picked each other up. Together we made it to the top.

It was almost completely dark now, but in the twilight we saw the outline of the cabin. I'd never been so relieved in my life. That, plus having Dex back, knowing we were both going to be safe, created an emotion that nearly brought me to my knees.

Dex twined his fingers into mine. With no gloves, my fingers were frozen but I could feel the heat radiating onto me.

"Come on," he said gravely. "It's not over yet."

We jogged up to the cabin and I realized we wouldn't be truly safe until we were at Rigby's. Still, we had to gather our stuff from there while we could and get ready for the final journey back, a journey we would be making in the dark.

The cabin was cold as we entered it and had a stale smell but it felt something like heaven to have a hard floor to step on and a wooden roof over our heads.

Dex closed the door behind me and locked it. Then he took the couch and pushed it right up against the door for extra protection.

"Let's do this fast," he said, walking over to the kitchen and lighting a kerosene lamp. He did the same to one hanging on the wall in the living area and finally the one in our bedroom.

I followed him in there. "Too risky to build a fire?"

"Too risky and no time, kiddo," he said. He picked up his duffle bag, putting it on the bed and started shoving his stuff inside. I did the same, and smiled once I felt my fingers close over my cell phone. I was smart this time to leave it behind. Unfortunately it still had no service but at least I wasn't going to have to replace it, not like we were going to have to do for Dex's camera. No wonder he chose to bring the more "expendable" equipment along.

"Dex?" I asked as I searched for my bottle of Advil.

"That's me."

"Could you hear me?"

He stopped packing and raised his head to look at me. His eyes danced in the lamplight.

"When you were calling me in your head?"

I nodded.

"Yeah, I could hear you. I heard you loud and clear."

I smiled softly, glad that I reached him somehow. "What happened to you?"

He shook his head. "I wish I knew. One minute I had ground beneath my feet, the next minute I didn't. I woke up buried under some rocks. I don't know how long I was out for but your voice got me up. It just took a while. There was one slab across my leg that took forever to get free of."

I dropped the bottle and went around the bed to his side, eyeing his leg with concern.

"Are you OK? Is it broken?"

"Kiddo, if it was broken I wouldn't be here. It hurt a lot at first but now I feel fine. I don't know. Maybe this whole crazy dimension thing made me heal faster or something. I'd believe anything at this point."

"Maybe."

"You know I thought about calling Pippa," he admitted. "I thought maybe she'd appear. Maybe, like, the gateway would materialize or something. But I was afraid to go back in there. I thought maybe I wouldn't come back out. And if I did, what if I brought something else back with me. If that's where we changed, Perry, we can't assume that the changes will always be good."

I had thought that too. I placed my hand on his arm and gave it a squeeze.

"Thank you for trying to find me," I whispered, feeling strangely small and awkward.

He raised his brows, his ring glinting in the low light. "Thank you for-"

He was interrupted by the cabin shaking, a deep rattling noise emanating from the living area.

I gasped in a panic and we quickly made our way out of the bedroom.

We froze.

The front door was shaking on its hinges, the couch being rattled back and forth like a bucking bronco.

I swallowed hard, unable to take my eyes away from the scene, from the scraping, scratching sounds on the wood, the way the handle tried to turn. It didn't help that the cabin had very little light in it, casting everything in limitless shadows.

"Maybe it's Rigby," I whispered.

A low, guttural moan crept in through the cracks in the door.

"No," Dex said slowly. "It's not."

I felt like I was getting tunnel vision, blackness closing in on all sides of me, but Dex grabbed my hand, hard, and brought me back to life.

"Do you remember if there were any guns left behind?" he asked, turning me so I'd look at him. "I can't remember if Mitch packed them all."

I shook my head, my brain too slow to latch onto any memory. Dex was acting as calm as he could but I could tell from the cracks in his voice, he was close to panicking as well.

He narrowed his eyes at the door, then looked around the cabin.

"It's injured, so I don't think it can get through there. That lock should hold it back, and if that fails, the couch should do the job."

With shaking limbs, I silently thanked him for barricading the cabin so well.

"We have to do something about the windows though and we need to defend ourselves. Perry, stay with me here."

I nodded, swallowing thickly. He pulled me toward the kitchen and we walked as quietly as we could. There was no doubt the creature knew we were inside, but the kitchen had a window, a window that offered no protection.

Dex quickly opened a drawer and brought a bunch of knives. I winced as they clattered against each other and only started breathing again when I heard the door continue to rattle. As long it was there, it wasn't here.

He handed me a long sharp hunting knife and kept another one for himself.

"Are you ready to do some hand-to-beast combat?" he asked, almost smiling.

"No!" I whispered harshly, the knife feeling foreign in my hands. Oh, how I wished I had that shotgun back.

His smile washed away. "Good. Neither am I. Let's get these windows covered. Help me with the armchair."

I doubted he needed my help, but it kept me busy and

not focused on the blood-thirsty monster outside the door. Oh who the fuck am I kidding, of course I was focused on the God damn monster outside of the door. I had blown half his shoulder away and he was pissed off as hell.

We got the armchair up on the kitchen counter. I didn't see how the beast couldn't just topple it over, but Dex got a broom and managed to wedge it between the corner of the wall and the chair. It looked like a feeble barricade but it might be enough if the creature wasn't at his full strength.

Next, we scampered over to the other window, unnervingly close to the door. The creature wasn't giving up and the thumps were getting louder, heavier and more spaced apart. It was throwing itself against the door now, perhaps getting desperate. The lock snapped off and clattered to the ground.

"Oh shit," I swore, eyes glued to the broken lock, unable to move.

"Perry, hey." Dex tried to get my attention while he picked up the kitchen table.

I couldn't look at him, couldn't move.

"A little help, please," he repeated. I finally tore my eyes away to him at the sound of the utter pleading in his voice. He was trying to turn it on its end so it would stand up high enough to block the window.

With legs made of cement, I joined him at the window, moving the heavy table back so it was covering most of the pane.

Then a silence cloaked us, settling around the whole cabin. I could hear my breath, ragged and wheezing as it came out of my lungs.

My eyes flew to the main door. The rattling had stopped. The door was still. The place was quiet. Too quiet.

We exchanged a worried look over the expanse of wood

and with a final thrust, pushed the table back. There was only a foot of space on my side that was uncovered and I had my head close to the darkness, contemplating if we needed to cover it up more when a head appeared beside me.

The beast was at the window, inches away, only a thin pane of glass between his swarming, liquid black eyes and bared fangs, and me.

I screamed.

And I screamed again when the window shattered. I leaped back from the rain of glass just as its muscled arm and snipping claws came flying in, making a grab for me.

I couldn't stop screaming, so Dex whisked me back into his arms until the beast's arm retreated back into the night, leaving a narrow hole of broken glass that let the whistling wind inside.

"The bedrooms!" Dex yelled.

We booked it to ours just as the glass shattered there, spewing fragments all over the bed. The monster had both arms inside, including the arm whose shoulder I shattered, it's bloody wound dripping down the wall as it tried to pull itself up.

Dex made a run for the bed, his sleek body low as he got ready to flip it up against the window. He had flipped the bed in the motel room the other night, so there was no reason why he couldn't do this.

Except when Dex got down, his arms straining underneath the edge of the bed, he could only lift it up a few feet. He struggled, face sweating and growing redder as the monster was almost in the room with us, only it's lower half was dangling outside. In the crazy glow of the kerosene lamp, I saw the creature closer than I ever had before. If it was a missing link, it was a bizarre, twisted one, a savage, animal face that couldn't possibly be related to us. Yet when I thought about the faces of evil I'd seen in my life, from Mitch's lustful, demented gaze earlier, to the depraved, haunting face of Abby, I knew that the link from man to monster wasn't too far off.

"Perry," Dex cried pitifully. "Help."

My heart sank. He couldn't do it. His strength was fading by the second and we didn't have seconds. We would have nothing if the monster finally made it into the room with us.

And it wasn't a question of if, but when.

I joined him at his side, getting into a low crouch and trying to push the bed up like I was in a weightlifting competition. The bed moved a bit and together we were able to move it up a foot.

But it was too late.

As we lifted, side-by-side, our arms underneath the bed, our chins on top of the mattress, we saw the rest of the glass shatter away. The monster was perched on the window ledge, perched like a snake with arms, like a raptor, ready to strike. There wasn't any time to think or act, except that I saw in its tar-filled, alien eyes that it had us. It had us right where it wanted us.

And it wanted revenge.

There was a flash of movement, its fur-covered muscles tensing to pounce, claws extended, when a huge blast shook our ears and the room.

We blinked hard at it, confused when it didn't move. The creature looked down at its leg and that's when we saw a stream of blood erupt from it.

Then it fell backward, falling out of the window and into the winter outside.

I was stunned. In my confusion I let go of the bed and it

slammed hard into the floor. It didn't matter. What the fuck had just happened?

Dex and I walked cautiously over to the window and peered out of it, the night breeze whipping back my hair. There was nothing below us except a patch of blood and a corresponding trail that led off into the woods.

And Rigby.

He was running toward us with a rifle in hand, his flashlight bobbing up and down.

"Are you all right!?" he yelled up at the window. "Stay there, I wanna see if I can kill this thing for good."

And then he was gone into the trees, following the bloody trail.

Dex and I looked at each other. I was dizzy from holding my breath and leaned against the wall for support. He took me by the shoulders and pulled me into his chest, embracing me. He held me like that until I felt I could breathe again, until my heart stopped thudding in my ears. Until we heard two more gunshots ricocheting into the night.

I pulled away and looked up. He was gazing down at me with an expression I couldn't read, made all the more mysterious by the glow of the lamp.

"What do we do?" I whispered.

He cupped my face in his hands and for a second I thought he was going to kiss me. I wanted him to kiss me. I needed it.

But he only lowered his eyes till they were at my level and said, "We're going to try and flip this bed up again. And then we're going to go out there and get those knifes. Then we're going to wait."

We didn't have to wait long. We managed to get the bed up. It took as much effort as before, but as least the window was blocked. Then we picked up the knives from where we left them and were about to test the couch for solidity when there was a knock at the door.

I jumped, nearly dropping the knife.

"Dex, Perry, it's me," Rigby yelled from the other side of the door.

"Oh thank God," Dex exclaimed and began to move the couch out of the way. We stood back as Rigby pushed the door in, gripping the rifle like an angry farmer with a rabbit problem.

"I couldn't find it," he said, staggering into the cabin. "The trail ended. I think I got his leg pretty good though. He won't be back for a while."

He looked back and forth between our relieved faces. "What happened to you guys? Where are the llamas? Where's Mitch?"

I exchanged a glance with Dex. He gave Rigby a grave smile.

"It's a long story and I don't think we have a lot of time. How about we tell you on our way out of this hell hole?"

Rigby nodded grimly, maybe knowing what was to come. Dex and I quickly gathered up our packs and we ran out into the night. It was starting to snow again but I was willing to put up with it for this last journey.

Rigby had come on his horse and Dex insisted that I would ride the horse back to give myself a rest from walking. My protest was weak and being the gentleman that Rigby was deep down inside, I was thrust up into the saddle. I held tight to the saddle horn, my eyes scanning the dark forest for anything unusual. I could never fully believe that the beast was gone for good.

While I rode, Dex and Rigby walked in front of me, leading the way. Dex explained everything from the moment that Rigby and Christina had left us. Rigby just kind of nodded, not saying much. I think he was in shock from the whole thing, not only finding out that at least one but possibly all of the llamas, his livelihood was gone, but that his hunting partner was gone too. I didn't know how close Rigby was to Mitch or if he knew what kind of person Mitch truly was, but he didn't show any emotion. Just a faint, "oh," after Dex told him I found his severed arm.

It was interesting though how Rigby almost had to argue with Dex over what the creature looked like. He was adamant that the beast had red eyes, though I knew for a fact they were eerie pools of black. He also thought the head would be rounder, that the fur would be darker. I guess that's how urban legends got started in the first place. One person sees only what they want to see, not what's really there. To Rigby, red eyes were the most frightening thing to see in the woods, but it wasn't necessarily the reality.

When we could see the lights of Rigby's house through the trees, he stopped and pulled back at the horse. He eyed both of us seriously.

"The reason I came out to the cabin…," he said, his voice low. His eyes darted to the house lights and back. "I came because I found out what Christina had done."

Christina?

He lowered his head a little, as if in shame, and continued, "This morning she had gone out for a ride. I was looking for a ledger in her room and I came across a bag. Inside were two transmitter circuits. From the walkie talkies she gave you."

I breathed out slowly.

"I questioned her about it. She broke down in tears… said that she took them out because she didn't want you to reach us. She thought that it would make the whole thing scarier if you felt on your own. I couldn't believe it, ya know?"

He rubbed at his face and I could see the strain on his brow. I would have felt sorry for him but at that moment, all I could think about was how God damn angry I was that Christina had done that. We could have all been saved if it weren't for that!

"Why?" I asked, trying to keep my emotions under control. "Why would she do that?"

"She thought that if you made a really scary show, then people would come here. That the business would get going again. Stupid, stupid girl...she even thought it would make for a better movie if the motion detector lights didn't work. When we were in the woods that time, she went on the roof and covered up the solar panels. She didn't think she put you into any danger, but she's going to find out the hard way exactly what she did. She put..." he closed his eyes and struggled for words, "she's going to have to live with what happened. And so will I."

I looked over at Dex. His hands had balled into fists and he was biting his lower lip hard. I wasn't the only one who was livid.

"We're going to have to bring the police into this," Dex said in a flinty voice. "She may have not meant for any of this to happen. But we almost died out there and we were the lucky ones. You don't fuck with people's lives like that."

Rigby looked up at him, tears glistening in his eyes. "I know. I'm so sorry for what she did. I know she will be too."

"Sorry doesn't even do anything in this case," I said to myself. He looked up at me and gave me a short nod.

"I know Miss Perry. I know."

I sighed and Rigby began leading us back to the house, to the lights, to a nightmare that didn't seem to end.

23

The night stretched on in a blur. Once we got back to Rigby's, we discovered Christina was gone. She had taken Rigby's car into town, I guess trying to avoid what she knew was coming. Luckily we had come up in the Highlander and within seconds, we had crammed ourselves into the car, its comfort and familiar smell easing my heart, and we rode it all the way into town. When you lived miles away from the cops, it was usually better for you to just go to them.

It was in the car as we approached the lights of civilization that my phone sprang to life. I had numerous texts from Ada and my voice mail box was full. I texted her back quickly to let her know I was alive but I couldn't respond to anything at the moment. All of that seemed inconsequential next to the severity of the case we were about to get involved with.

Not surprisingly, the police station in Snow Crest consisted of a couple of officers and that was it. There was only one guy in the jail cell, and he was just the neighborhood drunk who started fights at the bar.

We were prepared for the cops to laugh at us as we explained our story. Rigby went first and they knew about him and his zany ways. But when we started telling them what we saw, that's when the cops thought we were really full of shit. The most we could do was pop the memory card into their television set and though there wasn't much proof of the actual beast, there was proof that something terrible had happened out there.

Dex and I even had to concede that the whole thing could have been caused by a "mangy bear", that damn bear always being used as the scapegoat when people tried to debunk Sasquatch sightings.

While we were talking – for hours and hours until our throats were sore – one of the officers had left with Rigby to go pick up Christina.

When they brought her into the station, I couldn't even look at her. I just couldn't believe that someone as young and seemingly innocent as her could do something so dangerous and so irresponsible. It didn't matter that she did it in order to help her dad's business – her actions got Mitch killed and it nearly killed us as well.

Thankfully, at that point we had explained all there was to explain. The cops wanted to keep the SD card as evidence and Dex only agreed to it if they promised to give it back. But I was beginning to wonder if it was even a good idea to air the show after all. A man died. He actually died during all of this and now that we were back in the real world, faced with real consequences, showing the scene of a murder for profit seemed downright wrong.

I voiced this to Dex as we left the station, his arm wrapped firmly around my side, trying to prevent me from going after Christina in a flurry of hateful word vomit.

"I'm thinking the same thing," he admitted. We walked

together down the darkened street to the Highlander. It sounds strange, but I wished I could have kept walking. I needed to clear my head. I was all messed up inside and I couldn't seem to get a handle on anything. The creature, Mitch, what Christina had done. It was way too much for my tired brain to handle.

"I really don't want to go back there," I told him, folding my arms across my chest. Because it was so dark out, the cops were getting some extra enforcement from the town of Cranbrook and initiating a full-on search in the morning. We were going to have to go back up to Rigby's and maybe the cabin. I hoped Rigby and a map would be able to take the team the rest of the way because there was no way we were reenacting our journey for them.

"We won't," he said. "This isn't a murder investigation, this is an animal attack and if anything I'm sure we're going to be suffering from PTSD soon. Anyway, I have a plan if they do try and make us."

"What's that?"

"We cross the border," he answered and the streetlights gleamed in his cheeky eyes. He shot me a look. "Are you sure you don't want to go to the hospital?"

I shook my head and got in the car. "The hospital here is probably administered by a vet. I'm fine. I'm just sore. I'm just tired. I just want to eat, then eat some more and pass out. I want to sleep in a warm bed and I want to sleep for days."

We turned the corner into the familiar glow of the motel.

"I can promise you food and a warm bed," he told me. He eyed the hot tub as we pulled the car up beside it. "And it's never too late for a dip in the hot tub."

That was probably the best idea I had heard in days.

We checked back in, the front desk lady eyeing Dex down like a criminal. She hadn't forgotten about the incident with the mirror and he had to promise – swearing on a random bible that she plunked out on the counter – that we weren't going to cause any more trouble. He swore with utmost sincerity but I knew that look in his eyes all too well. He was enjoying the fuss.

Once again we got two separate rooms. And once again, my heart dipped a bit. It was the right thing to do, for both of us, but I knew it was going to be harder sleeping away from him. It had to be done, though. It's not like we'd go back to sleeping together once we got back to Seattle. It would be me in my room and he in his. The room next door.

I plunked my bag on the springy motel bed, so tempted to just pass out on it, face down. But Dex was knocking at the adjoining door before I could. I got up and answered it.

He grinned at me and I was struck by how much I loved it when he smiled. I mean really smiled. White teeth, tanned face, black hair. It was perfect.

"Pizza is on the way," he announced, not coming in.

"That was fast."

"I have fast fingers." Another grin.

My eyes shot up to the ceiling and I hoped the heat creeping up my neck wasn't noticeable.

"It's handy when you're dialing for takeout," he continued, in mock earnestness. "Should we go in the hot tub now, or wait until after we eat?"

"Can we eat the pizza in the hot tub?" I asked.

He winked at me. "That's my girl."

He closed the door, leaving me alone in my room. Which, at that moment, was actually a good thing. I had the vision of him saying a very similar phrase the day before, our naked bodies on the silver space blankets, him coaxing me to another orgasm.

Holy shit. That was an image that wasn't leaving my head anytime soon. It felt wrong to be mildly turned on after everything we had been through. I began to think maybe I needed a cold shower instead of a dip in the hot tub.

I didn't have much time to contemplate it. I got into my black Slayer t-shirt and black booty shorts and was covering myself up with the thin motel robe when Dex knocked at my door again.

"Pizza," he called out and opened the door, walking right in. He was dressed in the same robe, the box of pizza balancing on one hand, a 2 liter of Coke in the other.

"Hey, I could have been changing," I warned him, wrapping the robe tighter.

"That was the idea."

"You're the worst pizza delivery boy ever," I said, pushing past him through the door into his room.

"I've heard I'm the best."

I shot him a wry look as he shut the door behind him and followed me back. "Don't tell me you worked as a delivery boy once."

"Only for a day," he said, handing the box to me and picking up two glasses from the counter by the coffee machine.

"Let me guess, you were fired."

He nodded at the door, for me to get going. "No, I wasn't. I was just trying to pick up a girl who lived down the street."

I opened the door and stepped into the cold mountain air. It was almost beautiful when you knew you had a warm place to protect you from it

"Did it work?"

He smiled at me and locked the door. "I told you. Best pizza delivery boy ever."

We walked side by side toward the hot tub, the icy breeze blowing back our robes. Our pace quickened when we saw the steam rising from the metallic gate, the low green light of the tub.

"Is there anything you won't do to get laid?" I asked.

A wash of sadness came across his eyes as he looked down, trying to open the gate. He cleared his throat and the melancholy was gone.

"I guess not. I'm a pig, as you say Perry."

I smarted a bit at that comment. I felt a tad bit ashamed. I locked the gate behind us and laid the pizza at the edge of the tub, conscious that he was watching me.

"You're not a pig, Dex," I reassured him. "You're just..."

"Me?"

"You're definitely you." *And you can be wonderful.*

We stood a few feet apart, both of our robes still on, waiting for the other one to undress first. So silly when you thought about it.

So I disrobed first. And Dex gasped at the sight of me. Not in lust, but in balls to the wall concern.

"Jesus, Perry. You're hurt." He sounded hurt as he said it.

I looked down. In the pool's wavering glow I could see a multitude of bruises and scratches covering my legs and arms.

"I'm not hurt," I told him quickly. "I'm cold."

I reached for the metal railing and eased myself into the hot pool, the scalding water burning my skin wonderfully, stinging at any wounds I had until the pain was gone. A trail of shivers and sparking nerves followed in its wake, rushing up as the water rose around me.

I looked up. He was still staring down at me, like he was caught in something I couldn't see.

"Get your ass in this hot tub right now," I told him. "I'm fine and getting better with every second."

It was true. Now that I was leaning back in the water up to my neck, I was overcome by extreme pleasure and a rare feeling of relaxation.

Dex continued to hesitate, then he finally dropped the robe. I swear, he had to make everything so dramatic, including getting into a hot tub. Not that I blamed him with that body. I tried not to stare at him in his grey boxer briefs. It was hard not to. It was damn hard.

He came in the water beside me, gasping at the heat as he went. Eventually he settled on the other side of the tub and leaned his head back against the edge. "Oh my God, please just leave me here."

"That can be arranged. You'll be really pruney though."

He straightened up and lowered his gaze at me. "Will you go to the hospital tomorrow?"

"I told you I'm fine."

"Will you?"

"We'll be busy tomorrow if we have to help them with the investigation."

"Will you?"

"Argh fine. Now give me pizza." I knew I had no choice to comply because Dex usually asked as a formality. If he really wanted me to do something, he'd find a way to make me.

"Done," he said and opened the box for me. I picked out a couple of slices and shoved them in my mouth, completely ravenous. I washed it down with the cold Coke that was the sweetest, most precious drink I had ever tasted.

We ate in silence for a bit. There was no talking, not with

our appetites, and it wasn't long before we both polished off the whole box. In hindsight we should have ordered two pizzas but Dex warned me that it would have been too much of a shock to our system. He was right, as usual.

With the food out of the way and there nothing else to do but talk or stare at each other, our conversation turned to more serious topics. We talked about Christina. We talked about Rigby. We talked about Mitch. And we talked about the beast.

It felt good to just lay it all out there with him, all the things I'd kept to myself about the whole ordeal. He could only hear my thoughts sometimes and it felt good to have a direct interaction with him. To know he was listening. We were in this together as we always had been and he was always going to be that person who understood. No matter what happened in the future, he had to stay a part of my life. If not for just being that one person in the world who understood what I had to go through, the things I saw, the way I felt when I was faced with something impossible. He went through all of it too. We really were cut from the same cloth.

We were both starting to get quite wrinkly from the water when I brought up the dilemma with the episode.

"Do you think Jimmy will be mad if we don't air it?" I wondered.

"We're not airing it, kiddo. You know that. It wouldn't be right."

I nodded, feeling a weird mix of disappointment and relief. "And he'll understand?"

"Definitely," he answered. When he saw the puzzlement on my brow, he went on, softly, "Your priorities change when you almost lose the person you need. Jimmy will be glad that we're alive and have both our arms."

I looked down at the frothy water. "So much for my first gig as a cameraperson."

"You did great. You're welcome to the job if you want it."

I offered him a half-smile. "Don't tell me you want to take over my position now."

"Oh it's your position again is it?" he finished off the rest of the Coke and wiped his mouth. "Well baby, I don't blame you. You're much prettier than I am."

"It's the boobs," I said modestly.

His eyes crinkled softly at the corners and I gave him credit for holding my gaze and not glancing downward. A beat passed, then he looked at the gate. "Well, I think I'm going to head back. I'll fall asleep in here if I stay any longer."

"OK," I said. My chest pinched. I didn't want him to leave. I wanted him to stay in the tub with me. I wanted to keep talking to him. I wanted to keep looking at him.

Plus, he had just called me baby again. I needed to hear more of that.

He got up slowly but once out of the tub, he scrambled to wrap himself in the robe and picked up mine, holding it out for me.

It was hard leaving that heat but I got out as quickly as I could. He wrapped the robe around me, picked up the garbage and the glasses and we did a quick jog through the parking lot toward our rooms, steam rising off of our bodies, dissipating in the starry sky.

We burst through his door and I walked toward the adjoining one to my room. Every step I took felt long, felt heavy. I ran a million reasons through my head of why I should stay. I thought of a million things I could say, including "I was wrong."

But I couldn't say any of them.

I just didn't have the words.

I reached for the door knob in slow motion and he called after me.

"Perry?"

I paused. A hope ran through me. I turned to look at him.

I'd never seen him look so...lost.

"Sleep well," he said in a strained voice. "If you need me, you know where I am."

The room next door.

I swallowed hard and gave him a grateful nod. Then disappeared into my room, the door slowly closing on his solemn eyes.

I DID NOT SLEEP WELL. I did not sleep at all. It was 2am and I was still tossing and turning on the bed. My mind was racing and it wouldn't stop. But it wasn't about the beast. It wasn't about Mitch or Christina or any of the shit that tried to kill me in the last 24 hours. As fantastical as all of that was, it no longer mattered. It had happened and we made it out alive. It was done.

And so were Dex and I. After everything I had said to him the other day, there was no way we couldn't be done. The man opened himself up to me for the first time and I was so pig-headed, so stubborn, that I threw it away. He practically gave me his heart and I turned my back on it.

I was hurt. I was so hurt by what he did to me. But now I was just hurting myself. I was starting to wonder if this was even about Dex after all. Was it he that I couldn't forgive? Or was it myself? For the things I had done to him?

He was right. He had been wrong to hurt me, to treat me

the way he did. But he wasn't alone. I lied to him. Right to his face. Because I was too scared to admit to him that I had been in love with him. I had lied to him, I had messed with his medication and I was acting like I could do no wrong. We were both at fault and I was starting to see the light that I apparently was.

I gripped the corner of my pillow and swallowed back tears of frustration. I had lied because I was scared. I had thrown love away because I was scared. All because I was scared. And I was still scared, no matter how deep I fell into my self-loathing, I knew there was a new chord of terror waiting to emerge. It was the fear of losing myself all over again, of letting go and never getting my soul back. It was the fear of learning to love again and having my heart broken. It was the fear of being a fool.

And it was the same fear that millions of people faced every single day. The fear of loving someone. The fear of being loved. Yet people did it anyway.

So why couldn't I?

I rolled over and looked up at the ceiling. A pale light from the motel's awning filtered in through the window. I was alone, lying in bed, feeling like my heart was breaking into a million pieces again, and there was no one to blame but myself. The agony slowly spread from my center out into my bones. It ached. I ached.

But it wasn't over. It wouldn't be over until I tried to make it right.

I had a feeling it wasn't where I lay.

It was in the room next door.

I pulled back my covers and padded my way through the dark over to our adjoining door. My hand hovered above the knob as last minute thoughts of pride ran through my head. I decided to risk being a fool.

I opened the door, then opened the other door.

The bathroom light in Dex's room was on, bathing it in a slant of low light. I saw his silhouette on the bed turn over and he slowly sat up.

"Perry?" he asked, the sleep clogging up his throat. "Are you all right? What's wrong?"

"Nothing," I said softly. "Maybe everything."

He sat up a bit more and reached over for the bedside lamp but I cried out, "No. Please. Leave the light off."

He paused then took his arm back. I could feel the bewilderment coming from him, it made the silence heavier as he thought of what to say.

"I just want you to stay there, please," I told him.

He swallowed hard. "OK."

I walked over so I was at the foot of his bed. I could see half his body lit in the grainy light. I knew I looked the same. Half of me in light, half of me in dark.

I stood there, staring at him, and slowly gripped the bottom of my t-shirt. I raised my arms above my head and pulled the shirt right off, dropping it to the ground beside me. I was completely topless and though I couldn't read his face properly I could hear him take in a sharp breath of air.

I tugged at the edge of my underwear and deliberately slipped them off. Once they were at my feet I stepped out of them and crawled onto the bed.

"Oh my God," Dex whispered as I came closer.

I didn't let myself feel modest. I just went with it. I wanted to give it all to him.

I crawled very, very slowly, like a big cat, giving Dex time to slide forward under the sheets and lie back.

I stopped when I was hovering somewhere above his waist and with one hand I peeled the cover away from him. He was completely naked under there and when I saw just how hard he was, when I felt him pulsing hotly underneath my palm, I made sure he saw my smile.

"Why are you doing this?" he whispered.

"Because I don't mind being a fool," I answered slyly. "And I want to make you come so hard, you'll be begging me to stop."

I caught the widening of his eyes before I grabbed his cock firmly and eased it through my wet lips into my mouth.

His moan was immediate, so I took that as a good sign. I continued for a bit, sliding my mouth up and down his shaft, working my tongue along the ridge, when he gasped and grabbed me up my arms.

"Stop," he said through his heavy breathing. "You're always first."

With raw passion, he flipped me over onto my back, my breasts jostling as I bobbed on the mattress. He went to town on me, eating me out until I came. I covered my face with the pillow, conscious of being in a motel, when he reached up and ripped the pillow away from my face. He continued and I cried out until I couldn't take it anymore, his fingers digging into my ass and driving me forward into his face.

Seconds later he was peering down at me, wild lust in his eyes. "I need to hear you. Never hide that from me."

"Don't boss me around," I answered, gathering my strength. I wasn't done yet. I sat up and pushed him back onto the bed, then I hopped on him, already wet and throbbing. I made sure I rode him until it was obvious he couldn't hold back anymore. I bit at his neck and earlobes and when he asked me to bite harder, I obliged, pleased at the mix of pain and pleasure I was giving him. He brought his thumb to my clit and started rubbing me and didn't let go until I did.

I leaned back as he filled me up, feeling his cries, feeling everything inside me. I was whimpering, overcome with the feelings that were pouring through me and then the whimpering turned into shaking and I couldn't hold myself up anymore. I couldn't do anything but swim along with the current, the warmth that coated my body.

I lay forward, resting my head on his chest, my fingers tracing his tattoo. His heart was beating wildly beneath it, his breath was tired, hot and rushing out of his lungs. I tried to move so that he'd slip out of me, but he placed his arms around me and held me tight.

"Don't," he said gruffly. "I want to stay inside you. I don't know how long I'll have this."

I raised my head and looked at him. His gaze was enthralling and I found myself lost in his eyes, lost in my feelings and in his.

"I want to be in you, be a part of you," he went on, voice growing lower with each word until he was whispering. "Let me be that part."

I smiled shyly and rubbed down at his chest. I wanted to reach in and soothe his heart. "You are a part of me Dex. You're every part of me. Always have been. Always will be."

He studied me with great intent, searching my eyes, searching my soul for signs of the truth. I returned the look. I wanted him to know that I meant every word of it. That and more that I didn't even know how to express yet.

A smile slowly spread across his lips and I saw that glorious mix of teeth, dimples and crinkly eyes. He didn't say anything, just smiled and held me tighter. I lay my head back down and he kissed the top of my forehead hard.

"I love you Perry," he whispered, mouth moving in my hair. "I love you so fucking much. And I'm losing myself. I'm losing myself to you and I don't care anymore because there's never been a better feeling in the whole fucking world. I love you. So much. Too much. Always."

My heart swelled at his words until I thought my ribs weren't big enough to contain the feeling. I thought it might spill out of me and never come back. So I let Dex hold me as the night went on. His arms stayed wrapped around me, keeping me together, keeping me to him as we slowly succumbed to sleep.

I had never felt so safe.

I had never felt so terrified.

ACKNOWLEDGMENTS

Much thanks to Elizabeth Henze, Matt Schiariti, and Amanda Polito for their last-minute editing work on this baby. Also, have to thank my fabulous beta readers, Kelly St-Laurent, Emmy Franke, Megan Caffery and Janice Pia for their enthusiasm and feedback as I spoon fed them this manuscript, chapter by chapter. Of course I wouldn't have readers if I didn't have such amazing book bloggers such as the one and only Maryse, Megan from The Book Asylum, Kristen from Seeing Night Reviews, Laura Moore from Little Read, Kara from Great Imaginations, SupaGurl Heather and Reading in Winter's Kristilyn for all your love and support! I know I'm forgetting a bunch of others, so if you've read and EIT and told your friends about it, this book is for you!

Oh, and I should thank Scott MacKenzie for cooking, cleaning and doing everything short of dressing me as I neglected him, myself and the world while trying to get this book done. It'll be worth it, baby!

WHAT'S NEXT?

Thank you so much for reading Into the Hollow, book #6 in the Experiment in Terror series.

If you want to connect with me, you can always find me on Instagram (where I post travel photos, fashion, teasers, etc, IG IS MY LIFE and the easiest place to find me online)
    -> or in my Facebook Group (we're a fun bunch and would love to have you join)
    -> Otherwise, feel free to signup for my mailing list (it comes once a month) and Bookbub alerts!
    Up next? Book #7 COME ALIVE (told from Dex's POV! It's...salacious, just so you know).

What's next?

ABOUT THE AUTHOR

Karina Halle, a former screenwriter, travel writer and music journalist, is the *New York Times*, *Wall Street Journal*, and *USA Today* bestselling author of *The Pact*, *A Nordic King*, and *Sins & Needles*, as well as over fifty other wild and romantic reads. She, her husband, and their adopted pit bull live in a rain forest on an island off British Columbia, where they operate a B&B that's perfect for writers' retreats. In the winter, you can often find them in California or on their beloved island of Kauai, soaking up as much sun (and getting as much inspiration) as possible. For more information, visit
www.authorkarinahalle.com

ALSO BY KARINA HALLE

Contemporary Romances

Love, in English

Love, in Spanish

Where Sea Meets Sky (from Atria Books)

Racing the Sun (from Atria Books)

The Pact

The Offer

The Play

Winter Wishes

The Lie

The Debt

Smut

Heat Wave

Before I Ever Met You

After All

Rocked Up

Wild Card (North Ridge #1)

Maverick (North Ridge #2)

Hot Shot (North Ridge #3)

Bad at Love

The Swedish Prince

The Wild Heir

A Nordic King

Nothing Personal

My Life in Shambles

Discretion

Disarm

Disavow

The Royal Rogue

The Forbidden Man

Romantic Suspense Novels by Karina Halle

Sins and Needles (The Artists Trilogy #1)

On Every Street (An Artists Trilogy Novella #0.5)

Shooting Scars (The Artists Trilogy #2)

Bold Tricks (The Artists Trilogy #3)

Dirty Angels (Dirty Angels #1)

Dirty Deeds (Dirty Angels #2)

Dirty Promises (Dirty Angels #3)

Black Hearts (Sins Duet #1)

Dirty Souls (Sins Duet #2)

Horror Romance

Darkhouse (EIT #1)

Red Fox (EIT #2)

The Benson (EIT #2.5)

Dead Sky Morning (EIT #3)

Lying Season (EIT #4)

On Demon Wings (EIT #5)

Old Blood (EIT #5.5)

The Dex-Files (EIT #5.7)

Into the Hollow (EIT #6)

And With Madness Comes the Light (EIT #6.5)

Come Alive (EIT #7)

Ashes to Ashes (EIT #8)

Dust to Dust (EIT #9)

The Devil's Duology

Donners of the Dead

Veiled

Made in United States
North Haven, CT
01 April 2025